Robert Fannin was born in Dublin in 1954. His previous careers include working as a fisherman, a deck hand on yachts, a cartoonist, playwright, signwriter, radio presenter and house painter.

Also by Robert Fannin

Shooting the Moon

ROBERT FANNIN

Falling Slowly

HACHETTE
BOOKS
IRELAND

First published in 2010 by Hachette Books Ireland
A division of Hachette UK Ltd.

1

All characters in this publication are fictitious and any resemblance to real persons, living or dead, is purely coincidental.

A CIP catalogue record for this title is available from the British Library.

ISBN 978 0340 98020 0

Typeset in Sabon by Hachette Books Ireland
Printed and bound in the UK by CPI Mackays, Chatham ME5 8TD

Hachette Books Ireland policy is to use papers that are natural, renewable and recyclable products and made from wood grown in sustainable forests. The logging and manufacturing processes are expected to conform to the environmental regulations of the country of origin.

Hachette Books Ireland
8 Castlecourt Centre
Castleknock
Dublin 15, Ireland
A division of Hachette UK Ltd.
338 Euston Road, London NW1 3BH

www.hachette.ie

To Marie and Bob

One

Doyle slips through the swinging doors and walks to a round table under a photograph of a beached black boat. He sits and hauls into focus the repeated patterns of the tables and their coverings. Hard to believe that only an hour ago it was a clatter of cutlery and tongues.

In time he will get up, leg muscles tightening for the frantic dance. It is as if they only know one remaining gear. To confuse them, he will walk slowly to his coat and ascend to the street up the spiral steps. The colour of the sky will depend on how long he has sat, and on the season. If it is summer it may be covered with a membrane of grey or blue. It will fill every crevice on the street with a light that is delicate and shadowless and as thin as soup. In winter it could be one of many things, or a mixture of many things. It may be still, cold, starless black, or wild with moon-filled clouds.

For almost a year he has walked up the same steps, up the same street, across Stokes Croft, up Nine Tree Hill and into the realm of the tall, poker-faced buildings inside which the men and women, children, dogs and cats of Cotham, unaware of their warmth, sleep.

*

The front door of the house surrenders to the turn of his key. The door to his flat can be stubborn. But, once open, it leads to two rooms connected by a corridor. A straight-backed chair stands in the centre of the main room facing the window. Small circular compression marks are dotted about the carpet.

From the chair the orange diamonds of the streetlights can be seen on the hill opposite. And, in this hourless time, Doyle sits. Ribbons of streets converge at roundabouts, their wet surface reflecting the antics of traffic-lights. The streets, as silent now as a ceasefire, are lined with leafless trees. But as the light leaks in, the silence splinters. First with birdsong, then with church bells and then into this traffic pours.

The curtain that Daphne made is thick and black. No light can pass through it. It is corded like the rig of a Chinese junk. Three nylon strings run up from a cleat attached to the window frame, through blocks separated evenly along the top, then drop to the curtain's hem. When it is raised, every corner of the room is rinsed in brightness.

Because of the curtain Doyle always wakes to darkness. Sounds offer the only clues as to time. He lies awake and waits for one. He pretends to forget he is waiting. He could follow, say, the tonal changes of a trapped wasp drilling for freedom. He could turn and check himself for parts but that might lead to masturbation, which, in turn, would lead to sweat and that would awaken the smells of the previous night, smells that had, until now, lain undisturbed in his pores.

He is waiting for the hammer-blow accuracy of the Polish church bell. Unlike any other timepiece, it reveals its knowledge in a long, slow sequence through which he can follow his movements: first bell – one a.m., cleaning up, smiling goodnights; second – two a.m., drinking at the counter with Geoff and whoever else; third, sitting, all people gone; fourth, home; fifth, sitting, staring; sixth, bed; seventh, unheard, also eighth, ninth and tenth. Will there be another? There it goes. Eleven – awake now. More? No.

Compute amount of sleep had, then hold position. Do not feel for parts and do not turn. Turning begets turning, which would disturb the stillness beneath his duvet where last night's cocktail of odours has released itself in long, slow-moving fingers – fried flesh and organs, wine, beer and sweat. They gather like fog in a jungle – the price of feeding the tubes.

This is how Doyle has come to see the people who use the restaurant. Flesh-covered tubes with legs that carry them from table to toilet and back. Arms to spoon or fork food into the hole at the top and wipe clean the hole at the bottom. They are obsessed with taste. Likes and dislikes are argued, using words padded fat with syllables. A tongue that can discuss, connected to a digestive system that can labour under the constant downpour of soups, sauces and sorbets, is said to belong to a palate that is discerning. The words that are launched and the tastes they describe are manufactured in the first of the tube's chambers. Once the food is chewed and swallowed, little interest remains. Any reference to what lies below the mouth, if not scientific, is said to be, 'distasteful'.

The restaurant is situated in a part of town that once heralded a boom. Professional attention drifted across the invisible border of the A38, one of the arteries into the city, and focused on an area that was rich with cultural diversity. That it was overshadowed by St Pauls, a place where that diversity occasionally caught light, added to the challenge.

The interiors of many tall buildings were emptied into skips that appeared on the pavement outside them. Rendering was hammered away, revealing fields of stonework. When work finished the buildings lay empty. Prices fell and were watched falling.

By then Doyle and Daphne had moved to Bristol from London. They rented the two-room flat in a house that overlooked a raised rectangle of grass with a solitary evergreen. Daphne charged at all the openings in her profession. She saw the move to Bristol as a way of slipping through the back door. There were two major television companies in the city as well as one of the best theatres outside London. There was also an energetic flock of independent theatre companies. So, she argued, with every opening in London bombarded with CVs and phone calls, a recent graduate of drama college was much more likely to find work in Bristol. Besides, the city was small enough to get around on a bicycle. And it throbbed with every kind of live music.

Doyle had little interest in the move. He was making enough money from selling his papier-mâché heads to hat shops around the city. But Daphne was dancing to images that blossomed overnight. Bristol was the answer to all her problems. One Saturday morning, hung-over and still wet from sex, Doyle was about to slip back into sleep but the persistent tapping of her talk prevented it. He opened his eyes and said, 'OK, we'll go.' She hugged him, then launched into a list of things that would have to be done straight away.

Three weeks later they moved to Bristol. Doyle found a job in a vegetarian shop that was close to the flat. His manner was perfect for serving food. He was tall and slightly built and had dark eyes that appeared attentive to every word. Most of the customers were thin shadowy strokes. They talked of their aches, their bones, of homeopathy and therapeutic massage. They spent money on vitamins and vegetables.

The owner of the shop was a fiery blond in his early thirties, prone to fits of dissatisfaction. 'Jesus!' he would say, sneezing into the dust that rose from the bags of brown rice he was filling. 'This stuff is pure poison. I hate this business.' His name was Geoff and, when asked, he said he was Polish.

Geoff liked Doyle because the customers liked Doyle.

Daphne decorated the flat with black and white prints, orange and yellow cushion covers and furniture she bought for half nothing at local auctions. She auditioned for the Bristol Old Vic, and later for some of the smaller theatres around the city. All agreed she was good and they would like to help her but nothing was offered. She borrowed money from her father and spent it on more photographs and postage. Her agent suggested voiceovers but her tapes were sent back. A memo on one said, 'Her voice lacks enough guttural ingredient to make it sexy.' Doyle found the note on the table among the breakfast things when he got in that evening. She was still in bed.

One day Geoff came into the shop excited by a property he had just seen. 'I'm going to call it Wet Willie's Sausage Factory,' he said, showing Doyle photographs he had just taken on his phone. One was of the interior of a restaurant and the other of a three-storey building in Picton Street.

'Why?' Doyle asked.

'Why what?'

'Why are you calling it Wet Willie's … whatever?'

'That's the marvellous thing. We won't sell any sausages – not one.'

'We? Geoff, what am I going to do in a restaurant?'

Geoff looked at him. 'You'd make the perfect waiter.'

'But I've never done anything like that before.'

'Piece of cake. Someone orders sausage, you bring them sausage. Couldn't be simpler.'

More and more often Doyle found Daphne in front of the television when he got home. She'd be sitting on the floor close to the screen mouthing replies to questions asked by the bow-tie-adorned host of a late-afternoon quiz programme, her striped dressing-gown shooting ripples from the bend at her knees. On occasions he had sat and tried to talk. If she replied, it was with a grunt, her eyes never leaving the screen.

Later he ignored her and went straight to the kitchen to cook. He was becoming acquainted with the vegetarian food from the shop. Daphne accepted whatever he presented without apparent thought or thanks. Once Doyle watched her spoon a bowl of seaweed into herself before she mumbled that the spaghetti had been undercooked.

One evening he came home to the boom of the TV but no one in front of it. He heard whimpering and followed it to the bathroom. She had squeezed herself into the space between the toilet bowl and the wall. She was naked. Her eyes were wet, bloodshot and unfocused. She drew in rushes of air, then murmured as she exhaled. Doyle went close and knelt down to hear.

'Help me,' she was whispering.

'Daphne – Daphne, I'm here, it's me.'

She turned towards him, stared at him, her eyes registering confusion, then anger. 'Stay away from me! Go on, get away from me.' It was a strong, defiant demand.

Doyle stood up and wondered what to do. All he could tell for certain was that his presence was making the situation worse. He stepped out into the corridor. Within minutes, wearing her dressing-gown, she appeared. She went straight past him into the bedroom and closed the door. When he checked on her later she was lying face down on top of the duvet, asleep.

Daphne never made any reference to the incident and neither did Doyle.

The few minutes' walk between the shop and the flat was the

only time he felt he could breathe. Between Geoff and Daphne he felt used – abused, even. To Geoff, he was an ingredient, one of many, in a scheme that would allow Geoff access to a fantasy that involved food, money and power. To Daphne, he had become as important and as ignorable as air. Her treatment of him was painful but he did not take it personally. She had turned her back to the world; she no longer registered him. He knew he should do something to shake her out of it but he did nothing. He walked past the red-brick walls of Kingsdown Parade, wanting to fall, like Alice, down a hole. He wanted to find himself somewhere he could laugh and shout and complain.

Doyle knew that Geoff was in talks with the present owners of the restaurant and could tell they were going well by his changing attitude to the shop and its customers. One lunchtime he came in eating a burger, the meat glistening pink and brown between the buns. He walked behind the counter and greeted Doyle. As he spoke pieces of partially chewed burger shot out of his mouth. A man Doyle had been serving looked at the large blond man, then turned and left the shop.

'Fuck him,' Geoff said. 'In a few weeks we'll be serving raw beef to Bristol's ulcerated business community.'

One evening Doyle coaxed Daphne out for a walk on Clifton Downs. The clocks had gone forward and the evenings were starting to get a little longer. She squinted in the low sunshine. 'God! Summer's coming and the days will just drag on for ever.' Doyle did not know what to say to that. He thought of kissing her. He had an image of them embracing, she leaning against the bark of a sloping tree, her mouth moist and open, her skin smelling of milk, the hum of bees drowning the distant city noises. When he bent down, her lips were clenched tight and she smelt of TCP.

They walked down Blackboy Hill hand in hand, the light

flaming the upper storeys of the red-brick buildings. They found a pub in a side street that looked as if it belonged on a fifties film set. The characters drinking at the bar wore shabby suits with wide lapels, their hair cut short. An upright piano that stood too close to the dartboard was gouged and scarred. Daphne drained her first vodka and tonic, and was on her third when Doyle was ready for his second pint.

'I'd prefer it if we could just go,' she said.

He looked at her and was aware that the only thing they shared now was the emptiness that lay between them. He had been talking about the restaurant, expressing doubt at his ability to be a waiter. He knew she had not been listening. He wanted to smack the conversation in the face, splintering every bloody syllable to see if she'd react. He didn't. The monotony of his words carried him to their conclusion.

A few days later Geoff came into the shop, bright with smiles. 'Come on,' he said, 'I'm taking you to lunch. Red-blooded flesh from the flanks of a young calf.'

'If that's supposed to be a joke your humour is not appreciated here,' said a woman with hennaed hair – she had been telling Doyle about a friend of hers who had been shot. The bullet had gone through the arm severing an artery and had just entered the lung when Geoff had burst in with his invitation for lunch.

'Drop in next week, love. We're getting a fresh shipment of baby seal from Greenland, guaranteed free range.'

'Sicko,' she said, took her change and left.

'So, what's the reason for this?' Doyle asked in the car.

'Just been to the bank. They like the business plan, said with my excellent – I repeat, *excellent* – track record they don't think a loan will be a problem. He said pop back at four and they'd have the paperwork ready. It's in the bag, Doyle, in the fucking bag.'

Doyle asked Geoff if they could stop off and try to tempt Daphne into joining them.

There was a strange quality to the silence in the flat, as though the air had thickened and was smothering every sound. He called her name. The word hung in the air in front of him. He walked through it to the bedroom. The bed was empty. Her dressing-gown lay on the floor forming a perfect C. He called again, then left the room. The bathroom door was closed. He stood in front of it and this time whispered, 'Daphne.' But the syllables twisted in his throat giving the word a high-pitched ending. He knocked. 'Daph, you in there?'

He opened the door. The bath was pale yellow, which clashed with the bright red liquid that filled it. The tip of her nose peeped out from behind the curtain of her dark hair. Her knees were matching islands of stone in the sea of red. A perfect image of her toes was reflected in the water. The mirror above the bath was streaked with blood, which shot across the wall like tropical vegetation. On the floor it lay in thick pools.

He felt his stomach swell. A rancid taste filled his mouth. He walked across the floor and held the side of the washbasin. The yellow eggcup of the toilet waited in the corner. Saliva raced around his tongue. He dropped to his knees and held his face over the bowl. The water at the bottom was the exact shape of a slice of bread. He could see the reflection of his head but could not make out features. A thread of saliva dropped from his mouth, almost making contact with the surface of the water. It detached itself and fell, causing two miniature ripples to run to the sides of the bowl then it resurfaced as an island of tiny bubbles. Suddenly Doyle's head was forced against the cistern as vomit erupted out of him. It was as though some giant had wrapped both hands around his middle and was squeezing hard. A second spasm thrust him forward again. The power of it astonished him. He waited for another.

Daphne's toes did not move. Neither did their reflection. They were as still as the taps above them. Doyle wrapped his arms around the bowl and rested his forehead on the rim. He heard the sound of a horn. The marmalade he had had with breakfast that morning was in the mixture beneath him. Another spasm drove him forward. This time it produced nothing but saliva and left him with a film of sweat that covered his upper lip and forehead, then turned cold.

A drop of water, a big globule, falling, tear-shaped, through a clear, empty sky, towards earth. On landing it spread outward and upward, for a moment a bejewelled crown, then collapsing into a dust-covered oval blob.

He heard footfalls in the corridor. Leave me alone, Geoff. Can't you see this is an awkward moment? Daphne's not looking her best right now and, to be frank, I'm a little under the weather myself.

Three words, each separated by a gap that is endless until it is broken by the next. 'Jesus . . . fucking . . . Christ!'

Doyle hears himself say, 'It's all right, Geoff.' Absolutely A O-fucking-K, buddy boy. Suicide's all the rage now. Two a month off the Clifton Suspension Bridge, six last year in Horfield Prison, so just a run-of-the-mill occurrence, really.

He felt hands come under his arms. They guided him to his feet. Doyle moved his head to view Daphne's face. Very white, eyes not quite closed. It had its own perfectly upside-down reflection through which tiny islands of scum floated.

In the blood by the side of the bath Doyle saw the blade of a Stanley knife.

*

He stared through the living-room window. The rooftops that climbed to the horizon resembled steps. So many, and beneath each a family lived. Hard to believe. Geoff was on the phone, his tone perfect, emotion restrained by adherence to duty but threatening to fill this spring day with shrapnel and flak.

Geoff filled the kettle, turned it on and looked around for tea-making paraphernalia. But the label he was seeking was lost in a cupboard full of labels. Finally he tried an earthenware container marked 'Tea' and there, nestled at the bottom, was a cluster of teabags. Geoff smelt them. Something about the way they sat there enmeshed in one another suggested to him that they might have been there for a very long time. He shouted to Doyle, wanting to know if he took sugar. The response was not a word he recognised. He took it as a negative.

'There you go,' he said, putting a cup in front of Doyle. He glanced at Doyle's face – it was the colour of uncooked pastry – and a thought surfaced within him, one he wished hadn't: That bitch has ruined my day. No, more than my day. She's ruined so many things it's incalculable. Ha! Ha! Look at me, I'm dead.

Wanting something in the room to change, Geoff leaned forward and turned on the television. A newscaster talked about a threatened rail strike.

'Turn it off,' Doyle said, then tried to raise the cup to his lips. It wobbled in his hand and crashed back to the table. They both stared at the pool of shining liquid.

Geoff turned off the television. 'Look, let's get out of here. The police said they wouldn't be long. We can wait for them outside.'

Doyle stood and followed him to the steps that led up to the front door. When Geoff sat he, too, sat. It was then he noticed the blood: it was on his shoes, had soaked into the knees of his trousers; it was even on his sleeves. 'How could she have done that?' he asked.

There was nothing Geoff could think of to say.

'What happens now?' Doyle asked.

'I don't know. For the moment we just sit.'

Doyle drove his long fingers through his hair, then interlinked them at the back. 'Geoff, tell me a story.'

'What?'

'Yeah, you know, a story.'

'Oh! For fuck's sake! I don't know any stories. Look, I'm sorry, I can't think of one right now.'

'What about *The Ugly Duckling*?'

'What about it?'

'Tell it to me.'

'For Christ's sake!' Geoff stood, walked down a number of steps then turned and faced Doyle's black-eyed stare. '"There once was an ugly duckling."' He stopped. 'Look, I don't know that fucking story, OK?'

'That was the song. The story doesn't start like that.'

'I don't know how it starts, then.'

'Do you know how it ends?'

'Yes.'

'How?'

Geoff had a strong desire to lean forward, grab Doyle by the collar and shake him. Instead he sighed and said, 'The duckling is not a duck, it's a swan, a young swan, a cygnet, and it grows into a beautiful white swan and it's over the fucking moon about the whole process.'

'Geoff, you really have a real knack with stories.' He smiled and realised that these moments with Geoff were special, like the time spent around a campfire after a long day's hike.

Between the roofs of parked cars a police car moved in silence.

Only after it stopped did a blue light start flashing. Two officers got out, and came in through the front gate where they saw Doyle and Geoff sitting on the steps.

Doyle was surprised by their youth. Surely this was a case for more senior men.

As they approached they removed their caps and looked up at the building.

'She's inside. It's the ground-floor flat,' Geoff said, shading his eyes as he peered up at them.

'Who lives there?' one of the policemen asked.

'I do,' said Doyle.

'And the girl, does she live there too?'

Doyle nodded. The policemen shared a look. One put his cap back on and started to climb the steps to the front door. Doyle began to get up.

'Stay where you are, please,' said the policeman standing in front of them. 'My colleague will first make an assessment.'

'She's in the bath,' Geoff said.

As the first policeman entered through the front door, an ambulance pulled up in front of the police car. Two green-uniformed paramedics got out and came through the gate. The policeman standing in front of Doyle and Geoff nodded at them and pointed to the door. They mounted the steps and disappeared inside.

Less than a minute later the first policeman emerged and walked down the steps. He tapped his colleague on the shoulder and the two moved towards the gate. Geoff and Doyle watched them. The one who had just come out of the house was talking in whispers. The other listened, shaking his head, furrowing his brow. They parted, and the one who had been talking continued towards the gate, now muttering into a small radio that was strapped to his shoulder. The other resumed his position in front of Doyle and Geoff. They waited for him to say something, but he didn't.

They hadn't heard what the guy at the gate had said into the radio but they caught a crackled reply: 'We'll get on to CID. Better bring them in.'

He turned and walked up to them. 'I'm arresting you both on suspicion of murder. You do not have to say anything but it may harm your defence if you do not mention when questioned something that you may later come to rely on in court. Anything you do say may be given in evidence. Do you understand?'

Geoff stood and roared into the man's face, 'What? Are you fucking nuts?'

'I repeat,' the policeman said, 'I am arresting you on suspicion of murder and have cautioned you both. Do you understand?'

Geoff spun on his heels, holding the sides of his head. 'I don't fucking believe this.' He focused on the policeman. 'Listen, it's you who doesn't understand. We came here to pick Daphne up and take her to lunch. I have a business to run. I'm trying to open a restaurant. I didn't kill anyone and neither did he.' He pointed at Doyle, who was still on the step.

'Just come nice and quietly down to the station,' the policeman said.

Geoff was moving in semi-circles, his arms held out as if he were a Baptist preacher. 'You simply do not understand. I have business that cannot be postponed. I have to be at the bank at four. It's absolutely vital. How could you possibly think—'

'Sir, resisting arrest will not help the situation. Do you understand?'

'Stop fucking asking me if I understand. All I understand is that you, whoever you are, have made a completely wrong assumption here and it's going to cost me my restaurant. Look at us, for Christ's sake – do I look like a murderer? Does he?'

'Please calm down, sir. Your co-operation will go a long way to speeding matters up.'

Doyle stood. 'Geoff, come on, let's just do this.'

Geoff looked as though he was about to reply but then stopped himself. He took a breath and looked at the policeman. 'Is there even the slightest chance we'll be finished by four?'

'I very much doubt it, sir.'

Two

This was not a dream. It had none of the hallmarks of a dream. The pavement beneath his feet was too hard and the wind had a slight chill. Somewhere in the evergreen, magpies were bickering. This was not a dream.

In the back of the car Geoff examined the tips of his fingers. When he found some stray splinter of nail he'd bring it to his mouth, clasp it between his teeth, then twist his finger and his face until he'd removed it. Doyle watched him, then tried to focus on what was outside the window. He had an image of his brain as a bird's nest floating on a lake. It should sink, disappear beneath the surface and find a home for itself in the soft mud below but somehow, against all odds, it stayed afloat.

The journey to the police station brought Doyle through parts of the city he had never seen before. They drove through a housing estate, then turned into the side entrance of a long, red-brick building. It had a forest of aerials and discs on its roof and barbed wire around the top of the railings outside.

Inside, the two policemen, Geoff and Doyle stood in a bright blue room, waiting, as a uniformed woman behind a screen in a hatchway finished typing. Sounds came from the interior of the building – an ignored telephone, a distant siren – but they were muted.

Geoff was still ripping bits of himself from the ends of his fingers but was quiet. Eventually the policewoman beckoned Doyle. The sign 'Custody Sergeant' faced outwards from the edge of the counter. Looking into the screen and typing, she dribbled out a long series of questions in a voice heavy with boredom. Name, address, occupation, date of birth, next of kin. When she looked up, Doyle saw that she was well into her sixties. 'You have been arrested on suspicion of murder,' she was speaking like a child repeating a rhyme, 'and as such you will be held incommunicado. Do you know what that means?'

Doyle shook his head.

'That you are not allowed to make contact with anyone. No phone calls, texts, emails. Is that clear?'

Doyle nodded.

'Are you likely to self-harm?'

'Self-harm? I don't know. I don't think so.'

'Do you have a solicitor?'

'No.'

'Right. You'll be appointed one from the duty-solicitor scheme.'

Doyle didn't say anything. Then, after reviewing the information she had collected, she said, 'If you can place the contents of your pockets in here . . .' and indicated a square grey plastic tray. Doyle emptied his phone, wallet, change and keys into it.

'Thank you,' she said, and nodded to the policeman. Taking Doyle by the elbow, he guided him through a door that was to the left of the custody sergeant's counter. It led to a small corridor off which there were three more doors. Everywhere the walls were the same vivid blue. The policeman took him into a room where several box-like metal structures had been placed in a line on a shelf about three feet from the ground. He slid open the doors of one and told Doyle to press all four fingers firmly on a glass plate inside. There was then an almost imperceptible flash. He had to do the same with his thumb and then was told to stand by the wall and look directly at the camera. There was another flash, after which the policeman told him to come over to a stainless-steel trolley. There, Doyle was asked to open his mouth while the officer took a DNA swab. He scraped the end of what looked like a cotton bud across the inside of Doyle's cheek and placed it in an oblong plastic container, which he wrote on and left on the bottom tier of the trolley.

'Right. If you'd come with me, please,' he said, and walked into the corridor. He took a transparent plastic bag that contained something white from a cupboard and then held a door open for Doyle. It led to a small bare room. Both men stepped into it. 'Please remove all your clothes and put this on.'

Doyle looked at him. He was young, smaller than Doyle, stocky and impassive. 'Why do I have to do that?'

'(a) To make sure you're not concealing any contraband on your person, and (b) so your clothes can be examined by Forensics.'

As he was taking off his clothes he thought of Geoff's reaction when they asked him to do this. He folded each garment and dropped it on the floor, then stood and took what the policeman had removed from the bag. When he opened it he found it was a white paper boiler-suit. It had a hood and a zip that pulled up the front from the crotch. The policeman asked him to place his own clothes in the plastic bag and hand it to him. They then went back out into the corridor where the officer opened yet another door. This led to a wide corridor, its walls tiled in white. The floors were painted grey and it was lit with neon bulbs. Another policeman approached. He simply nodded at the one who had escorted Doyle so far, then Doyle heard the door behind him close. He was alone with this new man.

'Come with me, please,' he said, and walked down the neon-lit corridor. Doyle heard a shout from behind one of the many blue doors that lined it.

'Shut up, will you?' the man walking ahead of him shouted back. He then stopped outside a door that was open. 'Here,' he said. 'Home.' Doyle looked at him, expecting more information.

'Well, go on, you might have all day but I certainly don't.'

Doyle stepped in and the door closed behind him. The room was tiled in white, except the floor, which was painted the same grey as outside. In front of him, at about knee height, was a shelf with a blue plastic-covered mattress, about an inch thick, on it. To his left was a wall, and behind it a stainless-steel toilet without a seat.

Doyle walked to the mattress and sat. The whiteness was everywhere. After several minutes the door opened and the policeman who had escorted him to the cell asked him if he'd like tea.

Doyle said he would.

'Milk, sugar?'

'No sugar, just a touch of milk.'

The door closed again.

He felt unclad in his boiler-suit. He sat up in the corner putting his back against the tiles, and folded his arms. He shut his eyes and the image of her face appeared, eyes almost closed. Every detail of the bathroom was there, the blood, the blade, photographically perfect. He opened his eyes. The brightness of the neon hit him. A headache pierced the back of his skull. And, suddenly, he felt weak.

*

The door opened and the policeman entered, carrying a white plastic cup that he handed to Doyle, saying, 'There you go. Just a cloud of milk.'

Doyle stared at him. The policeman stared back, straightened and left the room, the door banging closed behind him. A cloud of milk – had he really said that? There was something wrong with this place: policemen don't talk in poetry to a man wearing a paper suit whose girlfriend lay dead in a bath miles away. But the walls around him were solid, bright and silent. They were part of a world he knew to exist. It was just that he had no business being there. And the dainty policeman with his clouded tea was a jester wearing words.

The lines of the Philip Larkin poem ran through his head, like a train from far away. It sounded more like a line from a rap song than something from a sixties poet. Was it true? Had his parents fucked him up? Had Daphne's fucked her up? Was that why she had raised the blade and made a hole through which her life had leaked away?

Doyle waited for the tea to cool and wondered when emotion would thunder into his head. All he felt was numbness. That, and the headache.

Maybe what had just happened was too large to be squeezed into a single mind between twelve fifteen on a Tuesday afternoon in spring and one thirty on the same day. Spread it out and maybe he'd have a chance to gather his wits and have a look at what had happened. Spread it out over, say, a couple of months. They'd be hard, those months, but he'd get an angle on it. It would overwhelm him now and then but at least he could hold some sort of perspective in view, most of the time anyway. But this, this sudden rush from life to death, from freedom to sitting in a room with grey floors and shiny tiles and a locked door, from Daph to no Daph, it amounted to wrongness.

And yet such things must happen all the time, the routine day-to-day running of catastrophe. A child comes in from harvesting crops to see his father beheaded, his mother burning and his sister being raped by men with uniforms and machine-guns. A barrel is pointed at him. How, at that moment, does he feel? The trigger is pulled. How does the gunman feel? There had to be chambers in the mind where the coping mechanisms for horror were kept. And chambers too where it was created.

He sat forward, parking his elbows on his knees, and Daphne's mother came to mind. Would they have told her? And what about her dad? He would react not unlike Geoff. Once out, the news would run like a disease through everyone who knew Daphne, everyone who knew him. The reaction would be disbelief, and when acceptance came, so too would grief. Her mother, Doyle thought, would be swamped by it. Theo, her father, would walk across its surface like a great angry Christ. Her sister would run wild from it. But who was he to say how all these people would react? And what of me? he thought. How do I react? Do I sit here losing myself in this mesh of analysis and daydreams? In the last hour and a half everything has changed for ever, and it has planted within me something big that I will now have to run through my system. The problem with running something this big through it is that it will change that system – turning it into what? A weakened, sadder version of what it had been before. That is what this will do to us all.

He passed the next half-hour beneath an unpleasant curtain of daydreams that drifted above him but never fell. When the door opened it was the cloud policeman, followed by a black man in a suit with a bulging, battered briefcase.

'Good afternoon,' the man said, putting down his case and extending his hand. 'Martin Midwinter. I'll be looking after you – legally speaking, that is.'

Doyle shook his hand. The man had clear eyes and a broad, confident smile.

Doyle introduced himself. The solicitor thanked the cloud man and then stood waiting for him to leave. When he had gone, the solicitor sat on the mattress and hauled the briefcase up beside him. He reached into it and pulled out several pieces of printed paper. 'Can I call you Desmond?' he said.

'You can but, apart from my mother, no one's ever called me that.'

'OK. What, then?'

'Doyle is fine.'

'Right, Doyle. Good. OK, well, first things first, may I ask how you are? They have you on a murder charge.'

'I murdered her?'

'Mr Doyle – sorry, Doyle – it sounds tough but what happened to you this afternoon is standard procedure in cases such as this. The police have to presume the worst and then work backwards. Do you follow? If they imagine that the slightest possibility exists that you two … There were two of you, right?' Again he searched the sheet of paper he was holding.

'Yeah. Geoff is my boss. We called in to find out if she wanted to come out to lunch.'

'And found her dead? Right. The police will presume the worst, hence your arrest and presence here. But you didn't answer my first question. Do you need a doctor, medical assistance, anything like that?'

'No, I'm fine.'

'You sure? You're on no medication, nothing like that?'

Doyle shook his head.

Midwinter smiled slowly. 'This must all seem very strange and confusing to you, Doyle, but we'll get it ironed out, I assure you.'

'How does it get ironed out?'

Midwinter looked up from the pages he was reading, about to smile, but didn't. What he saw was a man who knew nothing of the system he was now immersed in and had not the slightest idea how to deal with it. His question was a fair one, and it was also unanswerable. 'You'll be interviewed shortly and then most likely bailed.'

'I haven't any money.'

The solicitor looked at him.

'To pay a bail, I mean. I have no family to speak of. How…'

'What you're talking about is a surety. That's an entirely different thing. Bail just means that you'll have to report back here in a week or so. It's a way of letting you loose but on a rein, if you see what I mean. No money will change hands.'

'Oh.'

'If you fail to turn up they can arrest you.'

'They arrested me anyway.'

Midwinter looked again at his client. 'Look, Doyle, this has been an awful thing to happen to you. You're most probably in shock. But what we have to do now is to concentrate. I need to know what happened and how it happened. Once the circumstances are clear to everyone, it will be up to the custody sergeant to decide on bail and that is what we want. To get you out of here so you'll be able to begin to put this thing in perspective. Do you follow me so far?'

Doyle nodded. He couldn't speak because he was overcome with a sudden urge to cry. It was a snake winding through his guts. Oddly, the solicitor seemed ready for it. He produced a small packet of tissues. Doyle took it and held it tightly. He was frightened of what might happen if he allowed himself to cry. A whole volume of feelings would erupt with such force it would tear him apart. But as suddenly as the urge had appeared it left him. He blew his nose several times and then waited, staring at the grey floor, for Midwinter to continue.

'Can you tell me what happened?'

Doyle twisted his arms around his waist and crossed his legs. 'I went into the flat to get Daphne. Geoff had asked me to lunch to celebrate getting the loan for his restaurant. I wanted Daphne to come too. But when I got there she was in the bath. The water was red and she was pale and Geoff came in and called the police and now we're here.'

'So you came home and found Daphne in the bath?'

'Yeah.'

'This morning when you left, what time was it?'

'I don't know – a quarter past nine, something like that.'

'And she was alive.'

'She was asleep – or, at least, I think she was.'

'She was in bed?'

'Yeah.'

'And she didn't say anything to you, or you to her, this morning before you left?'

'I can't remember. I don't think so. She's not a morning person.'

'OK. Is there anything else I should know?'

'I don't know what you should know. I don't know what anybody should know. I don't know.'

'Are you OK?'

'Stop asking me if I'm OK. How can I be OK?'

Midwinter didn't reply. He looked at Doyle, then glanced about the room as if he was searching for a phrase he needed. He must have decided it was elsewhere. 'So, I'm going to tell the man outside that we're ready. When that happens we'll be taken to an interview room and when we're there it's important to listen. Remember, the onus is on them to prove whatever they suspect.'

'Suspect? But I didn't do anything.'

'So we'll go and listen to whatever they have to say. We don't have to say anything. If you get tired or confused just stay silent. Think before you speak – that is, if you want to speak at all. OK? Ready?'

Doyle shrugged.

Midwinter smiled. 'These guys are just doing their job. They have to make sure they know what happened. That's all. You'll be fine.'

Thirty minutes later they sat in a small room in front of a blue Formica-covered table that was rimmed with a thin strip of untreated pine. Deep holes had been gouged in the wood. Initials had been written in Biro and the word 'cunt' had been scraped with something blunt towards the corner. A black recording device sat on the end of the table propped up on a copy of the *Yellow Pages*.

Two men entered the room, one small, plump and in his mid-fifties, the other younger, thirties maybe. They both wore suits. The older one gave Midwinter a nod of acknowledgement as he sat down. 'Afternoon, gentlemen,' he said, then leant over and turned on the tape recorder. 'Time is fifteen twenty-one. In the room is the suspect, Desmond Doyle, his solicitor Mr Martin Midwinter, Sergeant Garry Streker and myself, Inspector Harry Kneebone.' He looked at his colleague, who had some scribbled notes on a piece of lined paper in front of him.

'Mr Midwinter,' the inspector continued, 'your client has been cautioned and has agreed that he understood the caution. As it now stands, he is a suspect in the murder of Ms Daphne Palmer with whom he shared the ground-floor flat at twenty-three Victoria Walk, Cotham. A phone call was made to the police at twelve twenty-seven this afternoon from a landline at that address, informing us that a girl was in the bath, the apparent victim of a suicide. On arriving at the premises at thirteen oh five, PC Coles and PC Williams confirmed this was indeed the case. The paramedics who arrived there several minutes later pronounced Ms Palmer to be dead.'

Midwinter had been studying his notes as the inspector was speaking. Now that the detective had stopped he nodded.

There was silence. It carried on for so long that Doyle wondered if they were not all waiting for him to speak. He stared at them but they seemed unburdened by it. Eventually the inspector raised a curled fist to his mouth, coughed into it and then said, 'Everything here, at first glance at least, appears straightforward. But,' he glanced at his colleague, 'take a closer look and certain oddities start to appear, things that imply other things, and those things need answering.' He directed himself back to Doyle now. 'You know what I mean?'

'If you have a question, please ask it,' Midwinter said, paying attention to the inspector now.

'There's a slight complication. Only slight, mind, but none the less it has little bells ringing in my head.'

Midwinter straightened in his chair.

'I'm no expert, Mr Doyle,' the inspector continued. 'In fact, the more I see, the more I realise that. And, of course, the coroner will do a full post-mortem later and we'll see then, but if you could give me some explanation of the bruising evident on your girlfriend's wrists and ankles.'

'You don't have to answer that,' Midwinter said, in a rush. 'Inspector, I'm calling an end to this interview. I should have had this information before now. I'll need to take further instruction from my client.'

The inspector regarded Midwinter for a moment. 'Is that strictly necessary, Mr Midwinter? We all want to get this thing sorted.'

'Then I suggest you change your tactics. This drip-feeding of information is unacceptable.'

Doyle, who had been staring at the section of the floor he could see between his thighs, looked up. 'It's OK,' he said to Midwinter.

There was a long silence.

The inspector broke it: 'Well, Mr Doyle?'

When Daphne first asked him to tie her to the bed he had used silk scarves and tied them loosely. Making love to her like that made him feel self-conscious and it also prohibited casual movement. This, to Doyle's mind, took a great deal of joy from it. When he told her so she said that when she was tied he could do what he liked with her – he could bite her or even slap her if he wanted. 'Treat me like a bitch,' she said, 'cos I am one.' A few nights later, after a bottle of wine and a joint, Daphne suggested that Doyle tie her face down and slap her bottom with his open palm.

The furrow of her back had caught the shadow. Her buttocks had risen in two perfect orbs, one mirroring the other. He ran his hand up her leg, over her thigh and then over the smoothness of them. She inhaled. Was she expecting it now, the slap? If so, how hard? Slowly he circled the orbs, allowing his fingers run down the crack between them burrowing into the heat that was gathering between her legs. Then quickly he raised his hand and slapped hard the buttock nearest to him.

Immediately regret rushed in to swamp him, followed by the urge to apologise, but her sigh of pleasure told him as clearly as a whispered instruction that he should do it again. He slapped her perhaps half a dozen times and then, to his astonishment, saw that her skin was reacting with a red glow. Instantly he tried to smooth it away and when his fingers slipped between her legs this time she lifted herself as far as she could to greet them.

'It was a game we played,' Doyle said.

'A game?'

'Yeah – you know, a sex game.'

'I see,' he said.

'It wasn't illegal.'

'Indeed,' the inspector said. 'And who instigated this game, Mr Doyle? You or her?'

'She did.'

The inspector nodded, as though that was the answer he had expected. 'So how rough did she like you to get?'

'I don't know – I mean, I've nothing to compare it with.'

'Did you ever draw blood in your sex games?' The question came from Kneebone's colleague, Streker. His tone was sharp.

'No – yes. Once.'

'Yes?'

'She asked me to whip her. I didn't like any of this.'

'Why did you do it, then?' the inspector asked.

'It was for her. You don't understand – Daphne was a bit weird when it came to sex. She'd, like, be all uninterested and distant and then when we started doing the pain thing she came alive. But I didn't like it. I didn't want to hurt her – I never wanted to hurt her.'

'You didn't like to hurt her?' Streker said, smiling.

'Mr Doyle, we're trying to establish how far these games went,' the inspector said.

'Well, we weren't in a bondage club or anything like that. I'd say they were pretty suburban, really.'

Now the inspector smiled. He looked first at his colleague and then at the solicitor. 'Well, I don't know about you, Mr Midwinter, but from my experience the suburbs are the place to go if it's weird and strange you want . . . but anyway,' he turned back to Doyle, 'in your opinion these games of yours were tame, and by that I mean non-life-threatening.'

'Yes, completely.'

'So when was the last time you played them?' Streker asked.

Doyle inhaled deeply. Last night they had been watching the ten o'clock news when Daphne, who had not uttered a word since Doyle had come in, said, 'I'm going to bed. I'll wait for you.' She left and he sat there for the next ten minutes, watching a man talk about the fear of inflation being the cause of it. He decided the time had come to tell Daphne he was not playing these games any longer.

When he got into the room she was lying on the bed wearing what she called her 'Barbie dress' – a scant piece of purple silk. She had tied her ankles to the two bottom bed posts. Her hands were gripping the rail at the top. Two short leather straps lay beside her. Doyle sat down and said that this had all become stupid. They never had normal sex any more: it always had to be a game where he was forced to make her suffer. And in the process he was the only one who actually suffered because it made him feel bad while she liked it.

'Tie my arms up, then stick your dick into my mouth and I'll make sure you like it too!'

And that was the problem, because even as she said it he could feel a little pod of pleasure burst within the head of his penis. Yes he would get excited and that excitement would mount to the point of ejaculation for them both but afterwards he'd lie there feeling alone, worse than alone, as though the whole process had alienated him further from her and what was troubling her. And this was the way it went again last night. At one point he got so angry that he rammed his penis into her from behind while pulling her head backwards with her hair. This drove her wild.

'Last night.'

'Was it a particularly energetic session?' Streker asked.

'You don't have to answer that,' Midwinter said.

'Those marks you mentioned might have come from it,' Doyle said, 'but, really, they're more likely to be an accumulation.'

'How lovely,' Streker said. This brought a brief, diminishing glance from his superior.

'Well, as I say, we'll have the coroner's report after the post-mortem and we'll see then,' Kneebone said.

'I don't understand,' Doyle said. 'We'll see what then?'

'The coroner's report, Mr Doyle, is a document that will tell us in great and graphic detail how every scar on your girlfriend's body got there and how much it had, or had not, to do with her death.'

'You think I killed her?'

'I don't think, Mr Doyle. I compile information and from that I make assessments, and at this particular stage of this particular incident I am still compiling.'

'Your friend seems very agitated. Why would that be?' Streker asked.

'Again, you don't have to answer that,' Midwinter interjected.

'I don't mind answering,' Doyle said to Midwinter, then to Streker, 'He's trying to open a restaurant. He invited me to lunch today to celebrate getting the loan for the premises and I suggested we go and get Daph. Because of that he finds himself locked up here when he's suppose to be signing papers. Of course he's angry.'

'And you're not?'

Doyle felt cold to the bone. He folded his arms about himself, leant forward and stared down at the table top.

A long silence followed. Doyle was aware only of the inspector's breathing. He exhaled in long, almost soundless rasps. Doyle wished simply that he could go to sleep. Surely, whatever else, he could do that. They couldn't stop him sleeping?

'By the way,' the inspector said, breaking the rhythm of his rasp, 'you didn't happen to come across a note, did you?'

'A note?'

'A suicide note?'

'No. Should there be one? I mean, is there usually?'

'Yes, in the case of suicide,' the inspector said. 'So, no note, and bruises about the wrists and ankles.'

Doyle looked at him.

'How would you carry a body, Mr Doyle?' This was Streker again.

'I beg your pardon?'

'Don't answer that,' Midwinter said to Doyle, then to Streker, 'Your insinuation is a deliberate attempt to confuse and/or anger my client. Cheap tactics, Sergeant.'

Streker turned to the solicitor. 'Oh, are they? Well, for your information I'm not making an insinuation. I'm making an accusation. It would take two strong men to carry Ms Palmer's dead weight. One holding her around the wrists, the other holding her around the ankles. Such action as to cause bruising. Is that what happened, Mr Doyle? You and your accomplice did that?'

'I advise you not to answer,' Midwinter said.

Doyle didn't say anything because there was nothing he could think of to say.

'What I would like you to do, Mr Doyle,' the inspector said, 'is to tell us not only what happened this afternoon but what you think led up to it.'

'I don't know why Daphne would kill herself. She had no reason to do that. I can't believe she did that.'

'The only thing we can be certain of here, Mr Doyle, is that Daphne Palmer is dead. That we do know.'

'Well, then, I don't know anything.'

'You mean you're refusing to co-operate?'

'Inspector, please!' Midwinter said.

'I'm only surmising here, Mr Midwinter.'

'My client is under a great deal of stress and I think you'll agree that under the circumstances he is being more than co-operative.'

'I opened the door to the flat and called her.'

'Why did you think she'd be in? It was the middle of the day,' Streker said.

'Daphne had been looking for work. She's an actress. That's why we moved to Bristol. She thought it would be easier here. It's not.'

'Go on.'

Doyle rested his forehead in the open palm of his hand and stared at the faint repeating pattern in the blue Formica. He tried, at several points, to begin speaking but the air leaked out of him before his tongue could catch it and turn it into the words he wanted. The result was a series of long exhalations that must have sounded like sighs. He was also aware that he was beginning to shake and tears were falling onto the table.

'I'll tell you what. Let's break for now. Interview temporarily suspended at fifteen forty-seven,' the inspector said, clicking the button of the tape machine.

By the time bail was granted it was past eight o'clock in the evening. Doyle and Geoff were taken in a police car to Geoff's flat. Geoff had been uncharacteristically quiet in the car and now in the flat he walked about turning on electrical equipment. Doyle took a seat in the living room by a pine table and stared at the paintings on the wall. They were all originals, the paint thick, bright and shining. They looked tropical. Eventually Geoff came in and put a mug of coffee beside him.

'Where did you get the artwork?' Doyle asked.

'Do you want anything to eat? What?'

'I was just wondering where you got the pictures.'

'The Caribbean, mostly.'

'I thought it was tropical.'

Geoff looked at him, then back at the paintings, then at his coffee.

'I went to art college in Camberwell, London,' Doyle said.

'You're taking all this a bit calmly, aren't you?'

'Am I?'

Geoff circled the table. Doyle sat tapping its surface with his fingers. 'Look, Doyle, I'm sorry, I really am. I'm sorry for what's happened and I'm sorry if I'm behaving inappropriately. I don't function well in conditions like these.'

'You're OK, Geoff.'

Geoff sat down and stared at him.

'What?' Doyle asked.

Geoff looked away.

'I don't know why she did it, if that's what you want to know,' Doyle said.

'I don't want to pry.'

'Pry away, you've every right.'

Geoff sighed and put his head in his hands. 'Holy fuck!' he muttered.

'That about sums it up,' Doyle said.

Three

Doyle lies in darkness. He has a headache. His heart has been pumping molten lead through his body and it is sore from the effort. Something is falling through the air above him. As he waits for it to land on him, he tries to turn himself into a platform, something shockproof to absorb the weight and the momentum. Here it comes. It is Daphne, as bloodless as a bicycle, dead as doornails, a penny-farthing for your forethoughts, my dearest, a dicky-bow for your daydreams. Is your body laid out now on a bench with the makeup boys putting colour to your pale face? Will they give you a smile? Will they cross your hands above your breasts? Will they sew up the holes you made in your arms? Honestly, the trust we place in total strangers when we surrender our corpses for our last appearance! And what will they dress you in, my pretty? Have they gone through your wardrobe already? Hope they pick something nice, not too revealing, something dark – it must be dark: what about the top you got for Aunt Alice's funeral? It's wine, but sombre. They'll know. Experts. Must be by now.

Doyle looks at the ceiling and knows no bicycles will crash through it. He will lie here hauling in and out of focus unfamiliar cracks and let thoughts descend on him, like a slow invasion of parachutes. Where does Geoff keep his toilet? As Doyle steps onto the carpet the knowledge of its whereabouts comes to him. Up a narrow staircase – watch for cats – and the light is operated by a soiled cord that dangles by the door. He looks at the bath. It is white, showing a line of faint grey a little more than three-quarters up its sides.

When he lies down again on the sofa-bed it dawns on him that, of all household furnishings, a bath has the most coffin-like characteristics. Could she be buried in it? Taps and all? Or could she be sent out to sea in it to be rinsed by the wash, turned into seaweed on your first anniversary so you can come ashore and let the sun dry you, the children's bare feet crackle you and the rain, finally, disperse you?

You never wrote a note, Daph. Maybe, lying there, you said to yourself, 'Well, I've fucked this up, can't write a suicide note with my wrists open.' You could have held the paper above your head so it remained unsullied. But then the blood would have run down your arms, got into your hair, your eyes. And even if you avoided that you'd have had to deal with the problem of ballpoints not working when they're upside-down. No, you'll think, I'll just lie here regretting the missed chance to make one last unanswerable remark. It would have been unanswerable, Daphne, except that after I die I'm going into the first bar I find just beyond the Pearly Gates and I'll say to the barman, 'Does a chick called Daphne drink in here? And he'll say, 'No, not any more. I had to ask her to leave three weeks ago and it wasn't the first time. Suicides, I tell you, bad news ...' 'Right,' I'll answer, 'any idea where I might find her?' 'Try the Harbour Bar. That's where most of them hang out. Turn left at Tesco – you can't miss it.'

Doyle turned into the pillow to let his tears soak into it. He felt heavy now – the bicycle had landed: it was grief. It was a good word for it. All the best words had just one syllable that started hard and finished soft. 'Dance' was one. And 'bruise'. And 'cough'. But think all night long if you like, my dear boy. The bicycle has landed, and it bypassed any platform you prepared for it and is now well and truly embedded.

Doyle sat up. What if his thoughts became bigger than his ability to handle them? 'Engulf' was now the word, engulfed in grief, swept into madness on a big warm wind and dispatched to a home to be dealt with by experts. Men and women who deal with the engulfed.

He thought of calling up to Geoff. But what could he say? There was a bicycle in him and he was well on his way to the wrong side of sanity? Geoff could tackle a fleet of bank managers and cook delicacies so delicious they'd be photographed as well as eaten, but he would run a mile from madness. Any sign of it and he would panic, run to the phone and call out into his motherless world for a sanctuary that no longer existed. Doyle would end up comforting him. No, leave the sleeping Geoff to lie, and wait until dawn comes to fade these ghosts.

Morning's entrance into Geoff's living room is delicate. It starts behind the curtains and spreads along the walls. Slowly, very slowly, objects begin to reclaim their colour and shadows begin to form, then to tighten. In the gathering light Doyle feels a gentle slush of fatigue run through him. His eyes are hot and heavy and his heart is thumping in a hollow it burnt for itself in his chest. Messages are running up and down his body, telling anything that will listen to close down. Everything will have to attend to itself because, for now, we're closing shop.

What he becomes aware of next is Geoff's voice. He is talking upstairs on the phone. The words are not clear but the tone is impatient and frustrated. Doyle imagines the reaction of the bank manager or supplier or whoever is at the other end. Geoff is up there now avoiding the truth. He may not want to advertise that he is out on bail on suspicion of murder, while trying to open a restaurant.

Later Doyle hears plates crashing and then Geoff walking into his living room and coming over to look down at the crumpled form on the sofa-bed. When Geoff sees that Doyle is awake he asks how he is, how he slept.

Doyle finds that, although his mind is doing laps around the inside of his skull, the rest of him is sluggish. Speech is difficult. What comes out of his throat is unrecognisable.

Geoff asks if he would like tea. The response ought to be simple but it is not. Doyle gives up and Geoff leaves the room. A few minutes later he is back with a green flared mug that he puts down by Doyle's head. The 'thanks' that comes out of Doyle is effortless. Perhaps that's the trick: don't think about what you want to say, let it run up and out of you, like water from the ground.

Geoff takes a seat by the table, still covered with the empty and half-empty bottles and glasses from last night. He turns to Doyle. Doyle stares back. Geoff says, 'Look, I have to go out. Will you be all right?'

Doyle sits up. A blister pack of pills is beside the mug. 'I've left you those,' Geoff said. 'My sister gave them to me because, believe it or not, I have a fear of flying. They're tranquillisers – just if you feel you want them.'

'Thanks,' Doyle says.

'You look awful.'

'Thanks,' he says again.

Geoff smiles briefly. 'Anyway, I'm out of here. If you need me just call. I'm busy today but that doesn't matter. Anything at all, anything. There's plenty of food in the kitchen, and there's milk in the fridge.'

'What are they?'

'The pills? Valium. Fives, I think. Nothing mind-blowing.'

Soon after Geoff had gone, Doyle got up and put the sofa-bed away. The day was now bright and the branches outside the window were beginning to unfold their parcels of green. He noticed Geoff had lots of books. In fact, he had lots of everything. Columns of DVDs, CDs, even albums. It was a short walk to the kitchen where the shelves of the cupboards were also crammed. The walls were busy, with spice racks, frying-pans and pots hanging from a frame by the back door and, again, there were books, all on cookery.

A cat crouched beside its empty bowl and gazed at him from the floor. Did it need to be fed? Maybe Geoff had forgotten. Should he? Where would he look for its food? Leave it.

The cat must have read his mind. In one movement it was up and out through the cat-flap, leaving behind it the sound of a dull plastic slap.

Doyle didn't know what he was looking for. Tea, coffee, breakfast? None of those. Biscuits, something sweet. He found raisins in a cellophane bag and brought them back to the sofa. They were too sweet, and their grittiness made him mistrust them. They might be ancient. He placed them beside his untouched tea, then picked up the pills. Two would do. He swallowed them with the tea and lay back on the couch. The sun was hot, uncomfortable on his face. If waves had been splashing on a shore, he would have enjoyed it – it would have been bliss – but he felt instead as though someone was holding an electric fire over his face. No – no thoughts like that. Stay on the beach. Lying on a beach or lying on a mattress in a prison cell, what's the difference? Your surroundings, that's all. They confirm where you are, and from them you extract sensations, pleasant, unpleasant. So there is a man holding an electric fire to my face. He wants to bubble and boil the skin off me, or I am lying on a beach in … where? Somewhere nice, somewhere that begins with B, all the best places begin with B – Barbados, Bermuda, Barbollocks. The sensation is the same: skin remover or beach bask?

But, no, I am lying on a friend's sofa-bed because my own home has been sealed off with white and blue striped tape printed with the word 'Police'. And no one comes or goes save the men and women in paper suits with blue-covered feet because they can unearth what happened there. Experts, bless them. No, they're sitting drinking tea, the telly on and a game of poker on the go. I'll see your triple vodka with a glum prediction of my own. Keep the sewers for the sinners, not a Saxon to be seen, and only dogs for dinner in that caff on College Green.

Doyle was woken by the phone. It was in his pocket and it vibrated before emitting a sound. It was Inspector Kneebone. He was curt and to the point. 'Where are you?' he asked. When Doyle told him, he wanted to know if Geoff was with him.

'No, he's out.'

'I see. Well, I'll call around in any case, if that's all right with you.'

Doyle looked at his watch: half past twelve. 'Right.'

He found it difficult to shake the grogginess, as though his mind was trapped in that moment of awakening. It was easy just to sit there and drift in soft, complicated daydreams. Perhaps two of Geoff's sister's pills had been one too many. And although the doorbell startled him, nothing else about the inspector's visit caused Doyle to fluster. The detective stood in the hallway between the living room and the kitchen and Doyle asked if he would like tea. Moments later he had forgotten if the man had said yes or no.

'Do you mind if I step inside and take a seat?'

'Fine. Sorry, I'm not a hundred per cent here today. Did you say you would like tea or not?'

'Don't worry about the tea.'

The inspector swept into the room and sat in the chair Geoff had occupied earlier. Doyle returned to the sofa-bed.

'Well, I just thought I'd tell you in person that you're free to go back to your flat.'

Doyle thought about this for a moment. 'Is she still there?'

'Your girlfriend?'

'Yes.'

'No, no. Lord above!'

'Where is she?'

'In the morgue. The coroner will be doing his preliminary report soon.'

'What does that mean?'

'It means that in the next few days I'll be receiving a report that will state his initial findings. Soon after that, if there are no complications, the body will be released to the family so that they can go ahead and make arrangements for the funeral.'

'They know about all this already?'

'Oh, they do.'

Doyle no longer wanted the chemical calm that he felt was stopping him getting access to what things meant. The words the inspector had spoken had meaning and context that were unavailable to him. He felt he was floating on oil, not knowing if he should be swimming.

Into the silence the inspector asked, 'Are you all right?'

Doyle wondered how he could answer that question. The thought struck him that the most common questions had to be the most stupid. 'What should I do now?'

The inspector scratched his chin and looked at him. 'Well, now, that's a question, isn't it? Her family live in Dartmouth, don't they? Perhaps you and your friend, Mr McAllister, should go down there and spend some time with them.'

'Geoff doesn't know them.'

'Well, you, then. Anyway, it's a bit too early for you two to be getting out the champagne.'

'What do you mean?'

The inspector stood. 'I'll see myself out.'

Doyle listened to the door downstairs slam, and then a car drive off. He felt as if his stomach had filled with a liquid that was foreign to it. He imagined it to be dark and pink. The vision was accompanied by the sound of droplets echoing. He needed, he thought, to eat, and wondered how he could organise that. Although the effect of the pills was weakening, his muscles were still too relaxed for him to press them into service.

He made tea, which he drank on the couch. He was snoozing when Geoff got back some time during the afternoon. When he woke again Doyle was glad to find that the mechanics of his mind seemed to be working. Feelings were sharper now, fears loomed, and his heart was beating in the hollow it had created for itself earlier.

Geoff saw that two of the pills were gone and told Doyle what he now knew: two was too many. Then he made an omelette, with bacon, mushroom and blue cheese. He brought it to the table still in the pan and cut it like a cake. He urged Doyle to eat a slice and then another.

It was only after the first that Doyle remembered the inspector's visit. 'He said that the coroner will have to make a report before they can release the body for the funeral.'

'I should fucking sue those bastards.'

'He said something I didn't quite get about it being too early for us to celebrate.'

'What did he mean?'

'I don't know. That he thinks we killed her?'

Geoff looked at Doyle. 'I'll sue their fucking arses.'

Doyle was suddenly full of omelette. He put his knife and fork down. I can't go on, he thought. I can't do this – this conversation, this business. Perhaps when I leave here I'll get a bus to Scotland, then another to a town I've never heard of and then I'll change my name and get a job.

'I'm sorry. It's like Daphne just did this thing and now the world's unhinged. Then just to add to it you get some creepy-crawly fucking copper making his way up your arse with the intention of camping there. Well, he can fuck off. I will sue, you know.'

Geoff had lost interest in the omelette too. It sat in the pan between them. Geoff eventually stood and lifted it from the table. 'Look, I'm sorry but that little fucker makes me so mad.'

'Geoff, getting mad at a copper is going to help no one.'

'Getting mad is the only option some people leave you.'

'He said I could go back to the flat.'

'Did he?'

'Yeah. They've finished there now.'

'Right. Well, do you want to go? I mean, are you ready?'

Doyle shrugged. The thought of going there seemed as impossible as stepping through a brick wall.

'I'll give you a lift.'

'Just like yesterday?'

'What?'

'You gave me a lift there yesterday too.'

'Jesus, was that only yesterday?' From the kitchen Geoff called, 'Only go if you want to.'

Doyle hadn't moved from the table. He didn't want to go to his flat. He didn't want to be here either. The pictures on the wall had begun to comment on him. His fingernails were dirty and he wanted a bath. A bath! He wasn't going to have a bath. Not here, not there. The mind should provide an envelope for itself to crawl into for times like these. That's what drugs are for ... No, fuck this, I have to go back there. If there's no refuge to be had here or there I may as well be there. It has the advantage of being the place where I live.

'I'll come in with you,' Geoff said, when they had parked as close as they could get to Doyle's flat.

'You know there's a bird called a chiff-chaff?' Doyle said.

'Yes?'

'That should be your name.'

'I'll come in with you.'

'No! No, I'll go by myself. I have my phone so I'll call you if I need to.'

'Doyle, listen to me, you've had a shock. It might not be a good idea to be alone right now.'

'You think I'll have a bath, don't you?'

'Sorry?'

'You think I'll have a bath, bring a razor . . .'

'Will you fucking shut up!'

There was silence in the car. Then Geoff said, 'I'm as freaked out about this as you are. It's all intensely disturbing and I don't like it. But I was born in this city and I've got friends that go way back. You're on your own. I'm worried about you. Not that you'll do what Daphne did. I just want you to be OK – OK?'

'I'm not going to kill myself.'

Geoff smiled. 'Glad to fucking hear it.'

The front door yielded easily to his key and closed with a quiet click behind him. There was an untidy heap of post gathered on the floor by the far wall. Fresh letters were thrown onto it every day by whichever of the flat-dwellers was first in after the delivery. There were two for D. Palmer: one was from a credit-card company, the other from the Bristol Old Vic. There were two for him as well: a mobile-phone bill and a catalogue from a shoe company.

He heard a door open upstairs and footsteps move quickly. He did not want to be caught here. But he would not have time to make it to his door now. So he studied the envelopes. The footsteps descended, then slowed. Doyle turned. It was the girl from upstairs. Daphne had known her name. She was small with blonde hair. Doyle had often heard her laugh in the hall late at night. She stood there, two steps up, looking at him.

'Hi,' she said. She was pretty. Had a round face and brown eyes and lips that were small and fat at the same time. 'I'm awfully sorry about what happened. We all were.'

Is this uncomfortable for her? Doyle wondered. Perhaps not. Perhaps he had now become an object of intrigue to her. Don't think like that. Don't think at all, he told himself. 'Thanks,' he said.

'If there's anything I can do. Anything at all.'

'Actually—' The word came from him without his consent.

'Yes?'

His inside began to vibrate – the forerunner of tears, or anguish, or some kind of emotional eruption. He took a breath. 'I was just wondering . . .' Doyle noticed how big her breasts were.

'You don't want to go in on your own?'

'Just in the door – I'll be fine after that.'

'OK,' she said. 'Shall I go first?'

'No, I'll go in, if you could stay around – just for a minute. Sorry.'

'Don't be, please.'

Holding the letters, Doyle crossed the corridor and opened his door. The view it gave was of the living room. It was dark because the curtains were drawn. He walked across the floor and opened them, then turned. She was standing in the entrance, looking at him. 'OK?' she asked.

'Yes, thank you. Look, just one more thing.' He went to the corridor that led to the bedroom and the bathroom. 'I won't be a second.' He looked into the bedroom. Again, it was dark but he did not open the curtains. The duvet was askew, its tail end trailing on the floor. The wardrobe was open. He went then to the bathroom and flicked on the light. The sound of the extractor fan came on with it. The bath was gleaming – everything was clean. He went back to the living room. She had taken several steps into the room. 'Thanks very much. I won't bother you again.'

'It's OK, honest. I'm just upstairs if you need anything. Remember that. Anything at all.'

'You're very kind. What's your name? Daph was good with names but I'm terrible.'

'Jasmine,' she said.

'Thanks again.'

'Really, it's OK. I work shifts so I'm around at different times. If you hear me upstairs you can always come up. It doesn't matter what time.' She paused. 'I lost my brother when I was young. I know what it's like.'

For some reason he found this comment irritating. He gave her a weak smile and told her again that she was kind. Then she left.

He looked at the letters in his hand. What would dead people want with credit? Maybe there was a scam in this. If he applied in Daphne's name, spent to the limit, then told them she was dead . . . Stupid. The date would be on the death certificate. Capital One, whoever they were, would figure it out. Is this what widowers do, stand in their silent homes thinking of ways to rip off credit-card companies with the corpses of their betrothed?

And am I a widower now, officially? Can't be – got to have been married first. Perhaps I should apply for the pension anyway. When I get refused I can take the government to Strasbourg, the Court of Human Rights.

He put the letters down and went into the kitchen. There he found the charger for his phone and plugged it in. Even before the feed of electricity pumped life back into it he noticed the light flashing on the answer-machine of the landline. There were thirteen messages. Fitting, Doyle thought. The first was from Daphne's mother, Margaret. Her voice came through the speaker as if from the darkness of a cave. She had had a visit from the local police and now she wanted to talk with him. She began to cry and the phone went dead. The next was from Daphne's father. He was subdued. From behind him Doyle's mobile phone vibrated on the counter top. He looked at the screen – eight text messages and eleven voice.

He skipped through the voices on the landline. They were all from Daphne's family and all began as though a sudden silence had robbed the caller of what they'd thought they wanted to say. When Doyle checked the message Daphne's voice bounced into the room: 'Hi, you're through to Daphne and Doyle, leave a message.' It was her voiceover voice and it was followed by a little laugh.

He played it again and again, until he wasn't listening to the words any more, just the tone and the specifics that had made it hers. He was startled when it was interrupted by the phone ringing.

'Where have you been? I've been trying everywhere to get you.' It was Ruth, Daphne's sister.

'I stayed at a friend's flat last night.'

'Doyle, you have a mobile. You didn't think to call me?'

'We were questioned by the police. I've just got back now.'

'Look, this is important. I've invited people here for tomorrow night. You've got to come. It's for Mum and Dad . . . for Daphne, a celebration.' She spoke in a flat voice. 'Seven thirty at Mum and Dad's.'

Doyle was silent. He saw the interior of the family living room: the piano, the stale air and the stale colours.

'You'll be there?' Ruth asked.

'Yes.'

'Will you get the train?'

'I don't know.'

'I can pick you up from Totnes.'

'I'll let you know.' He unplugged the phone at the socket, turned his mobile off, then walked to the table and sat. The second letter was from the Old Vic. He looked at the postmark on the letter from the Old Vic, then at the date on his watch. It had been posted three days ago. He opened it – a handwritten note.

> *Hi, Daphne*
>
> *Just thought I'd let you know that we'll be auditioning for the part of Portia in 'The Merchant of Venice' on the 16th and 17th. Nic and I have discussed it and we'd both really like you to try for it. It'll be a modern-day production, a lot of rap, graffiti and oodles of sex – something to get the punters in. Give me a call.*
>
> *S. X*

A lot of rap, graffiti and oodles of sex – had he just been given the secret of theatrical success? It was fitting that the one Shakespearian play they thought might suit Daphne involved cutting flesh with knives.

Doyle went into the bathroom, lifted the lid on the toilet and began to urinate. As he did so, he looked at the bath. Long, yellow and empty. Where had it all gone – her, her blood, the water, the stains and the scum? When he flushed the toilet he sat on the side of the bath, dropped the plug into the hole and turned on the hot tap. Out the water tumbled, cold at first but soon steam rose from it. He turned on the cold tap and let the urgency fuse in a battle of bubbles. When it was ready he removed his clothes. Then, ignoring the warnings from his toes, he eased himself into the heat. His head rested where hers had, his arms lay loose as hers had done, and his feet took up the position he had remembered hers had taken.

It's warm in here, Daphne – hot, actually. Do you mind? I need to feel you again and this is as near as I can get. Do you remember the day on the cliff walk? You were wearing the skirt with the dots – it opened like a parachute when the wind got under it. And the waves, Daphne, do you remember the waves? They crashed on the rust-red rocks below us and above the seagulls crackled and you said we should be otters. Do you remember that? I said, yes, we could be, having no idea what you meant. But you smiled your white smile and said we'd have to find somewhere grassy to lie down, and you climbed on ahead and I watched your thighs and the pearl of your crotch and I wanted so much to lick you there. And when you reached the top you stood and looked out over the bay, all grey and green with merchant vessels at anchor, waiting to come in, and I put my hand on you. I raised your skirt and you stood still. I rolled your knickers down your thighs, as though they were Plasticine. You held onto my arm to balance as you took them off and then we just stood there, looking out at the city of silhouettes, knowing it would be mad with fuckers rushing around chasing coin, and we stood there silent in motionless foreplay. And when I did touch you, you burnt. You clasped a rock with your hands and I pumped you from behind and you were shouting, 'Yes,' and 'Yes,' and I thought my heart would burst, and you sank to your knees and I after you. Then we rolled over and your face was hanging in the air above mine, you biting your lip and staring at me, then your eyes closing like you were in pain, and I wanted to laugh and say that, yes, this was easy, that, yes, we were otters, and you moving above me and seagulls moving above you. And then you got off me and said you wanted to see me come so you wrapped your fingers around me and you pumped me till I flooded up and out into the air. You watched the arc of it land on your hand. You wiping it on your skirt as you looked up at me to see if I saw. Do you remember?

Four

When Geoff got back to his flat he had trouble finding a parking space. This was not unusual but it angered him. Cleaning up Doyle's debris angered him too. His stupid fucking girlfriend had complicated life beyond belief. He had missed the meeting with the bank yesterday. His solicitor – who was meant to be with him – had had to divert to the police station. It had made Geoff look unreliable and unprofessional. His excuses on the phone that morning had sounded feeble, even to himself.

He knew Daphne's death would have many different connotations for many different people. But it had already shown a tremendous capacity to disrupt. It was a hurricane, except it would not move on, and defied prediction as to the damage it would do. Her death gave her a prominence she had craved in life; it enabled her to touch people beyond her reach. It was an act of egomania. No wonder suicide was illegal.

He had intended offering Doyle the job of restaurant manager over lunch. When Doyle suggested they stop and get Daphne, Geoff had been inclined to dissuade him. The business of the notes still lingered. But on second thoughts this might have been the perfect opportunity to bury that. The restaurant was going to make all of their lives better. Her sharing in this moment of triumph would show her that. Christ almighty, talk about the best-laid plans!

Perceived wisdom would suggest that Doyle was not restaurant-management material. But Geoff had been happy to ignore that. Despite the fact that it could not now happen he still wanted to keep Doyle involved, perhaps something peripheral but not utterly mindless. Doyle needed something to do right now – on top of which he had no income.

He had first come across Doyle out the back at Nuts 'n' Stuff. Geoff had gone out to sort the cardboard mountain that grew every week with the deliveries. It had been raining so the mountain sagged and folded over itself in a pile that Geoff knew would separate at the first touch and be crawling with worms. Geoff did not like worms. It was then he noticed a dark-haired man with a long and very pale face leaning over the wall, looking at him.

'Can I help you?' Geoff asked.

His question seemed to startle the man. 'Well, actually, I was wondering if you needed any workers. I've just arrived in Bristol. I need a job.'

There was something about this lanky screed of a human that intrigued Geoff. 'What kind of a job?'

'Anything, really. I did display work for shops in London, hat shops. But I'd do anything. I just moved here.'

'Display work?'

'Yeah, I made heads out of papier-mâché. They'd display their hats on them, you know, instead of mannequins.'

'I don't sell hats.'

'OK.'

'But I could use a general dogsbody.'

'I'm not fussy about the rank.'

'What?'

'General, general dogsbody ...'

Geoff studied the face again. The skin was porcelain, the eyes were deep brown. There was no hint of humour anywhere. 'OK, but if you ever get to deal with customers avoid the humour.'

'So I'm hired?'

'You are. You can start by cleaning this mess up. It's a recurring problem so if you can organise someone to pick it up weekly it would be better.'

'Sure, I'll look in the *Yellow Pages*.'

'You can look wherever you like,' Geoff said, and left him to it. The man hadn't mentioned money. Geoff thought that strange.

At the end of the first week Geoff handed him three hundred pounds in cash. He had worked for three days. He said thanks and put it into his pocket. He didn't even count it. He had arranged for a skip to be delivered and replaced every week so now the back yard should be clear of clutter. Despite his abstracted air Doyle was efficient, and the regulars seemed to like him. He could cut, wrap and package with surprising speed and yet there was always that distance.

Geoff had other staff. Sheila was the store manager, but she was part-time. Karen and Pat both worked the till, dividing the hours between them. He found himself relying more and more on the constancy of Doyle's presence. He was there for deliveries, he could chase up missing items, he'd stock-take when things were quiet and he enjoyed setting up displays, some of which were excellent. But Geoff knew better than to begin to depend on him. He viewed him much as one would a piece of rented equipment, knowing that the situation between them would exist only as long as it was of benefit to both.

But four weeks later, when Doyle was still there, Geoff found himself including him in projected plans, such as they were. The day-to-day running of the shop now bored him; the routines it demanded were dull. He had set it up and it was doing well, but now he wanted a new challenge.

He first heard of the restaurant through a friend of his mother, a woman called Marjorie. She was frequently there when Geoff dropped in to the flat in Hotwells. He thought it was a good thing: if his mother had a friend she'd be less dependent on him. Marjorie was saying that her son had finally got a job in a restaurant but – and wasn't it just his luck? – no sooner had he started than the owners were talking about putting it up for sale. 'And it's a gorgeous little place. It's just that it never makes any money.'

Those words had intrigued Geoff. He got the address and, two days later, drove down Picton Street to have a look. Straight away he could see why it was struggling. There was nothing on the front of the building to announce it to the casual stroller, and the entrance was shabby. What it needed was a proper swinging sign over the pavement and an inviting doorway. Downstairs it was clean and friendly. The menu was limited but what it offered was good, solid Italian fare. On a busier street, at ground level, it would be a gold mine. The challenge here would be to get people to come to a place that was off the beaten track and whose interior was not visible from the street. Again, conventional wisdom would have said no, but there was something about the place that Geoff liked. With a change of menu and décor, he might be able to entice people down here. And he was sure that if they came once, he could persuade them to return.

It was owned by two Italian brothers. One, the motivator Geoff suspected, had suffered a mild stroke and since then the place had been running on empty. Even though it had not yet been put on the market he made an offer. Two days later he got a phone call to say the offer was, in principle, accepted. Two weeks later the bank approved his business plan and that was the day he had asked Doyle to lunch, the same day that Doyle's girlfriend had decided to fuck everything up by killing herself.

Geoff was confident that he could turn the restaurant into one of those places that people would 'discover', and once they had, they'd treat it as their own personal refuge. With Doyle's friendly but abstract air, the place would feel understated and non-threatening, an atmosphere that would belie the professionalism and efficiency that Geoff would ensure came from the kitchen. It would be a delicate balance but, between him and Doyle, it would be a winner.

But now Daphne had taken Doyle out of the picture.

It could still happen. It *would* happen. It was just that a fundamental part of the chemistry had changed so other things would have to change as well.

Five

The strap of Doyle's overnight bag dangled above him. Ruth had said seven thirty and the train he was on would arrive in Totnes at five thirty-seven. Ruth had said she'd pick him up, which would give him nearly two hours with her.

It was raining when he stepped onto the long, narrow platform. He caught sight of her at the far end. She was alone, standing with her arms folded, staring straight ahead. As he walked towards her he told himself again that it was not his fault. No matter what anyone said, Daphne had done this on her own. He had lived with her but he had not created her mental state and he was not responsible for it. He told himself this yet, even for him, it was a paper flag blowing in a storm. He knew, as he closed the distance between himself and Ruth, that everyone would have their own version of the event and that he, most probably, would play a role in all of them.

Tears were streaming from her eyes, and her mouth was twisted into a downward smile. He put down his bag and wrapped his arms around her. She buried her head in his shoulder, and as he held her, he felt her body heave. When they separated she took his hands. 'I'm sorry, I didn't want to ...'

'It's OK.'

She shook her head. 'No,' she said, 'that's the one thing it's not.' Then she looked up at him. 'Thanks for coming, though. Mum and Dad so want to see you.'

Looking into her eyes, he was struck by how much like Daphne's they were. It robbed him of what he had been going to say. He just wanted to gaze into them. She was not Daphne, nothing like her, but if he focused on the eyes she might have been.

'Come on,' she said. 'The car's outside.'

It was a large, dark blue jeep with the words 'Dartmouth Yacht Charter Co' written small and in white along the side. The interior was tan and spotless.

'How are you?' she said, turning the key.

'Ruth, I haven't got a clue.'

'Yeah,' she said.

They drove through the evening traffic in a complicated silence. Ruth wanted to extract all the information she knew Doyle must have that might explain why her sister had killed herself. That would be the simple and reasonable object of a conversation with him, but getting information out of Doyle was like trying to catch fish with your hands.

Doyle peered into the cars ahead and envied the occupants their normality and destinations. He wanted to be heading home to a two-up, two-down back-to-back with nothing more pressing on his mind than whether to go to the pub or stay in and watch television. He wondered then if life was ever that simple for anyone.

The road was familiar to him from previous visits. He had been to Dartmouth four or five times over the years with Daphne, but although it was a pretty town, he had never felt comfortable there. He did not get on with Theo, her father, a tall, powerful man who always spoke as though he was reading a telegram. At first Theo had been keen to introduce Doyle at the golf and yacht clubs. Doyle had accompanied him on one outing and ended up standing for two hours listening to men who had decorated the same conversation so many times that words were hardly needed. When Doyle's reluctance to join Theo again became clear, the older man had dropped him.

Between Theo and his wife, Margaret, there was a persistent tension that deteriorated at times to little more than childish squabbling. On his first visit Doyle noticed she had trouble walking. Then Daphne had told him her mother suffered from ME. Its effect on her health varied: at times she moved about almost unaffected by it, at others she used her wheelchair and sometimes, if it was really bad, she stayed in her room with the blinds closed, insisting on silence. Doyle liked Margaret – despite her disability there was a sprightliness about her – but he found the atmosphere in the house draining.

And Daphne was never herself around them. With her father she was either flirtatious or dismissive, but mostly dismissive. Towards her mother she was tolerant, but an anger or resentment lingered. It was hard to define but Doyle could recall times when Daphne had snapped at her mother with rudeness or even cruelty. Doyle had tried to stay unentangled and was always glad when the time came to leave.

They had cleared Totnes and were on the open road. The rain had stopped.

'And how are you?' he asked Ruth.

'Numb. That's the only word I can use. Numb and angry, if that's possible.'

'What are you angry about?'

She shot him a look. 'My fucking bitch of a sister!'

'Something happened.'

'Exactly! What happened? What could have possibly…?' It was

hard for her to talk without tears moving in to drown what she wanted to say. 'What could possibly have happened to make her do that?'

'There's not a lot I can tell you.'

'The last time I spoke to her she sounded ... well, she sounded like herself.' Ruth wiped away tears as she swept around curves.

'There were a couple of incidents,' Doyle said. 'I should have seen the significance . . .' He told her about the time in the bathroom when Daphne had squeezed herself between the wall and the toilet. He told her about the rejection slips and the all-day TV-watching but none of it sounded as if it might lead to suicide. Everything he said sounded slightly implausible.

Ruth continued driving fast.

'When I said something happened, I meant something a long time ago,' Doyle said in conclusion.

'What? You can't find an explanation for it during the time you and she were together so you think it has to have been something from the past?'

Doyle thought about this for a moment. 'Yes.'

'Daphne was spoilt. She always got what she wanted – but I refuse to believe that just because it wasn't going all her way out in the big adult world she topped herself. I mean, she might have been a selfish bitch but she wasn't stupid.'

'She wasn't a bitch at all.'

Ruth glanced at him. 'I'm just trying to get my head around this, and I can't.'

Theo stood framed in the front doorway, almost a mirror image of Doyle in size and stature. But unlike Doyle he seemed comfortable in himself. Even now he appeared cool and calm, his blue eyes lively, his smile solid, his suit impeccable and his handshake firm. It wasn't until he spoke that he gave away any hint of how he might be feeling. 'Come in. Good of you to get down.' The voice sounded tired and worn. As Doyle stepped inside he noticed that Theo had paled and the skin around his jaw hung loose.

The hallway was brittle with reflected light, which bounced off the glass-covered paintings, the mirrors and even the broad leaves of the potted plants that stood on ornate plinths. Theo led Doyle down the carpeted centre to the living room. This, too, was bright, made so by a vast window that overlooked much of the garden, the houses on the hill beneath, and the river, where boats in their hundreds were moored in long lines. It was a room full of art, books and ornaments. Doyle wondered how anyone could live in a place that might have been arranged for a photograph in a Sunday supplement.

Margaret was on the sofa. He went to her and kissed her cheek. When he straightened he held on to her hand. Her face was heavy with pain and pleading. What could he say? Nothing – and that was the problem. Daphne had created an emotional situation from which there was no delivery so no words could comfort. 'I'm just so sorry,' he said, 'so sorry ...'

'I know,' she said. 'I'm very glad you're here. Sit down.' She indicated the space beside her on the couch. Doyle sat. Margaret didn't seem to be moving much today.

'Will you have a drink?' Theo asked. 'I have a malt you may like.'

Margaret turned her head towards her husband. 'Just because he's Irish it doesn't mean you have to ply him with whiskey.'

'Don't be so bloody silly, woman.' Theo walked to the cabinet and poured. He handed Doyle his drink, then sat in an armchair opposite the sofa. Doyle noticed the wheelchair against the wall in the far corner.

'Where's Ruth?' Margaret asked.

'She's gone down to get Garry,' Doyle replied.

'That boyfriend of hers is a brick, but I must tell you, she's not taking this at all well . . . I suppose you saw that.'

'How is she supposed to take it, for God's sake?' Theo said.

Margaret ignored this. 'She seems very angry at the moment. Don't be surprised if some of it's directed at you.'

Theo sipped and stared at Doyle as though he was waiting for him to start talking.

'I wish there was something I could say, something that would explain it,' Doyle said, 'but I know as much as you do.'

'That simply cannot be true,' Theo interrupted.

Of course it wasn't true, but how could he unearth here and now the details of living with their daughter? Did they want him to describe the disengagement he had seen her go through from him, from herself, from living? Did they want him to tell them that when he and Daphne were in London she had been sustained by friends and by the things she did? That there they had had lives that were as interdependent and as separate as railway tracks but in Bristol it had all stopped. In Bristol it had been nothing but hard graft and rejection. Looking into the eyes of her father, Doyle began, for the first time, to grasp this.

'No, you're right. You want to know what happened but I don't know what to tell you.'

'But I mean – damn it, man – was it drink, drugs, what?'

'None of that. I got a job in that health-food shop, as you know. The owner wants to open a restaurant and I've got a little involved with that. He and I were going out to lunch together to celebrate him getting the loan for the place the morning I found Daphne. I went by the flat to see if she wanted to join us.' He stopped: nothing he was saying sounded relevant.

There was silence.

'Why won't they release the body?' Margaret asked.

'The inspector told me that the coroner in Bristol is—'

'They suspect foul play,' Theo interrupted.

'What do you mean "foul play"?' Margaret demanded.

'If they don't release the body it means they suspect there's been hanky-panky.'

'You're being ridiculous.'

'No, he's right,' Doyle said. Their bickering was a drill through his skull. 'They treat suicide as suspicious until the coroner is completely satisfied that it's not.'

'Oh, dear God!' Margaret said, bringing a hand to her mouth.

Theo drained his glass and stood. 'I'm going to show the boy his room.' He walked towards the door. It was only then Doyle realised that meant him. He got to his feet and glanced at Margaret. She was lost in thought. He picked up his bag and followed Theo, who was waiting for him at the foot of the stairs. 'Not good to bother the old girl with too much detail,' he said, then mounted the stairs – rather too fast for a man of his age.

He brought Doyle into Daphne's old room. It was much as she had left it when she went to college in London. The walls were covered with huge posters of lone males: Kurt Cobain, looking moody, and a grainy close-up of Ian Curtis the lead singer from Joy Division. Colourful feather boas and scarves hung all over the walls and, over the bed, a large Native American dream-catcher. It was all stuff Doyle was familiar with, but seeing it now somehow gave it an importance and permanence it had not possessed when Daphne was alive.

Theo walked to the single bed and sat. Doyle put his bag down by the wardrobe.

'I don't get it,' Theo said. 'I've thought about it and thought about it and I can't see why a girl like Daphne would do something like that. And I keep on thinking, When was it we last spoke? It was on the phone – it must have been. But, you see, I'm not good on the phone – pass the girls on to their mother when they call. Don't know why . . . generational thing, I suppose.'

Doyle sat in front of the dressing-table on a kitchen chair that had been painted pink to fit in with the general theme of the room. He was not used to seeing Theo like this, introspective, uncertain. It robbed him of the ability to respond.

'Did she say anything?' Theo said.

'What do you mean?'

'Say what was bothering her. Christ, there must have been something – the girl killed herself!'

'I'm not aware of any big issue, if that's what you mean.'

Theo was still staring at him. 'Well, that's good – I mean, it's good that she wasn't tormented – but it only adds to the confusion. Why did she do it?'

'Mr Palmer—'

'Theo, please.'

'Theo, I don't know what to tell you. She was really excited about the move to Bristol, too excited, as though it was going to be the answer to everything. She was convinced she'd be working in the Old Vic or one of the other theatre companies. She said that lots of TV was filmed there. I know she applied for everything, but I think that, bit by bit, it dawned on her that there was as little access in Bristol as there was in London. She despaired, I guess.'

Theo was looking at the floorboards. 'All right, I can see that. I understand that – but I just don't get why she would react so ... so violently?' He looked up and, for a moment, Doyle thought he saw the pleading he had seen in Margaret's face. What Daphne had done had left no grey areas, no nook or cranny where something small might lodge, settle and later grow. In front of him Doyle saw a man who would never again experience idle moments: Daphne had claimed them. Nothing for him would taste the same, look the same or feel the same. In killing herself she had killed little bits of everyone around her.

The front door slammed and they heard voices. 'We'd better go down. I think we're expecting a few.' He stood. 'I realise you didn't have to come – it must be difficult. I do appreciate it.'

For the first time Doyle felt warmth towards the man. For all his pomp and bluster he was just another human being, and now a broken one. 'I'm glad to be here.'

Theo smiled.

There were several people in the living room. Ruth was pouring drinks and handing them to Garry, who delivered them to whoever was in need. He had just returned from a couple who were sitting on the sofa with Margaret when he saw Doyle and Theo enter. He embraced Doyle. 'I'm so sorry, really.' When they separated he said, 'I'm not going to talk about it, all right? You bearing up?'

Doyle smiled, nodding, noting that Garry's hair was an awful lot tamer now than it had been when they'd first met. 'I'm OK.'

'Good.' Garry glanced at the sofa. 'You remember James and Alice?'

Doyle shook their hands. He had met Alice on several occasions in Dartmouth. She and Daphne had been friends at some stage but Doyle had never been able to work out when. Alice seemed suitably subdued, as did James, whom Doyle had no recollection of meeting before.

'Will you be all right up there?' Margaret asked.

'Up where? He's not staying in Daph's old room, surely,' Ruth said. She was still pouring drinks.

'Why ever not?' Margaret said.

'That's just too weird.' Ruth turned and handed her father a whiskey. 'Doyle, what are you having?'

'I don't know – gin and tonic?'

'Since when did you become a ponce?' Garry said, and winked at him.

He had first met Ruth and Garry – Theo, too, for that matter – on a summer's day in London three years ago. Doyle and Daphne had decided, over a lunchtime pint, that it would be much more fun to go to bed for the afternoon than head back respectively to work and college. Daphne and Ruth shared a garden flat their father had bought for them while they were studying; Daphne said it would be empty all afternoon and it was only a short tube ride away. Once they were there, she went straight to the kitchen. She sat on the table and drew Doyle into her. They were kissing hard, unbuttoning one another, when the front door opened. Ruth walked in, smiled and began unloading shopping, as though she wasn't at all surprised to see her sister in the process of seducing, or being seduced by, a total stranger. Daphne made reluctant introductions and Ruth then asked if they would like to help her set up a barbecue. Doyle, embarrassed, said he'd be delighted to. He and Daphne disentangled and took instructions. It wasn't until they were in the garden, sipping white wine and passing a joint, that Daphne seemed to come round to the idea of a barbecue. By then they had been joined by Ruth's boyfriend, Garry. He was tall, broad, of mixed race, and wore his hair in a perfectly round Afro.

Doyle lay stretched on a sun-lounger, listening to the birds and the laughter of the two sisters. Ruth was telling Garry how she had found them when she walked in and was now implying that Daphne had a seriously tarty streak. 'Honestly if we were to invite all her exes round right now we'd fill the whole fucking garden,' Ruth said.

'I can't help it if I'm admired and adored, can I?' Daphne said, as she sat on the side of Doyle's lounger. Doyle was unsure whether he was supposed to comment on this or not. He felt very stoned.

Suddenly the banter stopped and Doyle peered through the sunshine to see a tall man in a suit coming towards them. Both girls said, 'Daddy!'

The man smiled as he perched on the edge of a garden chair. 'So, this is what you two get up to on a sunny afternoon, is it?'

'Have a glass of wine, Daddy,' Ruth said.

'It's four thirty in the afternoon.'

'Party pooper!' Daphne introduced Doyle. He struggled to string together what he thought was the right combination of words but, fortunately, Theo was too focused on his daughters to notice any oddities in Doyle's speech. After a few minutes Daphne whispered to Doyle, 'Christ, we picked the wrong day to come.'

'Here,' Ruth said, handing Doyle his drink. 'Get drunk, stay drunk, that's what I've been doing.'

Margaret winced. The two beside her sat frozen. Doyle remembered Ruth driving earlier: she hadn't smelt of drink at the station. He took a chair by the dining table. Either Ruth or Garry was on permanent door duty, letting people in. The younger ones would have known Daphne from her schooldays. Some were neighbours, friends of Margaret, it seemed, and there was a host of older men, whom Doyle presumed to be Theo's associates. Whatever else, the Palmers were not going to be shy about telling the world that their little girl had killed herself.

Everyone seemed awkward when they first entered and most were glad to take refuge in drink. Doyle had had several gin and tonics, but they were having no effect. Fortunately Garry, between his trips to the door, sat next to him and, true to his word, didn't mention Daphne. Doyle asked him about the business that Ruth and he had started – a bareboat charter business – last summer and were preparing for its second season. 'So here we are, up to our tonsils in debt, in a major recession, and now this.' He looked to Ruth who, at that moment, was staring at him. 'I'm not sure what will happen.'

'Well, the banks can't start demanding their money back when they've all gone bust,' Doyle said.

Garry smiled. 'If only it worked like that …'

While waves of drunkenness, laughter or tears rolled through the rest of the room, Garry remained outwardly calm and pleasant. Looking at him, Doyle thought that in many ways he was the exact opposite of Ruth. The drink she was lowering into herself was heightening her agony. She was throwing glances at the two of them and Doyle felt that she, probably like most other people in the room, thought that he must hold the clue as to why Daphne had done it. Surrounded by the pale colours and eggshell sheens of this Dartmouth living room, he felt they would be happy to lynch him. But maybe the drink he was consuming was doing to him what it seemed to be doing to Ruth: poisoning his thoughts.

With a great deal of effort Margaret stood and thanked everyone for coming. She then looked as though she was about to continue, but did not. She said simply, 'To Daphne,' and raised her glass. Under the circumstances it was as dignified a speech as Doyle could have imagined. Soon afterwards she went to bed and Doyle wished he could do the same. Not because fatigue was hauling him in that direction but to be away from this room where strangers were pouring on him what he perceived as a rancid mixture of scorn and pity, where names and faces merged and all, as the drink loosened them, found their voices. Theo, in some odd way, seemed to be enjoying it. He stood, thin and tall, listening, talking, a hand on a speaker's elbow, a wounded man playing his role. Doyle looked at his watch: a quarter past eleven, an acceptable time to depart. He slipped out as though heading for the toilet, but then went upstairs.

Six

Doyle had grown up in a terrace house in the centre of Wexford town in southern Ireland. His father worked in a factory across the road, attaching handles to spades, and drank in the local pub three doors down from the house. His only excursion outside this triangle took place at a quarter to eleven every Sunday morning when, in a suit that flapped about his thin frame, he'd walk the half-mile to mass. Doyle's mother was a slight woman – Doyle couldn't remember ever seeing her eat but she smoked constantly and raged about the evils of alcohol. Her own father had liked his drink and sometimes Doyle would catch something in his mother's sunken eyes that made him think they'd seen things she did not want transferred to memory.

He had two older brothers, Kieran and Sean, who had gone away to England, which, as his mother often reminded him, was a swamp across the water where few surfaced and from which fewer still returned. But after his father's death he and his mother went there too. Doyle was eleven when they had arrived at Aunt Eileen's door. She was his mother's sister and lived in a council flat in Portsmouth. Aunt Eileen suffered from the same affliction as her father and, after almost two years, Doyle and his mother were housed by the council in a flat across the harbour in Gosport.

He went to the local school, Bridgemary High, where life was eventually made bearable when two attributes he was previously only half-aware of came to light. One was that he could play defensive football well enough to be welcomed into any team and the other was that he could draw. This put him in favour with two separate groups, which was enough to let him slide through the years without attracting the hard-core resistance that existed towards foreigners. Although he was only ever addressed by his surname – he had been christened Desmond Edward Doyle – it didn't bother him. In a way it even seemed to fit.

By the time he had got to Camberwell College of Arts he had come to believe that first names were the gates through which people entered your life and, as such, should be used sparingly. Presenting himself by surname alone kept a distance between the world and him, a distance he felt he needed to get perspective on life.

By the end of the first year at Camberwell he considered that he might be touched with the same disease that plagued both sides of his family. During the last two months of his first year he had gone on a bender, sucked into a cycle of drunkenness and hangover so that the days merged, becoming nothing more than clouds that swept overhead. It seemed an oddly familiar and comfortable place to be. When the binge ended – he had spent every penny he had and could borrow – he was amazed by how his brain reacted. It was nothing but a frightened mass of nerve endings contorting everything he imagined he saw into three-dimensional horrors. He stayed locked in his room for three days, relieving himself into supermarket bags that either burst or spilt.

When he recovered he went to an AA meeting. As he sat in the smoky room, listening to the stories, he thought it odd how keen each speaker seemed to be to nail him- or herself up in front of their fellow sufferers. They seemed eager to compare wounds. The stories they told had a humdrum tragedy that, to Doyle, seemed too lazily scooped under the umbrella of alcoholism. He decided instead to see if he could become a moderate drinker. He expressed this to Toby, the sculpture student from Camberwell with whom he had gone to the meeting. Toby smiled. 'You'll go through a lot of pain and then you'll be back. I just hate to see it but there's nothing I can do – your decision.'

As light leaked into Daphne's room Doyle found himself staring at the posters. Was it a coincidence that the two men on the wall had committed suicide?

He lay still, listening, but other than the birds outside, there was no sound. After a little while, he sat up on the side of the bed. He wanted to leave. There was no reason to stay. He had performed his function, such as it was. Anything else was beyond the call.

Downstairs and dressed, he looked about for a notepad and pen. The living room was awash with empty glasses and bottles. There were even some full ashtrays – for some reason, Doyle was glad to think of people smoking inside a house, like old times. He abandoned his search and decided instead to steal out of the front door and get a cup of tea somewhere in the town. It was a quarter to eight: somewhere was bound to be open.

As he approached the front door he heard Margaret call, 'Doyle, is that you?' Her voice had come from just the other side of the door to his left. It was the room she used when she was bad. He had not realised she was in there now.

'Yes.'

'Come in.' She was sitting up in a single bed with a duvet cover that matched the wallpaper. 'Sneaking away?'

'Yes.'

'Thought you might.'

'I'm sorry. I've been awake for hours and I really should get back.'

'It's OK. I'm sure we'll see you soon.'

'Of course you will.' Doyle wondered whether he should go over and kiss her, but somehow that seemed wrong so he smiled instead.

'I think you were very brave to face us all.'

Doyle closed the door and slipped out into the chilly morning.

Geoff sat at the back of the restaurant, thinking. If the wall that separated the kitchen from the dining area was gone, people could watch their food being cooked. A good hand-built pizza oven would be nice, and perhaps he should look into getting a spiral staircase. There was an area at the back that had potential as a courtyard – it would certainly do, for the moment at least, as a smoking area. With some plants and a canopy it could be a very nice feature. Looking about, Geoff knew he could have the place up and running for not too much at all. He could always close later on, say, in January, if need be, to make any serious changes. For the moment, though, he could see the place operational inside three weeks.

What he needed now was someone with a good eye for decoration – and then it dawned on him that Doyle might be his man. But, of course, that was the pre-Daphne Doyle. Perhaps it would be worth bringing him down here, though. Besides, Doyle needed to be kept busy. Thinking about him made Geoff uncomfortable – he could see him sitting in the police station, stunned and pale, an echo of the man he had been.

Still, that was in the past. What he was looking at now was the future and it might be that this little place could be of benefit to them both.

Later that afternoon he called Doyle.

'Geoff, what's up?' He sounded groggy but that was promising – it might mean he'd been sleeping.

'You OK?'

'Yeah, what time is it?'

'Two – you just wake up?'

'Got back from Dartmouth a few hours ago, had a snooze.'

'Look, when can you come down to the restaurant? I need to see you.'

There was a long silence. 'Today?'

'Yes, today. Jesus Christ, man, you live just up the road!'

'OK. Keep your hair on. An hour?'

'Thirty minutes – life's short.'

Half an hour later Doyle walked into the restaurant. Geoff stared at him. 'You don't look good. I'm going to get you something to eat.' He handed Doyle a coffee, then went back into the kitchen.

Getting out of Dartmouth by public transport had proved a lot harder than Doyle could have imagined and he was glad to be back in Bristol. Sitting there, listening to Geoff whistle in an empty kitchen, was fine: it was neutral, the kind of thing that happened every day. In Dartmouth he'd felt as if he was sitting in a car that had been driven over a harbour wall, feeling the cold water seep in and wondering could he hold his breath till the water had gone over his head and it was time to get out.

Geoff put several dishes in front of him, rich with seafood. Doyle found the smell nauseating but Geoff seemed excited; he told Doyle what was in each dish.

'Look, sorry, Geoff, I've kind of eaten already.'

'What the fuck does that mean, "kind of"?'

'I had some banana.'

'Banana?'

'Yeah.'

'Banana? You can't live off fucking bananas. Here, have a pancake at least.' Geoff was already putting one on his empty plate. 'Squeeze some lemon over it.'

He went on muttering about bananas.

'They're good for you, easy on the digestion, and you don't have to wash up after.'

'Fucking bananas! I asked you here for a purpose and it was not to talk about bananas.'

'What, then?'

'Have a look about. What do you see?'

'Geoff, I'm not really in the mood for games. Can you just get to the point?'

'OK. I've got big plans for this place, most of which are going to have to wait till the tills have been ringing awhile. Meanwhile I want it to look good, I want it to be interesting. Not some beyond-the-pale futuristic wank but good – you know.'

'Yeah?'

'Well, I thought maybe you might come up with something for me.'

'What – like an interior design?'

'Yeah, that sort of thing.'

Doyle had a look about the room. 'Are you serious?'

Geoff's face fell.

'I don't know, Geoff . . . I'm not really in the mood to take on a project. Paint the place white, change the tablecloths, some nice artwork . . . keep it simple.'

Geoff smiled. 'See? I knew I was right. What did you say again?' He had whipped a piece of paper out of his back pocket

– a letter with the Bristol City Council logo at the top. He glanced at it, sneered, then turned it over and started writing. 'White?'

'It's just a suggestion – it could be a cool blue. You just want the place clean and crisp. It's too fussy as it is.'

'This is good. So, white, right? And new tablecloths. What colour?'

'Dark blue.'

'*Dark* blue?'

'Yeah.'

'OK, and what else?'

'Well, get this crap off the walls.' Doyle waved at the small framed photographs of olive groves under blue skies. 'Get some fresh artwork. Big, original, but good.'

'How?'

'Buy it.'

'Oh, for Christ's sake! I'm not laying out thousands on some shit that I'd be stuck with – besides, I wouldn't have a clue where to go.'

'Ever hear of art galleries?'

Geoff stopped. 'Art galleries, that's it. We'll make this place into a fucking art gallery.'

'Geoff, it's a restaurant.'

'Yeah, but what's an art gallery? Only walls. And what have we got here? What's the one thing we've got here? Walls, acres of them.'

'Great!'

'No, Doyle, better than great. This could be fantastic, and with you running it, it would be.'

'What are you talking about?'

'This could be perfect – seldom are things so simple. OK, I'll be honest with you – totally honest. I want you involved in Wet Willie's with me but I realise you're in no fit state to take on anything managerial right now – but what if you took on this? It would mean you're involved, you'd be around, so when you feel you'd like to take on more full-time work you'd already be here. Perfect.'

'What is it you're asking me to do?'

'Find artists. Say we put on a show for a month and every month we change over. We have an opening night, wine, press . . . We'd become a little cultural enclave as well as a restaurant. This could work out very well for everyone.'

'And you'd pay me?'

'Of course. You could either work on commission of sales or a flat rate.'

'Flat rate, if you don't mind.'

'So you'll do it?'

'I didn't say that.'

'What have you got to lose?'

'Well, like you said, where do you get artists?'

'Ever hear of art galleries?'

'Oh, Christ, Geoff! They're not going to give me a list of their artists and say, "There you go. Poach them."'

'Doyle, my man, you'll figure it out. It would be a nice easy way of turning over some money, that's all I'm saying.'

'I don't know.'

'Have a think about it.'

When Doyle left the restaurant he had no wish to go home. Funny: in the little time he had spent there since Daphne's death he had discovered that the flat was a place he didn't like going to and yet, once he was there, it was difficult to leave. He had a vague idea of heading towards the waterfront. There, even on a dull day, he could get lost in the glisten of ripples, the swans and the boats. He walked across Stokes Croft and down Jamaica Street, past hoardings bright with graffiti. It caught his eye, the loud, colourful swirls, the areas of dark, the figures frozen in the brickwork. It was raw, cartoony, and fitted perfectly with the sound of sirens and the bleak endlessness of city life.

Is this what Geoff wanted? Should he hunt down these graffiti artists, have them paint on canvas and show it in the restaurant? Maybe create a kind of art zoo where graffiti artists could paint over each other's work like they did on the street so there'd always be something new and bright? No, graffiti had no business indoors. An art zoo would be no different from an animal zoo, cruel and unnatural.

Passing the museum at the top of Park Street, he noticed that inside there was an exhibition called 'Passion for Paint'. Most of the artists exhibiting had been dead for more than a hundred years. They had probably drunk in the same Parisian café. He wondered was there a café anywhere in the world today whose clientele would be collectively remembered a century and a half from now.

He walked into the building, across the wide, echoing hall and then to the stillness of the room where the paintings hung. In front of him was a large Cézanne. To its left a Van Gogh, then a Turner and a series by Francis Bacon – all people who spread paint on canvas. Some furrowed it, twisting it into grooves so thick the image almost became three-dimensional. Others coaxed it and courted it until it was so smooth that images emerged like shapes through fog.

The Bacon series was three portraits in a row. Each twisted a little more so that you got the feeling you were seeing something of the character behind the face. Was that it? Was that why people got excited by this stuff? Because the face we present to the world is a badge of our personality, and a mask to hide it? Perhaps that was what artists do, dive beneath the image and into the soul, then paint the image but in such a way as to reveal the soul.

Doyle thought back to his own days at art college and his attempts to paint. He could do it, and sometimes he could do it well, but he had to drive himself. He'd fuelled himself on books about artists and the images he saw in the books, then tear off down the alleyways of imitation, branching out from time to time with something original. Such an endeavour would last maybe six weeks at the most, and then he'd run into a lull, a period when nothing excited or motivated him.

People went from painting to painting, staring at each one in silence. But he did not have the concentration for that. As he turned to leave he was caught by a large picture hanging near the door. It was by Turner, and when he'd seen it on his way in, up close, it had looked a mess, a mass of swirls dominated by many shades of the same brownish yellow, but now he could see it was a seascape, one muddied by the weather. He walked towards it and, at a certain distance, the image dispersed. Then he backed away from it, waiting for it to click into place. It happened, but not uniformly. Bits on the periphery of his vision would appear to make sense but when he focused on them they'd disappear again, and the area his eye had just left would suggest shapes he'd not seen when he was looking at it. Two more steps backwards and it was there, the whole thing intact: a boat battling for survival in a storm. Odd to think that the painter had had to apply the paint up close yet still be aware of the effect it would make when it was viewed from twenty metres away.

Outside, he looked at the poster again. So that was art, or someone's version of it anyway. And in this city of almost half a million people there had to be some who were, at this very minute, producing it. All he had to do was find them. He could, of course, try to do it himself. Knock out eight or nine paintings every month in different styles and sizes and keep the cash if they sold. But if that was a plan it was a ridiculous one.

Five minutes later, when he was passing the window of an art gallery on Park Row, a painting almost stopped him in his tracks. It was more than a metre square. Two bright, larger-than-life magpies gazed at each other from across a red tablecloth. The magpies and the table were seen from above but somehow the artist had put in a dog drinking tea from a china cup and saucer that you viewed face on. The perspective had been twisted but not in any way that was detracting. The picture had a remarkable lightness, almost comedy, yet it was a serious piece of work, delicately executed. Doyle looked in through the window and saw more pieces in a similar style.

For some reason he was reluctant to step inside, perhaps because the gallery was empty, except for a man behind a desk in the centre of the room. Or maybe because he hadn't been into one since Daphne and he had cruised them in London in the early stages of their relationship. But then a man and a woman passed, stopped and went in. They seemed to know the man inside. Thinking their presence would cover him, he opened the door and entered.

The couple were odd. He was tall, with long, lank hair falling from beneath a straw hat, and he wore a silk scarf, while she was small and dark, with eyes that sparkled. She wore a bright lemon coat. They went straight to the man at the desk and a friendly conversation began in low tones. Doyle studied more work by the artist whose painting was displayed in the window. They all had the same lightness and humour and the colour was vivid. They could almost have been illustrations for a children's book, but before they slipped into the realm of fantasy something in them bit you. Perhaps it was the precision with which they were executed, compared with the playfulness of the subject. Whatever, they were exciting. They were signed 'Harding' in a childish scrawl.

'Can I help?' the man asked.

'Oh, I'm just looking. It's lovely work.'

'Yes – Gina's unique.'

'Is she Bristol-based?'

'I know what you mean,' the man said. 'They look like they were created in a hot climate, don't they?'

'Yes,' Doyle said. 'But they weren't?'

'No, and it's not even as if she's got a fiery temperament.'

'Right!' Doyle said, but couldn't think of anything to add to this and neither, it seemed, could the man. He smiled and backed away towards the couple, who had drifted to the far end of the gallery.

Doyle took one sweep around the walls and knew that Gina Harding's work would be perfect for the restaurant. Then he left the gallery and decided to go back to the flat. He was happy to have seen work of that standard: it meant there were probably people all over the city producing paintings and, some of them at least, would equal it. He wondered if she had a website.

The flat was bathed in a gloomy light. He plugged in the kettle, then went into the living room where he sat. He listened as the noise from the kettle rose in volume, full of heat and bubbles, then quietened and clicked off. It was his cue to get up but he stayed put. The chair he was in faced the window so he looked out at the hill opposite. The streetlights had just come on, illuminating it like a life-size three-dimensional map. He followed the progress of cars, watched them appear and disappear as rows of buildings, trees and other obstacles got in their way. Then he sat until the darkness had descended and all he could see were lights. They were many, of different shapes, colours and purposes, traffic-lights, house-lights, the flashing orange of pedestrian beacons. Finally he went back to the kettle.

Mug in hand, he went into the bedroom and turned on the computer. More noises, bleeps and flashings before it lapsed into the familiar solid drone. He typed in 'Gina Harding'. The pages filled. Five or six down he found 'Gina Harding; Artist, Bristol'. He clicked on it and the screen showed squares and triangles that, one by one, from the bottom up, filled with pictures similar in style to the ones he'd seen earlier. The area between contained text and at the top of the screen a button said 'contact'. He clicked on it and was looking at a picture of her with her details beneath it.

He wrote down her mobile and landline numbers, then lay on the bed. Gina Harding looked hard: the photograph was of someone who didn't like her photograph being taken. It would be easier to email her, but what would he say? It might be better to talk to her, although she didn't look like the kind of person who'd be easy to talk to.

His ability to talk to people had improved since he'd met Daphne but he still felt awkward engaging in casual conversation – especially a conversation he had instigated with a particular purpose in mind. He would make the world's worst salesman, he thought. With Daphne, talking had been easy . . . at the beginning, at least.

The first time he had seen her she was standing at a bar. He was with a drinking buddy he had met at Camberwell, a guy named Tommy. Doyle watched her, the way her skirt – it was long, in rich autumn colours – fell over the swell of her hips, the way she lodged a boot on the rung of a bar stool as she waited, money in hand, to be served, the way her dark hair fell in loose curls across her back. When she turned he caught a glimpse of her profile: her lips were full and her nose was small, upturned.

When Tommy noticed that he no longer had Doyle's attention he followed Doyle's gaze. 'Christ!' he said. 'It's the Daph!' and called to her. She waved at him and said she'd be there in a second.

'Who's "the Daph"?' Doyle asked.

'Daphne! You must know her!'

'I don't.'

'She's nice.'

'Lovely.'

Two minutes later she was sitting with them, explaining she was waiting for Mark, that they were going to see a movie. Tommy introduced her to Doyle, then continued talking to her as though Doyle was not present. Tommy was suggesting she should call Mark and tell him she had changed her mind: she wasn't going to no movie, she was going on the piss with them instead. Doyle was taken by her laugh, throaty and rich. 'Vivacious' came to mind, and 'sensuous'. Her dark eyes sparkled. Were they dark? In that light it was hard to tell – perhaps brown or hazel, maybe even green.

Between Mark, whoever he was, and Tommy, Doyle thought himself far enough down her chain of admirers not to be called to duty so he sat back to just enjoy the sight of her. The way she used her hands as she talked was delightful: she had the confidence to express herself without care as to what others thought. Her orange blouse was unbuttoned to a cleavage that promised softness within. He could have watched her for hours. Then Tommy excused himself and he was alone with her.

'So, who are you?' she said.

She had asked with such friendliness that he was caught off guard. 'I really haven't a clue,' he found himself saying.

She laughed with the throaty sensuality that made Doyle want to laugh too.

'But you're an art student, right?'

'Yes. Are you?'

'Good God, no, can't draw to save my life. Drama, me.'

'An actor?'

'Yes. And director, lighting, stage set, costume and makeup.'

Doyle noticed that Tommy had re-emerged but was in conversation on his way back from the toilet. 'Is your boyfriend an actor too?'

'Boyfriend?'

'Sorry, I meant the guy you're going to the pictures with.'

'Where are you from?'

'I started out in Ireland.'

'You sound like you dropped out of the sky.'

'Actually, I was dropped on the floor while my mother was peeling potatoes.'

That laugh again. 'Your mum added the placenta to the stew, I suppose?'

Life is rich, Doyle thought. Five minutes ago I was admiring her from afar, now this. 'She was Mammy, actually. In Ireland they're all mammies.'

'I've been to Ireland – Kerry, I think. When I was a kid.'

'Did you like it?'

'The Guinness was gorgeous.'

She was funny and he was enjoying this. Something about her made him forget himself. He sat back. 'So, how come you know Tommy?'

She and Tommy seemed to belong to a large but loosely connected gang. Doyle knew a few of the names she mentioned, could even put a face to one or two, but he was strictly on the perimeter. He discovered that Mark was a friend and not a boyfriend. This happened when she received a text from him saying he was caught in a bar across the river. By then Tommy had rejoined them but now he no longer dominated – Daphne wouldn't let him. And this seemed to irritate him. On the way to another bar he peeled off, saying he'd catch up with them in a while. Without him Doyle and Daphne cruised in one another's company. They drank and laughed their way through another three bars, and when closing time came Doyle knew only that he was in a rare state, drunk and happy. Walking towards a taxi rank, he stopped her in front of Gap and they kissed for the first time. Afterwards they walked arm in arm, like long-time lovers. When she told him he could sleep with her if he wanted to, he smiled broadly and said it would be wonderful.

After that they didn't want to be out of each other's company. But it wasn't a closed, sealed-off affair. It offered itself to other people. Daphne knew everybody, had slept with quite a lot of them, but seemed completely content with Doyle. In the back of his mind Doyle wished their relationship was less drink-sodden, but he was having more fun then he ever remembered. At the time he was sharing a small flat near King's Cross with two other art students. Daphne said it smelt and normally steered him towards her place at the end of a night. She shared a terrace house with Mark and Frankie, who worked for magazines. It surprised Doyle, shocked him even, that she would leave her room and walk naked to the bathroom at the end of the landing. He once lay in her bed listening to her having a casual chat with Mark, knowing that she was naked. He even joked about how big her tits were. She laughed and said it was all the man-handling. Doyle didn't feel he could say anything about his jealousy if, indeed, that was what it was. He doubted it was as simple as that. He feared something much more primitive, ownership, something like that, something she would rail against. So he kept quiet but it bubbled under his skin.

He found himself trying to engineer conversations so he could discover how many people she had slept with. Once, when it worked, she just shrugged and said, 'Who cares?' He acted as though he certainly didn't.

Their life became a little quieter when Theo bought the garden flat for her and Ruth. Within a few months they realised that Doyle had all but moved in so he stopped paying rent at King's Cross and instead paid it at Daphne's. It was fun to be with her, always exciting, even if they were just watching TV. But there was that niggling, the poison that had entered earlier in the affair. Sometimes when he was waiting for her to come back, at gone nine o'clock, the dinner cold under the grill, his texts to her unanswered, the snake of jealousy would slither inside him.

Eventually she'd burst in, starving, half-drunk, her apologies drowned by enthusiastic descriptions of whom she'd met in which bar, and Doyle felt himself, not the snake, recoil. On that Saturday morning when she mentioned moving to Bristol, his first feeling was relief. His first thought was: she hasn't slept with anyone there.

He walked into the kitchen taking Gina Harding's details with him. He picked up the phone and pressed the numbers – any other approach would have been fatal. It rang for so long that he was beginning to hope it would go to a message when a grey and smoky voice answered.

'Hello,' he said. 'My name is Desmond Doyle and I've just seen your work in the Hayward Gallery.'

'Yes?'

'I run a gallery myself and I was wondering if perhaps you'd be interested in showing your work there.'

'What gallery is it?' she asked.

'It's not open yet. It's being constructed as we speak.'

'Where is it?'

'Picton Street.'

'Picton Street?'

'Yes. It's a restaurant as well as an art gallery. It's going to be an absolutely—'

'Can I stop you there? Are you the owner of this restaurant?'

'No, I'm the curator.'

'I see.'

What did she see? Doyle wanted to hang up, go to the sofa and lie down.

She continued, 'I presume this is a new role for you.'

Doyle didn't know how to answer.

'Otherwise,' she said, 'you would be aware that artists are generally tied to the gallery or galleries that show them.' She was adopting the tone of a bored instructor, talking fast, getting impatient. 'I couldn't show in your restaurant even if I wanted to.'

He felt a door closing but part of him wanted it to stay open. 'OK. Well, I'll be honest, the owner of the place asked me to find artists to show and I took on the job because I'm interested in art and I know it would be a good place for anybody to show their stuff.' Why was he saying any of this shit? Why did he care?

'I can't help you.'

'Do you know any artists who might be interested?'

'No. Wait! My nephew, maybe ...'

'Yes?'

'He'll be here tomorrow, if you want to see him.'

'What kind of work does he do?'

'Graffiti, but lately he's taken to canvas.'

'That sounds interesting. I'd like to see some of his stuff. Where is it you live?'

She gave him the address, then said, 'This has nothing to do with me, you understand?'

'Yes, fine. I'll see you tomorrow. What time?'

'He'll be here all day. Why don't we say two o'clock?'

'Great.'

He put down the phone and went into the living room. Again, he stared at the view from the window. How do people live out these dead hours? What are they for? He smiled then. He had just done business – well, business of a sort. Was this how life would roll now? Telephone calls, meetings . . . talk, using lies and flattery. I am a curator, pleased to meet you. I am your curator, a little bruised but still here for you.

He closed his eyes. I am your curator and I dance to the tune of one Mr Geoff McAllister but, really, I'd rather seal myself away and tell myself tales about times of jolly plenty, about days of sun-glitter on water displaced by an oar and the silky progress of the bow. Listen, and you'll hear the click of the camera. Listen, and you'll hear the song of the robin, the scamper in the undergrowth of things furred, of faraway laughter, of leaking lagoons. Of thoughts that won't stop tumbling, pouring out onto the screen of the brain before release to the public in the form of words. Everything is designed to bring about change because change is good just as static is bad. Daphne had the right idea. Take a blade, a quick slit here and a quick slit there, then lie back and let the changes commence. The big one. The one we pretend will never happen.

He opened his eyes, went into the bedroom and looked for her among the forgotten garments in the laundry basket. He picked out the pinky-purple silk of the Barbie Doll dress. In it she had smiled. Its hem had lain across his thighs as she'd straddled him.

He let it hang in front of him. The there was an oval stain at the back. He spread it out on the bed. The straps were thin, frivolous. He took off his own clothes and stood before it. He tried to render his mind dormant, wall it out in white, then turn off the lights. It wouldn't obey.

He shivered, picked up the dress and held it to his face. In the softness of the folds he caught the scent of her. There and then there no longer. He scrunched the material into his fingers and inhaled. She was gone. He let it fall open and felt a pulse of pleasure as it passed his genitals. He tossed it onto the bed where it lay discarded and empty. He realised that he was cold so he slid beneath the duvet and curled up.

Daphne if you'd let me I would have protected you. I would have wrapped my long arms around you and held you and squeezed from you all the ghosts and goblins with their menacing squeals and high-pitched laughter and their mockery of you. You could have sat on my knee and we'd watch them flee and then we'd have danced like fairies on the summer lawns. We could have held hands shopping on Park Street on a Saturday afternoon or laughing as we fell out of a pub on the Gloucester Road looking for late-night delights on the way home. We could have done that. But nothing can be done now you see. That's the problem now. There is nothing of you left. Waves come ashore on empty beaches, rain falls into empty fields, high pressure forms to the south, drifting north, falling slowly . . .

The phone was ringing, its sound sending the images of a dream scattering. Doyle arose and raced to the kitchen.

'Hello.'

'Hi.' It was Geoff. 'Listen, I want to come over – that OK?'

'Come over? What time is it?'

'Ten past eight. You all right? You sound kind of groggy.'

'I was asleep.'

'Oh. Well, anyway, I'll drop by. I'm in the shit. We need to talk.'

'Yeah, OK.' He put down the receiver and went back to the bedroom. The dress was lying on the bed. You're in the shit!

Suddenly an emotion crosses him, it is anger and it's fleeting, it was there.

He was about to put Daphne's dress back into the laundry basket when he changed his mind. Washing it would mean she was utterly gone. He folded it around the stain and put it into a drawer, then got dressed.

Geoff arrived in a flurry. He placed a bottle of Jameson on the table along with two packages wrapped in white paper and then said he had to use the loo. From the smells and rising heat coming from the packages Doyle guessed Geoff was treating them to fish and chips.

The toilet flushed. It was odd to hear the sounds of another person in the flat.

'Jesus, just looking at that bath gives me the creeps,' Geoff said, walking straight through the living room into the kitchen. 'Any glasses?'

'In the cupboard above the washing machine.'

Geoff sat down, opened the whiskey and poured two measures. 'Cheers,' he said.

'Cheers.'

'Look, tell me if I'm offside here, Doyle, but wouldn't you be better getting the fuck out of here?'

'No.'

'Right. I'll mind my own business. Have some fish and chips.'

Doyle peered into one of the packages.

'They're banana-flavoured,' Geoff said.

'I'll get some plates.'

'And vinegar, if you have any.'

Doyle brought in everything he thought might be needed for the first meal anyone had had in the flat since Daphne's death. As soon as he was settled, Geoff got up and filled a jug with water, which he put in the centre of the table. They ate to a litany of Geoff's complaints about the problems in finding people to do the little work that needed doing. Everyone, it appeared – 'and this in the middle of a recession,' Geoff reminded him – was busy, and those who were available had quoted an arm and a leg for the job.

The fish was OK but the chips stuck in Doyle's throat, like sewage to a wastepipe. Geoff ate fast, swallowing and talking and sipping his watered-down whiskey in a flurry of movement that brought everything towards his mouth. 'Jesus, those chips are fucking magnificent. I wonder where he gets them.'

'So you're in the shit?'

This stopped him. 'Well, yeah, I guess, but who isn't?'

Perhaps the whiskey had taken the edge off his problems.

'So you're not in the shit?'

'I had the suits from the bank over today. Beautiful timing. It coincided with the hard hats from the building regs who are basically just putting the boot in. They want this and they want that and there's no fucking talking to them. The spiral staircase? They won't have it unless there's another exit out the back. And that can't be done without knocking into the lane for access, which, of course, would need planning permission and that takes time – and time is the one thing I do not have.'

'So it's not possible?'

'It's possible. There ain't nothing that's not possible. It's just the means to do it.'

'The banks?'

'Don't talk to me about the banks. They've spent years force-feeding us credit and now they have a seizure if you even thinking about asking for it.'

'Have they said no?'

'They stare about the place with expressions that would poison piss. I have a meeting with them on Thursday. Before that I've got to talk to an architect – can you imagine? Me and a fucking architect? – so I can give them some sort of plan. It's a wonder anyone bothers trying to do anything!' He refilled his glass. 'How are things your end?'

'I'm meeting someone tomorrow.'

'That's very good. Shit! I nearly forgot. I got two hundred of these made up.' He reached into his jacket pocket and gave Doyle a small box with a business card sealed onto the lid. It bore the dark blue and yellow Wet Willie's logo and, beneath it, Doyle's full name and under it the word 'Curator', then contact numbers and an address. 'I put your mobile on it. Hope you don't mind.'

'No, that's fine. This is very impressive. They're good.'

'Hey, you can't do business without a business card. Who is it you're meeting tomorrow?'

'A woman called Gina Harding but—'

'Never heard of her.'

'Geoff, I'm not going to be able to get household names into Wet Willie's.'

'Well, who is she?'

Doyle didn't feel like mentioning that Gina Harding herself wasn't a prospect. 'She's an artist. She has an exhibition at the moment in the Hayward Gallery.'

'If I could just convince the bank that this is going to be something more than your bog-standard eating-house maybe they'd see their way to putting their hands in their goddamn vaults.'

'How are you going to do that?'

'Singing waitresses, live music – create a place that's great to eat in *and* a platform for art. A hothouse for the talent in this city. I don't fucking know.'

'Geoff, it will be.'

'It will be what?'

'What you said, a hothouse for art.'

'A hothouse in which I'll slowly go broke – no, quickly go broke.'

'It's not going to be easy.'

'You can chalk it down.'

'I meant it's not going to be easy to get artists of the calibre you want.'

'Art's fucking art. No one knows fuck all about it and it's all shite anyway.'

'Have you just come from a class on how to inspire your staff?'

'Don't talk to me about staff, for fuck's sake. Look, Doyle, I'm sorry. I've had a day of fucking problems. Every time I turn around there's another waiting to be solved and I'm running out of ideas.' Geoff put the last of the chips into his mouth. 'I need something that will add a spark to all of this, something to ignite it.'

'Well, I said I'd find you art and I will. But beyond that I don't think I can help.'

'This opening, it's so important. It's got to be big. The place has got to be looking fantastic, some big-name artist paraded around the walls, a DJ, a fucking good one, a few celebs – OK, minor if need be – you know, an *atmosphere*, that's what I'm after, so everyone there knows it's the place to be, the finest there is.'

'That would be good.'

'It's going to happen.' He raised his glass, then swallowed the contents.

Seven

Gina Harding lived in a tall Georgian house in Montpelier. Doyle suspected it was on one of the roads he could see from his living room, one of the ribbons he watched in the dark. It was a street of steady steepness and her front door, like his, was red. He lifted the brass knocker and sent a deep, dull sound through the interior of the house. If he had been a bat he would be able to work out the hall's dimensions from it, as well as the contents. If he had been a flea he could have crawled through the letterbox and had a good poke about. But he was neither. He stood and faced the door.

He waited, then knocked again. He was just about to step back onto the pavement when the door was opened by a tall woman wearing an apron and rubber gloves. Her blonde hair was swept across her forehead and tucked behind her right ear. She was pretty, much more so than the photograph on the website suggested, but she looked harassed or perplexed, possibly both.

'Hello. My name is Doyle. We spoke on the phone yesterday.'

'My nephew isn't here. I would have rung you but I didn't have a number.'

''Oh, that's a pity, I was hoping ... Look, can I come in? Five minutes, no more. It's just that ...'

Gina Harding stepped back, making room for him to pass her.

'Thank you,' Doyle said, as he went into the hall. It was completely empty except for several coats hanging from the picture rail. The floorboards had been painted grey and there were gaps between them wide enough to lose a pencil. She closed the door behind him, darkening the place, then walked up the stairs. 'The living room is this way,' she said.

He followed along a corridor to a room that was small and crammed with objects yet gave the impression of space to wander in. The windows overlooked the entire north-west of the city. Doyle walked to them and looked out – somewhere in the midst of all that was his flat.

He turned to find that she was removing her apron and the rubber gloves. 'Would you like some tea or coffee?' she asked.

Doyle was hung-over. It was the kind of hangover that only whiskey brings, hot behind the eyes, dry mouth and a rose garden of nerves that blossom anew at every fresh thought or sound. 'Tea would be lovely, thanks.'

She seemed somewhat surprised that he had taken up the offer. 'Right,' she said, heading to the door. 'I suppose you want sugar and milk and all that, do you?'

'Well, milk would be nice, if you have it. I don't take sugar.'

'I'll see what we have.'

When she had gone he squeezed into a tiny armchair that was embroidered with roses. Everything about the room was in miniature, from the upright piano in the corner to the bookcases on the far wall, as though it had been designed for someone very small. Yet she was a tall woman.

What was he doing here? It would have been easier to become a waiter. All he'd have had to do was take orders and deliver them, follow a script that had been written centuries ago and played out by hundreds of thousands of people every day ever since. Anything but this. What was he going to say to this woman? She clearly didn't want to have anything to do with him, and her fucking nephew was off doing drugs somewhere. He had a strong urge to get up and leave.

But the door opened and in came Gina Harding, carrying a tray that she placed on a footstool in the centre of the room. On it were a mug and a cup and saucer. The cup was delicate and dainty, like the one in the magpie picture. The mug was green with a gold trim around the side. It was chipped. Both contained a brown-grey liquid. 'They're both the same,' she said. 'Sorry, I don't think you're supposed to put milk into Earl Grey.' She handed Doyle the cup and saucer.

'Thanks. I think you can put milk into anything you like.'

She smiled. It was a brief gesture with which her features seemed unfamiliar. She sat opposite him on the edge of another tiny chair, holding the mug in both hands. 'So what are you, then? A businessman, a restaurateur … what?'

Doyle scrambled for one of his cards and gave it to her.

'A curator! Well, fancy that,' she said.

He had just sipped the tea, which tasted of soap. 'I've been given a job to find artists for the restaurant.'

'Wet Willie's …' she read aloud. 'Why has the job been given to you?'

'I'm sorry?'

'Maybe I'm being rude, am I? I want to know why you particularly were given this job.'

'It's not rude, not at all.'

The light from the window was shining directly on her, illuminating strands of grey in her blonde hair and making her brown eyes sparkle. She had a well-constructed face, high cheekbones, full lips. He guessed she was somewhere in her late thirties – it was difficult to say. But there was something hard in her expression. Her voice, too – it was soft but had a heaviness to it as though the words were spoken through a process that was in need of repair. Despite this, Doyle detected kindness.

'So, are you going to answer my question?'

'Well, I would if I could. I don't know, is the answer.' Doyle smiled. 'Does it make any difference?'

'Well, yes, it does. Have you any background in art or have you just been chosen at random to go out and find a cheap way for this guy to decorate his restaurant?'

'I was at art school,' Doyle told her.

'Well, then!' she said, as though he had just found his lost membership card to her club. 'Which one?'

'Camberwell.'

'Oh!' That pleased her.

'I didn't finish my degree.'

She held out her hands like a pope on a balcony. 'The fact that you got into somewhere like Camberwell means you were serious about your work. Why did you quit?'

'It was a load of bollox.'

She reacted to this as though he had slapped her. Eventually she said, 'And do you feel the same about all art?'

'Your work lifted me. It made me smile. When I saw it I just thought, Wow! Something fresh.'

'Thank you.' She smiled again.

'Where do you work?'

'Upstairs.'

'I'd love to see.'

'I'm sorry my nephew couldn't be here. Some of his stuff is up there but I'm not sure he's that keen to exhibit – I think he thinks his street-cred may suffer.'

'I'm getting the impression that people, artists, don't like to be seen hanging in restaurants.'

'Gosh, no! There's nothing wrong with it. In fact, in many ways it's much better than a gallery – more people will see it, that's for sure, and usually the commission is a lot less.'

'But …'

'Well, if you want to get established it's not going to happen in a restaurant. Art galleries are about a lot more than just showing your work. They take an artist on, bring them forward . . . It's a game, I know, but it's a game you have to play if you want to make a living wage.'

'I see.'

'Don't be downhearted. You'll find lots of people who'll be very happy to hang their work in your restaurant.'

'At the moment it doesn't look that way.'

'Well, I'll show you my nephew's things – I'm sure he could be persuaded,' she said, getting up.

Doyle followed her into the corridor, which now seemed dark compared with the light living room. At the end of it was a narrow stairway. It looked new: the wood was untreated, its edges still sharp. At the top there was a door, also new and unpainted. She climbed up and held it open for Doyle. He had to stoop to get through.

The room was long with a pitched ceiling that had two large windows on one side through which light poured. There were paintings everywhere. There were also lengths of wood – for frames, Doyle imagined – and a fat roll of bubble-wrap. He walked slowly down the room viewing the paintings that were stacked against the walls. He could tell by the colour and fluency that they were Gina's. He looked at each one. This was what should be on the walls on opening night. She was walking behind him. At the end of the room there were two pieces, one on an easel, the other on the wall, of a different style. Perhaps the work of the elusive nephew. Then, in a stack against the wall, he came across what must be the nephew's work. Loud colour confined by thick black line. It was lively and raw, but nothing in comparison to his aunt's. 'Yes, they're Alan's paintings. Good, don't you think? Let's lay them out here so you can have a better look.'

As they were shifting the pieces, Doyle kept looking up at the two at the back of the room although he couldn't make out what they were.

When they had finished lining up her nephew's work, they stood back to view it. He definitely had a style and enough ability to pull it off. 'They're nice,' Doyle said, 'but I'd prefer yours.'

'Look, I've explained I can't—'

'What are these two about?' he said, walking to the back of the room. The one on the wall depicted water in all its shades of blue and green. There was something just beneath the surface that he couldn't quite make out. He looked at the other: there were lots of reds, with daring strikes of blue and bold black, but the subject was hard to define – until suddenly, as with the Turner he'd seen in the museum, it clicked into place. It was a woman, a girl: the reds were emanating from her hands. The blues and the blacks were a network of lines that tore upwards towards her face, which was hard to make out, lost as it was among the reflections of a bright light shining from somewhere unseen. But he could tell she was laughing, mad laughter, more hysteria than joy. Dark curls floated on the surface.

He started to back away. And as he did the first began to reveal itself. It was the same face but now, beneath the surface, the eyes, half closed, were on him, their expression unreadable. Looking from one to the other caused the images to dance in front of him. In one Daphne was drifting below the surface almost lifeless. In the other she was lifeless but laughing.

He turned and made for the door. Gina was in his way. He pushed past her. He grabbed the door handle, stumbled down the stairs and went into a toilet he had noticed on the way up. There, he fell in front of the bowl. He thought he would vomit but within seconds the urge had left him. He remained where he was, his head balanced on the rim of the porcelain. It was as if Gina Harding had come in just as Daphne's life was leaving her and begun making sketches. How could this have happened? What had he just seen?

There was a knock on the door. 'Are you all right?' The tone was concerned.

The queasiness came and went in waves, pasting his forehead with sweat. Questions formed but were swamped before he could consider them. Slowly he rose to his feet. It was an illusion, that was all – it had to be.

He ran cold water over his wrists; it encased them in a transparent bracelet that furled at the edges. Water, that's what would have killed her. She would have got drowsy, then weaker, until finally she'd have slipped under the surface and then it was over.

But this was ridiculous. When he'd found her she was sitting up. Or was she? He couldn't remember. It was a blank. How could something like that have gone so completely?

He looked at his reflection in the bathroom mirror. His skin was pale, almost green. It made the whites of his eyes yellow. A question prodded him, like a finger: 'Did I do it? Did I kill her?'

'Are you all right?' She was still there, standing just outside the door. Somehow he would have to get past her and out of this house. Even the air in here was wrong, heavy and impossible to breathe.

He turned off the tap. He didn't want to have to kill Gina Harding, absolutely no point. Just tell her you're unhinged, temporarily insane, she's a nice woman, she'll understand. No, just get out.

He dried his hands and opened the door. Her eyes widened when she saw him. She stepped back. 'What happened? What did you see? You look awful!' There was a gap between her and the wall, he stepped into it and was past her. He had a clear run now to the stairs and from there to the hall and the front door.

Outside, he ran. Down streets and around corners. He ran unaware of direction or of the people he shared the pavement with. He ran until he ran out of pavement and people. Then he staggered to a tree stump and sat. His body fizzed. His bones were light and his skin paper. He wiped his hair away from his sweating forehead, then leant forward and pulled up his socks. When, finally, he stood, his leg muscles felt dry and hard. When he tried to walk, pain sprang from the sinew at the back of his ankle. It made him limp. He hobbled to the corner of a large red-brick building, looking for something that might tell him where he was.

Around the corner was a broad empty street. On one side a row of terraced houses was followed by the concrete face of a large industrial building, a network of rusting fire escapes decorating the front. Then there was wasteground littered with broken glass and abandoned cars, some of which had been burnt out, stripped of their paint, the shells were coated with bright orange rust. Beyond, there were more houses, an earthy mud-brown. Weeds grew up from the road surface.

Doyle looked back down the street he had just come up. It was equally devoid of anything inviting so he decided to keep going. He would come out somewhere.

As he approached one of the mud houses – that was exactly what they looked like close up too – he saw an elderly man leaning on his gate, watching him. When Doyle got within a few feet the man nodded. Doyle nodded back. As he passed, the old man said, 'Day.' Doyle wondered what had come before it. 'Good day' or 'Nice day' or maybe even 'Friday'. Perhaps there had been no other word. Perhaps the man stood there saying 'Day' to passers-by when it was light and 'Night' in the dark. Perhaps if you stopped and asked, he would inform you of the season, the year or even the phase of the moon. Doyle looked back at him. He was still staring.

A couple of hundred metres further on the grey cement surface began to separate into cracks that became bigger until there was more gap than road. Some distance ahead he could see that a wide trench ran diagonally across and beyond a mound of earth. He'd have to turn back.

The old man, his eyes little black berries of merriment, watched him approach. He lifted his arms off the gate as Doyle got to within talking distance and stood up very straight. 'You're here about the rabbits, aren't you?'

Doyle looked at him. 'Sorry?'

'You're looking for rabbits.'

Doyle stopped. 'No, I am not looking for rabbits.'

The old man's smile broadened. 'It's all right, you can tell me.'

'I'm not looking for any bloody rabbits, OK? I'm looking for a way out of here, if you must know.'

'Well, that's simple. Just follow the route that got you here.'

Doyle regarded the man. The skin around his eyes curved like the grain in wood. His cheekbones were high and deep creases carved the skin that dropped from them. He was small and thin. His fingers were swollen and gnarled, the skin covering them a bloodless yellow. He was wearing lightweight rain gear and sandals. He was old but it was impossible to tell how old.

'To be honest, I don't know how I got here. I was running, not looking, just running.'

'Rabbit chasing?'

'Rabbits were the furthest thing from my mind.' Doyle looked at the house behind the man. It was a two-storey cottage covered with what looked like mud.

'They're made of straw and coated with clay,' the man said.

'Really?'

'Yes. That's why they have me out here on wolf duty.'

'Do they indeed?'

'Indeed they do. I thought that maybe you were a wolf when I saw you coming down the road. That's why I was wondering about the rabbits, see?'

'I don't follow.'

'Well, no wolf I ever met has turned up his nose at a rabbit.' The old man seemed pleased with this statement.

'I'm not familiar with the ways of the wolf but I'm sure you're right.'

'Why don't you come in?'

'No, thank you. I should try to get back to where I was.'

'That proves it.' The old man was becoming excited now. 'I'll put the kettle on.'

'What do you mean?'

'You're definitely no wolf. What wolf would refuse an invitation to the straw house? Besides, you can use the phone to call a taxi.' The old man turned his back and walked nimbly to the front door of the house.

Doyle had his own phone in his pocket if he wanted to call a taxi, but there was something intriguing in the old man's demeanour. He looked up and down the road, then opened the gate and followed him up the path.

The inside of the house was a surprise. From a small square hallway one set of wooden steps led up and another down. Doyle followed the old man as he ascended and found himself in a large, brightly lit room that clearly served as living room and kitchen.

The light came from a dome in the ceiling. The stairway continued up to a landing with several doors off it. In the living room, the walls were decorated with guitars, banjos and other stringed instruments. A sitar rested on a sofa.

The old man moved to a counter in the kitchen area. 'Sit down. What's your name? Not Peter, I hope.' He chuckled.

'Doyle.'

'Is that it? Bit short for such a tall chap.'

'It's Desmond Doyle, but I'm called Doyle.'

'Do I detect an Irish accent?'

'I was born in Wexford.'

'Ha! Ha! I never miss a trick.' He moved towards the table holding two cups.

'You thought I was a wolf.' The table was covered with newspapers and books.

'And perhaps you are. Who knows?'

'I'm not a wolf.'

'My DNA testing kit is in the pawnshop so we'll probably never know for sure.'

Doyle found himself smiling. 'And what is your name, may I ask?'

'Terrence Martin Hassler and I am presently the guest of my daughter and son-in-law. He's a musician, hence the ...' He waved towards the wall. 'My daughter is an artist, very good. Me, I can't draw a potato.'

'And they're not at home now?'

'No – Frank is on tour in the Far East and Eleanor has gone out to join him. She doesn't like to leave me on my own for too long. I don't know why.'

'Do they not have children?'

'Children! Of course they do. All at university – Edinburgh and Oxford, art and science. Covering all angles, see?'

'How far are we from the centre?'

'Well, that would depend on what you're talking about.'

'How far are we from the centre of the city?'

'Oh! That centre. Not far – two miles, perhaps. How do you take your tea?'

'Milk, no sugar.'

The old man went back to the counter. 'They wouldn't like this, you know.'

'Who wouldn't like what?'

'Frank and Eleanor. They wouldn't like me inviting in the wolf.'

'Is this house really made of straw?'

'Oh, yes.'

'I can't see any.'

'That's because it's rendered – rendered invisible.'

'It's an impressive building.'

'It's the latest, or was the latest, in alternative technology.'

'Whose idea was that?'

'Frank's – and Eleanor's. There were others but they baled out, if you'll excuse the pun. The council didn't clear the area. All a bit of a mess.' He came back to the table carrying a teapot. 'So, Mr Desmond Doyle, can you tell me what it was you were running from?'

'Something very odd just happened.'

'Yes?'

'Can I ask you how old you are?'

'I'll be ninety-seven in June.'

'My God!'

'My God indeed.'

'You're a fit man – how did you manage that?'

'I had a great friend once, a marvellous skier. He'd whoop it up in the nightclubs until two in the morning and then be on the first lift at nine in the morning. When I asked him how he acted like a teenager when he was eighty-nine he said the secret was to eat little, eat slowly and never worry. When I told this to my son-in-law he said, "In that case I have ten minutes to live."'

'So you took your friend's advice.'

'Me? No! Not at all. I've low blood pressure, which means you're always cold and tired but you live for ever.'

'I'm twenty-nine and I can't see much point in living.'

'There's absolutely fuck-all point in it but it's what we do.'

'My girlfriend's just killed herself.'

'Ah! You poor man.'

'I don't know what to think about it. I mean, I don't know if she was all that wrong to do it. People just automatically think it's a terrible thing to do but maybe it isn't.'

'You feel lost.'

'Well, I don't know what to believe. I don't mean about God or religion, I mean I don't know what I know. Everything I thought was there, everything I thought was real, has become vague. I don't know if my girlfriend is really dead because I don't know if she ever existed. I mean, are people who never existed dead? No, they're not, because death is when someone who was there is no longer there, right? So maybe I just invented her. I'll tell you something I think is odd. I can't recall her – I can't, you know, see her face. I have memories of her but they're slippery, and maybe they're slippery because she never existed. It is possible, isn't it, that I invented her and now I'm uninventing her? But then today, just now, before I came here, she appeared in paintings I was looking at, and the one thought I had was that I killed her.'

'Belief is more powerful than knowledge. What you believe you are is what you are.'

'What are you saying? If I believe it happened, it happened? And if I don't, it didn't?'

'I was captured by the Japanese at the fall of Singapore. I was very young and they held me for four years. In that time I saw a lot of things I couldn't believe.'

'So then, according to you, they didn't happen?'

'Who knows?'

Doyle looked at the old man. He had probably witnessed hideous brultality. Had it unhinged him? Maybe it had reduced his ability to reason, hence the rabbits and his general oddity.

'The phone is just behind you,' the old man said, smiling.

Doyle turned and saw it on the window-sill. 'Thank you.'

'What are you going to do?' the old man asked.

'I really don't know.'

'Well, that's a good point to start from.'

'Do you understand the concept of being overwhelmed? Sorry, of course you do.'

'You're answering for me, thinking of my time in the camps. Well, that was different. That was war, and in war life and death take on a different meaning. Now we treat life as a given, and we're amazed and upset when it's taken away.'

'Yeah, but she killed herself.'

'It's a brave thing to do.'

'Brave? Are you mad? It's not brave.'

'You said you thought you killed her?'

'Just now I went to see paintings, an artist's work, and Daphne was in them – she had got into the paintings. She was in the bath like she was when I found her.'

'Well, my advice to you would be to go back and see those paintings again.'

'Why? You think I was seeing things?'

'Lots of things can be seen in a painting.'

'There were two of them – she was in both.'

'My daughter's an artist. Me, I can't draw a potato.'

'You said.'

'Did I? That's the trouble with getting old – you repeat everything and your friends are all dead, which is probably just as well.'

Doyle took out his phone. 'I'm going to call a taxi now.'

'Yes.'

The taxi dropped Doyle at the flat. Inside it was silent. It felt like a place where nothing had ever happened or possibly would ever happen again. And yet it was heavy with an event, with an absence, something that was now no more, complete yet incomplete.

He put on the kettle and felt that it, too, had to struggle to boil. He made a cup of tea and went into the living room where he stared out of the window. In front of him he saw a segment of city, a hill that used its tiled roofs and strips of green like steps that climbed to the summit. And now, in the gloom of this late Saturday afternoon, all colours were fading, losing their vibrancy, so that soon nothing on the hill would be visible. And just as that thought came so did lights, a strip of streetlights that flickered and steadied, radiating a delicate orange to bathe the street beneath them in a loose imitation of sunlight. And lights came from the houses too. And soon the place had taken on an image of itself but now in negative. Although it was gaudy and without detail it had a strong beauty. It told a different story from the daylight version of itself. How would the painters he had seen yesterday tackle it? He would employ cubism because that was how it looked even now, especially now. How would Gina Harding paint it? Just as the thought struck the telephone rang. He wanted to ignore it but in the intensity of the silence it seemed to scream.

'Hello, Desmond?'

He knew immediately that it was Gina Harding. 'Speaking.'

'Hi.'

'Hello.'

'We need to meet.'

'Do we?'

'I don't know what happened here this afternoon. I need to know.'

Doyle was silent. He could see the two paintings as if he was standing in front of them. What had the old man said? Something about seeing in paintings what you wanted to see. Maybe if he saw them again ...

'I saw something in those two paintings. That was all.'

'What did you see?'

'I'm not sure now. Maybe if I could see them again?'

'OK. This evening?'

'No, tomorrow.'

They arranged that he would call in the morning, at eleven, and then he put down the phone, walked to the chair and sat again. He became aware that he was alone. He was expecting no one and the next person who would walk through the door would be some part of this thing that Daphne had set in motion and they would have an agenda that he was part of but only because he was linked with her. His life was now just strings of events that he could neither control nor alter. And how real were they? Daphne had existed. That was indisputably a fact. She had killed herself. Was that another? Yes: he had found her.

– Yes, you found her, but that doesn't mean she committed suicide.

– OK, then, who killed her? Cock-fucking-Robin?

– Maybe she staged it, and the police were actor friends who had access to uniforms, and Gina was an actress too. But what about Kneebone? One thing was for sure: he was no actor. No, it was nothing like that.

He couldn't do this – sit in a chair looking out of the window with his brain on fire. He'd go mad. Maybe he was already. And if he couldn't do it, why was he still doing it? Perhaps the answer lay in drink. He should float away in a sea of it. He had only once slipped into that ocean, gone far enough to see the place where monsters be. And beyond the monsters would be other, bigger, monsters. And what would lie beyond them? What had the old man said? 'We live because that's what we do.' Doyle thought he'd like the old man to be here now, making tea and repeating that he couldn't draw a potato.

But the old man was not here and neither was there a sea of drink to set sail upon. There was just the lake of his window and the view beneath its surface of people living their lives in all the robust rush that people do. He never really was one of them. He looked like a person, spoke like one, had arms and legs and a digestive system; he had wants, hopes and plans even, but somehow he had never seemed to connect with the world, even before Daphne had killed herself.

A society was made up of molecules; each one found others that it could connect with and together they'd make a cluster, which would perform something vital or elegant. But he, Doyle, had been engineered differently. He'd slip out of a connection, slide on to the next encounter and fail to connect properly there too. Was that why she had done it? She had got saddled with someone who couldn't connect and she couldn't leave, so she'd decided to take the bus?

He thought of the girl upstairs. She'd said that if there was ever anything . . . But what was her name? It would be good to have her here now, walking about and talking – and he could watch her mouth move as she chatted about her day and listen to her bracelets clink as she raised her hand to smooth her hair and see too far up her skirt when she crossed her legs, and watch her looking through the guide on the TV. But that was a girl from long ago, a girl who was left somewhere in Hammersmith or in the Green Angel on the Goldhawk Road. That Daphne had never come down the M4 to Bristol. But the body of that Daphne would go along the M5 some day to be buried or burned by her people. So maybe the girl upstairs was the answer to all his ills. Maybe with her I'll connect and she'll lie in my arms as the bulldozers tear away at the walls of our home . . .

Doyle awoke in the chair to the deep silence and darkness. He went to bed and spent the seven hours until dawn in turmoil. Several times he got up, twice to drink – once he even ate thinking that, although he didn't feel it, he might be hungry. All of it was documented and separated by the bell of the Polish church.

Eight

Early on Monday morning Gina Harding walked into her studio, carrying a mug of tea and a slice of toast. Ever since she had spoken to Doyle the previous evening she had wanted to come up and look at the two pictures. But she hadn't wanted to make a point of it. The two drawings had emerged from her fingers at a speed much more rapid than normal but she would not allow them to dominate her. She had started the first one evening last week. She had almost finished for the day when she'd pulled out a sheet of heavyweight cartridge paper and clipped it to the easel that lingered unused at the back of the room. Beside it, on the table, was a box of pastels and she realised, as she picked up the first stick, that she had no idea what she was going to do. This was fun. She had been working from sketches and painting in oils for an exhibition next September but this was an outing into the unknown.

She was aware of the vibration of the pastel in her fingers as she passed it over the rough paper. She was aware, too, of the dry sound it made and how its dust fell like exhaust from an engine. She made curves that seemed to have their own purpose. She chose colours that were strong, lots of reds, vibrant greens and blues. And black. She had always shied away from jet black, but here it was now in big bold strokes, sliding down the page, separating the blues and the reds and the yellows. She abandoned the colours and started using her fingers to move, spread and blend. She could see a water pattern emerge but it was interwoven with too much black. That didn't matter. She was enjoying herself. And when she had finished she stood back.

She could see it now. It was a picture of a girl. She was lying in a bath, an old-fashioned bath with a rim. She was very still, the water almost overflowing. But the water was red and the girl's black hair streaked through it like seaweed. The paper was completely covered, yet it didn't feel finished. She took it off, pinned it to the wall behind the easel and stuck up another piece of paper. This was crazy. This was an extravagant reaction to the tight work she'd been doing for weeks now. Leave it.

As she washed her hands in the sink at the far end of the studio she looked at what she had just done. She didn't like it. The style was too bold, too forthright, but there was something strong about it. She was tempted to go back to the blank paper on the easel when she noticed the time. It was almost eight o'clock: she'd been working on the pastel for nearly two hours. It had felt like minutes. It was time to cook. Alan was probably back already, glued to a screen, remote in hand, earphones wedged in place.

Her sleep that night was full of images that were garish and improbable. In the morning she decided she was coming down with a virus, a cold probably, and remembered that one of the images from her sleep was a little black dog curled up by the side of the bath in the pastel she had done the previous day. It had lain there curled up, relaxed but keeping an eye on her, and she knew that if she went anywhere near the figure in the bath the dog would launch itself at her.

She got on with her work as normal that day, waiting for

further symptoms to develop. They never did. But she was aware of the blank piece of paper at the top of the room and that on the wall just behind it there was a girl in a bath and, as a piece of art, it had nothing to do with anything else in the studio. She ignored them both but promised herself that later in the afternoon she'd do one more. That would be the end of it. But nothing she could do that morning was right: the oil on her brush would not smear smooth or rough on the canvas as it normally did, the colours weren't working and the perspective was wrong. She threw her brushes down, not even bothering to clean them, and approached the blank paper.

She was aware of witnessing herself step into a place in her mind where she felt calm. She picked up a pastel stick and again felt it in her fingers as it slid down the page. And this one seemed to complete her. When it was finished she knew that whatever internal mechanism had been at work it had expressed itself and now she could go back to her own work.

It was another girl in a bath. In fact, looking at it from a distance, it could have been the same girl, but it was a close-up and this time her face was below the surface of the water, but only barely, and she was smiling. No, that was too strong: she looked as though she was preoccupied with some amusing memory or thought and was happy to lie there, for the moment, in the silence. The water in this one was red too.

Nine

Harry Kneebone's mother-in-law was ill again, although this time it looked like the old lady might actually make her final bow. The result of this was that Jenny was spending more and more time out of the house. And the result of that was that the domestics had slid to a halt, which meant no ironed shirts, no proper breakfast, and this morning he had achieved something he had previously believed to be impossible: he had emptied the toothpaste tube. So, he had left the house in a crumpled shirt, the taste of last night's takeaway still gritting the back of his teeth and the knowledge of something he did not care to admit: he had, long ago, surrendered his independence for home comforts.

To add to it all, he had found a postcard from his son lying on the mat by the hall door as he was leaving. His initial reaction had been relief – it was the first time Chris had made contact in what must be five months. This, though, had quickly soured. Why did his son insist on putting them through this? Chris had abandoned his mobile – in fact, he seemed to have abandoned all the technical advances of this and the last century. Harry Kneebone read the back, then looked again at the front: the boy was somewhere in Chile. As he put the postcard into his inside jacket pocket he wondered at what stage parenting stopped. When you stopped caring, he guessed.

When he reached the office he sat at his desk and turned on the computer. As he waited for it to go through its routine before he could access it, he got out the postcard. In his almost illegible scrawl, Chris had said, 'Last night I watched the moon rise above the Andes. Now I'm watching the sun sink into the Pacific. Does life get better?' It was signed 'Chris, with love.' The postmark read 'Puerto Montt' and it was dated mid-March. So, four weeks ago, his son had had just the right amount of wine, marijuana and/or cocaine in him to scrawl this little reminder that he was still alive, still self-obsessed and still thought he had the right to parade his absence in front of them whenever he pleased. Jenny, of course, would not see it like that. She'd get excited, she'd be on the phone to her sister, then to Maureen from work. It would make her day, her week, and then, as time passed and the frustration of not being able to reply came to bear, it would leave her feeling empty. It was like getting postcards from the dead.

He put it back into his pocket and turned to the screen. Among the darkened drop of unopened emails was the coroner's report on Daphne Palmer. He clicked on it to discover it was headed with the word 'Preliminary'. By the end of the first paragraph it was suggesting the evidence, both physical and pathological, showed that the girl had taken her own life. He read through the next couple of paragraphs, registering nothing. He was wondering why this news disappointed him. Surely to Christ it was better that if the girl had had to die, that she did it at her own hand rather than someone else's. At least with suicide the victim and the perpetrator of the crime were one and the same person. So why, then, was he feeling uncomfortable? Maybe it was because if the coroner's 'Preliminary' report proved right, his instincts were not as sharp as he would have liked to believe.

He reread it. The inconclusiveness hinged around an 'inconsistency' in the execution of the wounds and the bruising, which was the result, it seemed, of repeated injury accrued over many months. If that was the case it would tally with the boyfriend's story. And his own investigations had borne out that the girl had been all over town looking for anything that would get her up in front of an audience and that she had been remarkably unsuccessful. So why, then, did he not believe what was in front of him and slide the report into the done-and-dusted tray? He didn't know. But what he did know was that if he insisted on ignoring what was in front of him he had better come up with a motive. All he had that was indisputable was a body. And it was the body of a young woman in her prime. Not that youth and beauty were protection against suicide: it was just that he didn't believe she'd done it. Something didn't fit. The boyfriend and his boss, McAllister, had ruffled his feathers. If there was any substance to what his instincts were suggesting, the answer had to lie with them.

He emailed the coroner's office, asking when the full autopsy would be complete. If, when they finally came out with their report, it stated emphatically that it was suicide, he would let it drop but until then he was treating this as murder.

He then emailed the planning office asking for a copy of the plans McAllister had submitted for his restaurant. It might be interesting to see exactly what sort of a restaurant he intended opening. Then a thought struck him: looking through the case notes, he saw that neither McAllister nor Doyle had been checked for previous offences. Why hadn't someone done that? He knew the answer straight away: no one believed it was anything other than a suicide.

Nothing came up on Doyle: the man had lived twenty-nine years and had never as much as farted out of place. McAllister, however, had a meaty little string of minor convictions from his younger years. It was mostly traffic – he had lost his licence in 1991 for speeding and dangerous driving. And there was one case of shop-lifting in 1988, which had led to an incident at the police station and a charge of assault on one of the arresting officers. McAllister had been fined two hundred pounds and given a two-year suspended sentence. And that, it seemed, had been the end of his little foray into the world of crime, at least until now.

Perhaps a visit to them both might rattle their cages.

Downstairs was a mess. A network of wires dropped from a scar in the ceiling. The sound of a saw blasted over the tinny radio that the workmen seemed unable to do without and there were people everywhere. Geoff stepped through it, hard to believe that all of this could have been created in one day, one morning. It hadn't looked so complicated on paper. He walked to the back of the kitchen and watched two plasterers at work. It just didn't seem possible that two men could get such a large surface so evenly flat and smooth. His presence, however, was making them nervous so he busied himself making sure that the pipes for water and waste were where they should be. He then went back into the dining area where the electricians had left the entrails of the new wiring system dangling from shiny metal boxes slotted into the wall. He stepped over a pile of timbers that stretched the length of the floor, wondering where it was all going to go.

He told himself it was the decoration that mattered, that and the furniture, but he would think about those later. Right now he had the kitchen equipment to worry about. From his conversations with the suppliers this morning, he was fairly sure of getting the heavy equipment, like the ovens and fryers, but now he needed to sit down and work out some details, the pots, pans, cutlery. Then there was the small matter of staff. Here, at least, the economic climate was in his favour. Lots of people out there were looking for work. One, a man whose CV read as if he should be applying for a job with the Roux brothers, would be in here within the next twenty minutes. When Geoff had pointed out his obvious over-qualification on the phone the man was honest enough to say he had been out of work now for nearly three months and would take anything. Geoff admired the candour. What he wanted in staff was honesty, hard work and a sense of fun. It had to be fun or it was a waste of time. That was the problem with the shop: it had become joyless. He had just come from there and was glad to be away from it. Everything about the place was dry and dull, and vegetarians could be such pious bastards. But they had given him a wage for the last five years and at the moment they were paying for this renovation so perhaps a he should cut them a little slack.

The building contractor he had pulled in at a moment's notice, and with good recommendation, was a tall, dark-haired New Zealander named Jim. He came through the door now, talking with a small, fat man, nodded at Geoff and said, 'This is Steve. He's going to give us a price on the tiling.' When Geoff continued to stare, Jim said, 'The tiling! In the kitchen.' When Geoff finally nodded, Jim laughed. 'You'd forgotten, hadn't you?'

He had, and that was a problem: this business was about detail and forgetting something as small but as important as the tiling in the kitchen scared him. What else was he forgetting?

He was about to start again on the list for the kitchen when another small, round man came through the door. This one was in a raincoat and looked out of place in the surroundings. Geoff recognised him at once. The man stood still, his eyes absorbing every detail until they fell on Geoff.

'Can I help you?' Geoff called.

The inspector gave an absentminded nod, then stepped over the timbers to join him. 'I say, this is going to be the business, eh?'

Geoff couldn't work out if the comment was sarcastic or not. 'That's exactly what it's going to be, the business.'

'Quite the entrepreneur, Mr McAllister.'

'Just trying to make a living, which, as far as I know, is not yet a crime.'

'Well, that would depend on the nature of the business you choose, would it not?'

Geoff exhaled. 'What do you want?'

Kneebone looked at him. 'When do you intend opening?'

'Couple of weeks.'

Kneebone raised his eyebrows. 'I expect there'll be a few late nights between now and then?'

'Exactly – so what is it? I'm busy.'

'What kind of place are you opening here, Mr McAllister?'

'What do you mean, what kind of a place am I opening? It's a restaurant – you know, a restaurant.'

'Thai, Cantonese, French, Spanish? There's a lot of different kinds.'

'A good restaurant is what I'm aiming for. I'd even say excellent.'

'Aim high, why not? Do you mind if I have a look around?'

'Be my guest, but take care you don't get your clothes dirty.'

Kneebone smiled and sauntered off in the direction of the kitchen. Geoff watched him. Jim stopped his conversation with the tiler to watch him too. When Kneebone went through the back door to what was to become the smoking area Jim looked back at Geoff. He smiled and shrugged but the sight of the little man wandering about was disturbing. When Kneebone came back, he walked into the centre of the dining area and stood there examining the ceiling. Geoff had had enough. 'Seriously, what the hell are you here for?'

'Rewiring? Very good.'

'So, you're a building inspector now, are you?'

'Remind me of something. How long did you wait in the car while your friend Mr Doyle was in getting his girlfriend?'

'You mean on the day he found her dead?'

'Yes, that day.'

'I don't know, not long.'

'Ten minutes?'

'I don't know, more like five.'

'One person can do a lot to another in five minutes.'

Geoff stared at the man. 'Look, Inspector, I'm busy right now, so if you don't have anything concrete why don't you wander off and let me get on with it?'

Kneebone came closer and stared up at him. 'How well did you know Daphne Palmer?'

'You asked me that before at the station. It's all in my statement.'

'Yes, and I've read your statement. In fact, the more I read it, the more it leaves me wondering.'

'Wondering what exactly? Daphne killed herself.'

'Oh, did she? Tell me, Mr McAllister, how could you possibly know that?'

Kneebone continued to stare at Geoff, then turned and left.

Doyle was looking for his keys when there was a knock at the door. It had to be someone from inside the building because they hadn't used the street-door bell. He didn't want any interruptions. He would be late even if he were to leave now.

He opened the door and, for a moment, failed to recognise the girl from upstairs. She was wearing a dark blue coat, and her nurse's uniform was just visible at the collar. Briefly Doyle thought she must be there in her professional capacity. But when her lips slid into a smile he found himself strangely pleased.

'Just passing, thought I'd check if you're OK,' she said.

'Fine, thank you. I'm on my way out, actually, but I'm good.'

'I've come off a night shift.'

'I'd ask you in but I'm just . . .'

'No, no, it's fine. I've been on a late shift. I just thought I'd check on you. Sorry, I'm being a bit nursy – I shouldn't do that.'

'No, do it as much as you—' Just behind him his doorbell sounded. It startled them both. 'Sorry,' Doyle said. 'I wasn't expecting anyone.'

When he opened the door it was Inspector Kneebone, smiling.

'Lovely morning, Mr Doyle. May I come in?' he asked, stepping into the hallway.

'I'm just on my way out.'

'Won't take a minute.' The inspector stopped when he saw Jasmine. 'Ah!' he said. 'The young lady from upstairs, if my memory serves me?'

Jasmine smiled weakly. She nodded and turned towards the stairs.

'Oh, don't go on my account,' the inspector said.

She looked back at him. 'I'm ready for some sleep – shift work.'

The inspector turned to Doyle. 'Well, I'll keep you company for a few minutes, if that's all right?'

'I was on my way out.'

'Like I said, it won't take a minute.' He stood back, allowing Doyle room to enter his flat. Doyle watched Jasmine climb the stairs before he passed Kneebone and went into the living room. Kneebone followed.

'Good friends with ...?' the inspector said, gazing at the view outside.

'Jasmine.' Doyle was happy her name had returned to him.

'Yes, that's right, the lovely Jasmine.'

'Look, I really need to be going . . .'

'Nice day for a stroll.'

Doyle noticed for the first time that the sky was blue – blue but tainted with high milky clouds. 'Can I help you with anything?'

'Oh, I'm sure you can, Mr Doyle. I'm sure you can help me with a great deal.'

'Inspector, I don't know what you want but whatever it is just say it, because I'm already late.'

'I was just mulling things over, Mr Doyle, and I wanted to see you again, see for myself the scene. Odd, isn't it? We have technology and digital this and digital that but there's nothing quite like a good old sniff about, let the senses bathe in it. That's what I like to do, if you'll pardon my choice of words there, Mr Doyle. Who are you to meet?'

Doyle watched him go down the vertical line of the CDs with his finger.

'Fan of Captain Beefheart, are you, Mr Doyle?'

'Daphne was.'

'Strange, for a woman. Still, mustn't generalise on grounds of gender, not allowed these days, apparently. Who else did she like?'

'A lot of different people. She had some strange tastes.'

'And in music, too, no doubt.' He had moved on to the row of DVDs.

'What do you want?'

'What I want is easy, Mr Doyle. I want to know what happened to your girlfriend. What do you want?'

'Right now, for you to go. I told you what happened to Daphne ...'

'You did, but you know what? I don't believe you.'

Doyle watched the crumpled little man in his living room. The inspector had never even met Daphne, never seen Daphne and him together. Why was he here doing this? Was it part of his job to ruffle the recently bereaved to see what happened? If it was, his job was a shit one. 'There's nothing I can do about what you believe.'

The inspector turned and looked at him, then smiled. 'Oh, I'd give yourself more credit than that ...'

'Look, I'm going now. You can stay here if you want.'

'It's all right, Mr Doyle. I've enjoyed our little chat. I can see myself out.'

Doyle stood back to allow Kneebone to pass. He then followed him to the front door where the inspector said he could drop Doyle anywhere he wished to go. Doyle said no thanks, went down the steps and walked off in the direction of Nine Tree Hill, aware that he was being watched.

As Doyle crossed the main road at the lights he wondered at the inspector's intention. If he had come to rattle him, he had failed. Doyle did not feel rattled. Or if he did, it just slipped below the surface of the numbness along with everything else.

It was nearly twenty past eleven when he got to Gina Harding's. She looked younger than he had remembered. Her face was handsome but there was nothing soft about it. It had to play host to a constant expression of concern that had long since robbed it of its softness.

'Hi,' she said, moving aside to let him in. Doyle stepped in, aware of irritation rising within him.

She went straight to the stairs and started to climb. At the top she unlocked the door and went into the studio. 'I don't know why I lock it – habit now, but I ...'

As soon as he entered he saw it. From this distance it was even more obvious. In the one where she was beneath the water she managed to look dead and happy at the same time. The other was less clear. She had cut herself but she was still alive, staring out from a bath of red water that was bouncing with the reflection of the overhead light.

The familiar sickness filled his stomach. He turned sideways and found himself staring at a mess of colour on a square wooden palette. Brushes pointed upwards from a jar. On a shelf he saw rags and bottles of oil and turpentine. The smells ignited an image of amber. He looked back at the two pictures. He was going to be sick.

'I haven't touched them since,' Gina Harding said.

Doyle went back down the stairs aware only of the physical weakness and lightness of head and fingers that were the forerunners to vomiting. On the landing he leant against the wall, sweating. He heard the door to the studio close and steps behind him descending. He became aware that she was standing in front of him. That look of concern would have deepened. He didn't know – all he could see was her feet. And they looked too dainty to belong to her.

'Why don't you go into the living room and sit down? I'll make us some tea.'

He didn't move.

'I'm going to make some tea and you do whatever you want to do. I'll be a couple of minutes.' With that the feet were gone, leaving him with the grey-painted floorboards. After some moments he went into the bathroom and sat on the side of the bath. Then, leaning towards the washbasin, he ran the cold tap, stood, splashed some water onto his face and looked in the mirror.

He saw a deformed version of himself, haggard, pale. Do a portrait of that, Francis how-do-you-like-your-Bacon. Another wave of nausea flushed through him. He sat. He was still sitting when he heard her pass outside, the tray rattling. He listened as a door opened, then closed.

He could get up, walk down the stairs and out of the house. It would be the most sane and sensible thing to do. In the room just above him there were two paintings, drawings, whatever she called them, of the woman who, six days ago, had bled to death in the bath from two slits in her wrists. These drawings/paintings were done by a woman who had not known Daphne, had probably never even seen her. What had sanity or sense to do with anything?

Eventually he stood and left the bathroom. He went to the living-room door, opened it and walked to a chair opposite where Gina was sitting.

His attention was taken once again by the dimensions of the furniture. Sunlight lit her eyes and lifted the highlights in her hair. It lit a rectangle behind her. But suddenly it was muted – a passing cloud. Then it came back, as if someone was playing with the brightness button.

She poured an amber liquid from a porcelain pot. He noticed the walls in the room were not evenly painted – there was a gap by the sofa where the yellow tapered into white. She picked up a jug and said, 'You do take milk?'

'Yes.'

The cup rattled in its saucer as she held it out to him. He took it and then, not knowing what to do with it, put it back on the tray. She sipped her tea.

'Would you like to tell me what's going on?' she asked.

The sun was strong now on his shoulders. He looked at her face, the light showing every mark, crease and crevice. 'You have no idea?'

She shook her head. Doyle was aware only that he wanted this conversation to be over.

'A week ago I found the girl I was living with in the bath. She was dead and her wrists were slit.'

Gina Harding's face froze.

'You've got a picture – two pictures – upstairs of my girlfriend.' His tone surprised him: he sounded contemptuous. Gina Harding was staring at him. He leant forward. 'My girlfriend committed suicide a week ago and you've been upstairs painting pictures of the happy event.'

She stood and walked towards the door, then turned and went back to her chair, aware that his eyes were on her. She sat. 'I don't know what to say.'

'How did you know her?' he asked.

'I didn't.'

He placed his hands on the arms of the chair, about to get up.

'I didn't know anything about this – not a thing!' she said.

'I don't believe you.'

'Just let me tell you about it from my side ...' She saw him draw breath and then told him how the pictures had come about. As she spoke she watched the rigidity ease from him. When she finished he said nothing and she wanted, at that moment, to walk over, take his hand and caress his head. He looked as if he was sitting on the last step of a stairway he had just tumbled down.

'You never knew her?'

'No.'

'I think I'll go now.'

'No, wait.'

'There's nothing else to say.'

'There's more going on here than you and I can fathom. There has to be a way to ...'

'I want nothing to do with any of this. I'm going.'

'Your girlfriend wants to make her presence felt – that much we can say for sure.'

'Can we? What the fuck do you know about it?'

'There's someone I think you should meet.'

'Who?'

'She's a spiritualist. She can help us.'

'You think I'm going to listen to some tea-leaf-reading idiot telling me a load of crap?'

'I understand you're upset. But this isn't easy for me either. There has to be a way to make sense of it.'

'Sense? There is no sense. There is nothing.' He folded forward as he spoke, perching at the edge of the chair, then put his head into his hands. She allowed the silence to gather around them. Outside a flock of seagulls burst into a squabbling riot that faded, leaving the muted drone of traffic. He didn't move.

'I have no idea what you're going through but there is a woman I know who might be able to help us.'

He lifted his head from his hands. 'I'm going now. What you do with your pictures is up to you.' He stood up.

'Look, I don't think—'

'I need to go.'

She rose. 'No – wait, please.'

'Don't say another word.'

'But you must understand what this is like for me.'

'I don't care. Do you understand that?' He pushed past her and swung the door open.

Ten

Geoff walked to the grocery shop at the end of the street. This whole fucking business was one of those things that came out of nowhere and floored you. And it had a tackiness about it that made him think it wasn't going to move on anywhere fast. What Kneebone was suggesting was lunacy – Doyle wasn't capable of killing anyone. But just how much, exactly, did that bloody inspector know?

Geoff had met Daphne on just three occasions. The first time was in the shop shortly after Doyle had started there. He had noticed her as soon as she came through the door. She was a serene, dark-haired woman with clear skin and brown eyes. But what was most striking was the way she carried herself, tall, erect, walking with broad-shouldered grace down the aisle to the counter.

Geoff was amazed that her sole purpose for being in the shop was to see Doyle. He watched them. You could tell they were a couple, yet there was nothing soft or intimate about the exchange. It was barely even civil. He gave himself an excuse to pass close and, as he did, Doyle introduced them. Geoff noticed the ease with which her face broke into a perfectly practised smile. He had never imagined Doyle with a cool, well-mannered beauty.

On their next meeting she had unravelled all his conclusions and left him envying Doyle. Geoff had invited them to his flat along with two other couples. He wanted to try out some new French cuisine and, also, he wanted to show Doyle what he could do as a chef. But primarily the evening was to be an indulgence in culinary experimentation with lots of side dishes, sauces and, of course, wine.

When he opened the door to Doyle and Daphne, he did a double-take. She was poised and she was breathtaking. And her smile was warm. Maybe that first time he had caught the tail end of a row. But here, now, she was funny and friendly, and he could see how good a partner she was for Doyle – he cruised in her wake, losing his awkwardness. They both relaxed into the evening in a way Geoff had not expected.

On the third occasion there had been a change in her. Again, it was in the shop. On his day off Doyle, accompanied by Daphne, had come in to pick up some odds and ends. Geoff tried to identify what had altered about her but couldn't. She seemed less vibrant. He wished he could reach into her and put right what was wrong. He knew Doyle would be sensitive enough to see it but the guy was so ineffectual he would never be able to help her sort herself out. While Geoff spoke to them he waited for something to ignite in her as it had during the evening at his place. It didn't happen. Later that afternoon he found himself writing her a note.

He didn't fancy her as such – well, that wasn't strictly true, he did, anyone would, but it wasn't like that: he had no desire to take her away from Doyle. He just wanted to make sure she got the kind of attention he doubted Doyle could give her.

Notes were something not many people used any more, unless to fire into their computers or their mobiles. And he could not now remember the exact wording but it was something like 'You seemed a bit down today, a withered flower. If there's anything I can do please let me know.' He signed it, then dropped it through their letterbox. He thought about the 'withered flower' bit – was it excessive? A touch of poetry was something he'd thought she would like. But why was he so keen that she should like him? He clearly, definitely, knew that he did not want to come between her and Doyle. He was certain of it. All he wanted to do, if possible, was to reach over Doyle and somehow smooth the ruffles from her life. But he did not go into any of the reasons why he would want to do that. Yes, the woman was beautiful but, Christ, beautiful women were ten a penny – well, two a penny, then. No, physical attraction wasn't an element: all he wanted was to protect her. He had perceived a vulnerability that Doyle, in his muddled way, wouldn't be able to do anything about and he knew he could. And, as it happened, he was right, about the vulnerability at least – the bitch had fucking topped herself. Christ!

He had pulled up outside the flat, double-parked, and run up the steps. He was just about to drop the envelope containing the note through the slot when a sense of dread passed through him – what the fuck was he doing? Images loomed of Doyle coming up to him with the note in his hand, demanding to know what he was about. It was like the hesitation you got before you pressed 'send' on an email. But a car had come up behind his and its horn beeped. Geoff looked at the driver: the bastard was banging his hand on the steering-wheel. Geoff slipped the envelope through the letterbox and went back to the car.

He had tried to think no more about it. But when three days had passed and there had been no response he began to wonder had the note got lost in the pile of junk mail that cluttered the hallway.

Then a letter with a handwritten address had arrived at the shop. Doyle himself had handed it to him, buried in a pile of other stuff. He had slipped it into his back pocket and waited for a quiet moment. Fifteen minutes later he opened it. There were just two lines in the centre of the page in small, neat handwriting: 'I find your concern as to my wellbeing touching but inappropriate. But as you have asked I'll tell you: I'm fine, a little down maybe. It happens.' He shoved it into his pocket and went back into the shop. It had been a stupid fucking thing to do. He had shown concern and been slapped by a haughty, stuck-up bitch.

Throughout the day he whipped out the letter and either got angrier or attempted to convince himself that there was a friendly touch at the end of it. But then he'd reread it and seen that the whole thing was squalid. Christ! What was he thinking? Writing a fucking note? And why write? Why not text or call – anything but a scrawl of ink across a blank page? All he had done was give her ammunition that could be used anywhere, any way, any time. And now, a week after she was dead, it had lost none of its power. Had it been behind Kneebone's visit?

As he walked back up Picton Street, it crossed his mind that she might have destroyed it. If she had, there was no problem. If she hadn't, it was a time-bomb. If Kneebone knew, then did Doyle? Geoff would have to tell Doyle – there was no other way. Yet if Doyle was unaware of it and Daphne had dumped the note, what was the point in unloading that sorry saga on him? Jesus fucking Christ! This was ridiculous – it wasn't like he'd shagged her, or even tried to shag her. He had done nothing but show concern. Yeah! Who was going to believe that?

Doyle was in the flat, pacing. Daphne was appearing in paintings done by strangers, Kneebone was hovering over him like a bird of prey and that mad artist woman wanted to call in the psychics. It was a floorshow of lunacy and it was distracting, but the weight he felt inside him was crippling. He couldn't bear it for much longer. It was a longing, a loathing, it was fear. It was an animal on the rampage in his head. It was more than he could put words to. He sat down but that was no use. There had to be someone he could talk with. That old man, if he could find him again. But what would he say to him? Jasmine! She was upstairs, asleep now probably. It would be so good to walk up there and slip in beside her, curl and cuddle into her, feel the warmth of her sleep breath on his face, the nudge of those big beautiful breasts and, maybe, if she'd allow him, to fuck this thing out of him. Maybe that was the thing to do: fuck himself raw and crawl off to the comfort of a coffin. Dear Christ! This was the problem: his thoughts. Nothing could stop them. No, that wasn't true: a bullet would do it. So, too, would some heavyweight tranquillisers.

He got out his mobile and called the taxi number. When it was answered he explained that yesterday he had booked a taxi and now needed to return to where it had picked him up but he couldn't recall the address: was it possible that they'd have a record of it and take him back there? She said that a call made yesterday would still be in the system but she was very busy right now and would call him back in ten or twenty minutes. He thanked her and hung up.

He made tea and turned on the television. A quiz show Daphne used to watch came on. He turned it off. A survey must exist somewhere investigating the link between suicide and daytime TV. It would be kept with the thousands of other surveys – humans compiling information about humans, all written in the language of academia, brilliant and boring and never to be read save by some other academic who will eat up a portion of their life, and their grant, proving or disproving it.

He knew he needed to sleep. But a river of thought flowed between him and sleep and it ran too fast even to consider crossing it. And the mad thing was, the lack of sleep fuelled the speed of the fucking river. That was the mad thing.

His phone gave him a fright. It was the woman from the taxi place. No call had been logged from his number yesterday. When he asked her if she was sure, she told him that all calls were logged automatically in the system. His number showed on 24 February but not yesterday. He thanked her and closed his phone. So he hadn't called a fucking taxi yesterday, not according to the system. Who knew? Maybe he was in the river already.

He had to get out of the flat. He stood at his door and looked up the stairs. She had said to do this, to call on her any time. She knew what it was like.

His thoughts were developing, like photographs in a tray, and he had no control over the images they were producing. His brain was a zoo of empty cages: all he could do was lock the gate, turn his back and let nature allow the fittest to survive.

He needed her now. He needed someone. He climbed the stairs.

He knocked and waited. Part of him was panicking, demanding that he turn, walk, run, get away. The rest stayed mute, as dumb as he was, standing there. He knocked again and decided on a compromise: he told himself he would count to sixty and then he could go. He couldn't get beyond five before a thought rolled in like a big wet snowball and crushed everything in front of it.

The door opened and she was there, looking a little perplexed, and everything in him ran into place to say what he would normally say to cover himself, except that he didn't speak. She smiled slightly and took a step back. He walked in and there he was, in the same four walls as his own, but these were different because they had different pictures, and the bookcase and the TV were in different places. She took his hand and just led him to the bedroom. When he was there she took off his jacket and took off her dressing-gown and told him it was OK, that no matter what happened it was OK. And then she moved the duvet and got in, and let him in, and he lay down beside her and she wrapped her arms around him and he was in the warmth, the silky warmth of her, and he held her tight, and she smoothed him, and he felt his eyes would crack if he didn't let the tears out. And she was stroking his head, saying words to him with syllables that melted, and the river no longer ran and he was in the strange land of sleep, and he went deeper and deeper until it was a dense dark blankness.

He awoke alone. He was aware that he was not in his own bed but could not recollect what circumstances had placed him in a stranger's. Then he heard music and knew where he was. It was Bob Dylan and it was something Daphne had remarked on: why did that girl always play Bob Dylan? Daphne had found it irksome, she said, it reminded her of an ex.

He lifted himself to a sitting position and stayed there, arms folded across his knees. He felt embarrassed: he had dumped himself on her. She had responded warmly, humanely, but he still should not have done it.

When he came into the living room she was ironing. She looked up at him as though this was something he did every day. 'Hi, cup of tea?'

He walked to an armchair and sat. 'I'm sorry to impose on you.'

'You weren't – you're not. Don't be silly.'

'What time is it?'

'Nearly half past eight, I'm back on at nine. I really hate night shifts.'

Her dressing-gown was white. Its length emphasised her smallness. It was open at the neck and he caught a glimpse of something black and silky. He looked away. 'I'd better let you get on,' he said.

'You're fine. Stay as long as you want. Did the music wake you?'

Doyle stood. 'No! I'll just go – there's things I need … Thanks, thanks very much.'

She left the iron pointing towards the ceiling and walked around the ironing board to meet him at the door. 'Come up any time I'm here – if you just want to sit in silence or to chat or whatever, OK?'

Doyle knew that all he wanted to do was ravish her, sprawl her across the table and bury himself in her. 'You're very kind, thank you,' he said, opening the door.

'Stop thanking me. Hope you have a good night. Do you want my work number in case?'

'In case?'

'Well, in case you want a chat in the night.'

'Is it me? My mind just tumbles out thoughts.'

'Like what?'

'Well, when you said that I thought, She thinks I'm going to top myself. Everyone thinks I'm going to top myself.'

She stared at him. 'People worry when they care.'

His flat was dark and cold. He sat watching the lights on the hill through his window until he heard her leave. Then he got up and turned on the lights and the television. The answer-machine was blinking. More caring people? The first was Geoff, 'We need to talk. Call me.' It always sounded American the way he said that. Next was Ruth, wanting to know how he was and asking him to contact her. There were two others from London friends, also wanting him to call.

Call me, call me, call me. Call me what? An arsehole, an egg, a niggling nocturnal nincompoop. They do not want me to call them: they want me to appease them. To acknowledge the courage they displayed in picking up a phone and calling me. To be seen to side with me in this, my bleakest hour. Well, no, sad man, sorry for your troubles and all that, but I'm keeping my bleakest hour to myself – selfish, I know, but what can you do?

He looked in his fridge. He wanted something to fry, something to turn crisp – bacon would fit the bill. There was nothing. He would have to go out again. Into the dark and the neon to find shops whose plastic-wrapped products reflected the overhead fluorescent lights, whose staff would stand behind the till, bored in blue with makeup, chewing gum and hoping only that time would pass.

He should make a list, he thought, but there was no point. He would buy or not buy whatever came to hand. He left the flat and turned right at the bottom of Nine Tree Hill but the shop he had pictured wasn't there. Had he imagined it? Maybe. It was cold for an April night but he walked on towards the centre of town. Several shops were open but they were on the far side of the road and, besides, his desire for something crisp had diminished.

He walked down steps into a tunnel that led out onto a submerged section of paved ground beneath a roundabout. He passed a collection of men and women drinking from bottles and cans. One approached him, swaying, with a hand out, a can of lager in the other. They both knew this was not a serious attempt to acquire funds. Doyle nodded at him and walked by, then heard, 'Wanker,' expressed in a slur. For a moment he thought of assaulting the guy. It would be easy – he was drunk and probably much weakened from an irregular diet of drugs and bad food.

Then it struck him that he was turning into something he didn't like: a bully, an advantage-taker. But why not? Why not go around beating the crap out of the likes of the unfortunate idiot behind him? It would rid the soul of angst and the streets of bozos.

Now he was sounding like a fascist. He walked up to street level, determined to be faithful to the person he knew himself to be. But why was he walking? And why in this direction?

He kept catching sight of his reflection and was surprised because he did not recognise himself. His walk, in these reflections, was a bawdy affair, full of a purpose and swagger that he didn't feel. Perhaps he was transforming into something or, worse, perhaps he had completely the wrong idea of the image he portrayed.

The centre of town was almost lifeless, but it was Monday and it was April and maybe, socially speaking, he was in a dead time of year. He went into a bar, one of a chain of bars that were decorated and named to look and sound Irish. To keep up the illusion he ordered a pint of Guinness. He was aware that he was the only lone drinker. The others were couples and a group of students in a corner. The barman, a plump individual of about Doyle's age, looked tired. His thumb danced about the buttons of his phone; he was either playing a game or sending the longest text in history.

Doyle was nearing the end of the pint and considering leaving when the female half of one of the couples came to the bar. The barman reluctantly left his phone aside to attend to her. She ordered wine and a pint of lager. Doyle had noticed her when he came in. She was all curves and a sideways smile that said, 'Make me laugh.'

She looked at him now but the smile had evaporated, 'Well, aren't you the life and soul of the party?' she said. Her accent was broad Dublin and the words, at once an accusation and an invitation, invaded Doyle, shattering an internal dialogue he had been unaware he was having.

He cleared his throat to give himself time to think of a reply. 'Is my presence offending you?' he asked.

She broke into laughter. 'Oh, Jesus, that's good, that's rich.' She turned to the man she was with. 'Hey, Hal, he wants to know if his presence is offending me.'

The barman placed her drinks on the counter. 'Just pipe down now, Rosy, right?'

'I was only after asking him how he was, for fuck's sake. Since when did a civil enquiry become a crime?'

'Since it came out of your mouth. That'll be six pound twenty.'

She smiled as she gave him a ten-pound note, then turned to Doyle. 'Your presence does not offend me. It's just, if you don't mind me saying, you don't look that comfortable sitting up here, staring into space like a convict.'

'Right. Well, there's little I can do about that.'

'You can come and join us, if you want. We're browned off looking at one another.'

'I'm only staying for one more.'

'You're Irish?'

'Yeah.'

'Ah, for fuck's sake, where from?'

'Wexford.'

'Wexford! You're joking me! I used to go there on holidays – Curracloe, do you know it?'

'Yeah, I know it well.'

'Imagine! Come on down and we'll have a drink.'

Doyle did not know if he wanted to join them but didn't see a way of refusing. 'OK. I'll just order my pint.'

She took the drinks back to the table and said, in a voice that seemed to fill the pub, 'Guess what, he's from Wexford – can you believe it? Wexford!' The man looked in Doyle's direction and grinned. He was in his forties and had an air of theatrical sophistication. She was much younger, although how much it was hard to say; she had an attractive face but it had seen a lot of life.

The barman was looking blankly at Doyle now. He ordered, feeling he had allowed himself to become trapped. He had to go over to the couple now when he would have preferred not to. It wasn't them – there was nothing about either of them that could physically threaten him: the man used a stick. It was that he would have to engage with them and he wasn't sure he was up to that. He took his pint and walked towards them.

The man watched his approach, still grinning. As Doyle sat the woman at first looked at him as though he had done so uninvited but then broke into a smile. 'Mr Wexford's here!'

'Hi, I'm Hal,' the man said, extending a hand. His voice was soft and he was well spoken. He appeared completely sober.

'My name is Doyle.' He shook the man's hand.

'Rose – Rosemary, actually, but no one calls me that.'

'You live in Bristol?' Hal asked.

'Yes, moved here recently from London.'

'I lived in Hounslow for years, hated the kip. Hal says we're going back but we're not.'

'Don't you like it here in Bristol, Mr Doyle?'

'I didn't say that.'

'Never mind him,' Rose said. 'He's a witch and he thinks he knows everything.'

Doyle was beginning to find the man's constant and somewhat strained grin irritating. 'A witch?' he said.

'Yes. Does that surprise you?'

'We all do what we can to earn a crust.'

Beside him Rose burst into laughter. Hal discarded the grin.

'Some may see us thus. I was born into the founding family of the House of the Old Ways and, although it may not mean a lot to you, I officiate within its circle as "Dubh Sidh", or Dark Fairy.'

Doyle wanted to laugh. 'Well, Duff Sid, why don't you do a spell for me?'

'Such as?'

'For a start you could dress the table with another round of drinks.'

'That, I believe, will be your job.'

'Oh, I see!'

'But my partner here, Rose, you like her? I can have her fulfil every darkest fantasy that lurks in your lured little soul, Mr Doyle.'

Rose banged her drink down on the table. 'Hal, will you stop it!'

'Spells, Mr Doyle, are only a small part of what I do and, between you and I, their power tends to fade. What do you do for a living?'

'Not a lot. At the moment I'm looking for artists who want to exhibit.'

'Hal's an artist,' Rose said.

Hal smiled at her. 'An illustrator.'

'Illustrator, artist, they're all the same to me. I'm looking for artwork for a restaurant a friend of mine is opening on Picton Street.'

'You could let him have those ones from *The Book of Cunning*,' Rose said.

'Rose, my dearest tulip, I very much doubt the diners at a restaurant will want to eat surrounded by that carnage.'

'You never know. What are they like?' Doyle asked.

'They are many scenes of necromancy, depictions of Pangenitor ...' He picked up his glass and drained it. 'I will now perform the first spell you asked of me.' He picked up his stick, and thumped on the floor with it, then smiled at the barman as he made a circular movement with his finger over the table. He then placed the stick to rest at the back of his chair. 'Soon,' he said, 'the table will be dressed but you, Mr Doyle, will have to pay.'

'And what if I don't?'

'There is no point in wasting our time deliberating on things that will not happen. Witchcraft may be all around you and you portray it to your own conscience as nothing more than a collection of coincidences. Coincidence!' He raised his eyebrows and smiled. 'No such thing.'

Doyle looked from him to Rose. She might be his daughter. There was a resemblance in the eyes. Their lips, too, had a fullness from slightly prominent teeth. Doyle turned back to the man. He had all the hallmarks of a failed actor, an idiot in search of a role, but there were certain small gestures and relaxed patterns in his speech that suggested something other than that. In either case it didn't matter. He was amusing, they both were. Doyle might have even gone so far as to say he was enjoying himself.

'Really?' Doyle said, when he realised that Hal was waiting to continue.

'Oh, yes. When you come across a coincidence, your path has crossed with someone or something else's.'

'Quite a few absurd things have been happening to me lately,' Doyle said.

Hal looked at him.

'My girlfriend appeared in two paintings done by someone who never knew her. She died days before they were done.'

'How did she die?' Hal asked.

'She slit her wrists. In the bath.'

The barman arrived with the drinks on a tray. Doyle began to reach for his wallet but Hal stopped him and said to the barman,

'On my tab, please, Gerard.' He lifted his pint. 'Rose, a toast to our friend.'

She raised her fresh glass of red wine. 'You poor man, when did this happen?' she asked.

'It'll be a week tomorrow.'

'And when did she appear in these pictures?' Hal asked.

'I saw the pictures yesterday. The artist did them during the week.'

'She's between worlds,' Hal said, almost to himself.

Doyle felt a flash of anger. 'She's between fuck-all.'

Hal dropped his head, then looked up at Doyle. 'I take it you're not a man who believes in an afterlife.'

'I know as much about it as anyone else. Zero.'

Hal glanced at Rose. He held her eyes for a moment, then turned to Doyle. 'After these drinks, Mr Doyle, I would like you to come with us.'

'Where?'

'You will have to trust me. And before you make up your mind, may I say I'm not on a mission to disprove what you've just said. I want you to come only because what you'll experience may make the immediate passage of your life ahead a little easier.'

Doyle picked up his pint. Rose was staring at him, waiting for a reply. Hal was wearing his irritating, confident grin once more. 'Fine. I'll come but I'll leave when I want to. Is that clear?'

Rose laughed. 'I don't think you'll want to, Mr Wexford.'

Over the next fifteen minutes he learnt that Rose was not Hal's daughter but his lover, although, as had already been hinted, it was not a relationship bound by any convention of monogamy. It also became obvious that Rose's hand was at the tiller of their affair, not Hal's.

As they were leaving Hal revealed himself to have a severe limp. His back seemed to curve forward and to the side, which might have accounted for it. They left together and walked down a side road that came out onto a main thoroughfare with a line of taxis.

Rose climbed into the first and gave the driver an address. She opted to sit in the middle of the back seat, leaving room for Hal and Doyle at either side of her. The taxi swung out into the road, made a U-turn and headed up Park Street in the direction of Clifton.

'Do I get any information about where we're going?' Doyle asked.

'A number of days are important in our calendar. One is, as you can imagine, Hallowe'en, the day that death comes out to play. And the second is Beltane, when it is life's turn.'

'And that is today?'

'Tonight is the first new moon after the spring equinox.'

'And what happens on Beltane?'

Rose's skirt was riding high over her crossed legs. Doyle noticed stocking tops. She noticed Doyle's stare and turned to Hal. 'He asked you what happens on Beltane.'

'You're right, my dear, he did.'

'Don't worry about it, love, you'll be grand,' Rose told Doyle.

'If I don't like it I leave, remember?'

'Just like in a dream,' Hal said, almost to himself.

'I don't follow.'

'During a dream that starts to turn nasty you force yourself to come awake – same thing.'

The taxi entered a driveway and stopped. The house in front of them was long rather than tall but somehow much more ordinary than Doyle had been imagining. Hal paid, then led the way to a set of steps at the side of the building that descended to an elaborate porch with a solid oak front door. The three climbed down, knocked and waited. The door was opened by a casually dressed middle-aged man. His eyes went from one to another and settled on Hal, 'You're cutting it a bit fine,' he said, and stood back to let them in. They filed past him, Hal first, into a hallway that was a jumble of furniture, pictures and rugs.

Hal stopped before a door, opened it and walked in. Rose followed. When Doyle entered he could see that this room continued the theme of chaos. A large, round rug with intricate repeating patterns, mostly in red, decorated the floor. High above it a weighty chandelier hung, and two large leather armchairs were parked at either side of an austere fireplace in which the remains of logs smouldered. To Doyle's right a long and highly polished dining table stood before a tall bay window and around it sat four people. From what littered the table, Doyle guessed that they had just finished a meal.

A large black woman in red velvet was sitting at the head. As it came up from her bust the material of the dress folded over itself so it resembled the leaves of a flower: her head seemed to emerge from a very large rose. A thin man in a suit and tie was on her left. His face was pale and his dark hair shot over his forehead in an arc. On the same side but several seats down, another man had long blond hair that framed his face in two perfect curves. He was wearing a black leather jacket and, under it, a T-shirt with Gothic script. Opposite him sat an overweight man with a mass of blond curls. He had on a tweed suit and had turned in his chair to watch the parade enter.

Hal went straight to the armchair that overlooked the table. Rose followed him and perched on its arm. The man who had let them in went back to his seat at the table, to the right of the rose woman. Doyle found himself stranded by the open door. His attention was taken by an intricately carved confessional just beyond the armchair that Hal was occupying. The wood it was made from had darkened over time so the many intricate carvings that framed its doors and sides were lost to view. Its presence gave the room a liturgical feel. He looked up: the ceiling was high and vaulted. Odd, Doyle thought, we are in a basement.

The walls were heavy with paintings – mostly portraits in oils, men posing to look important, stern or both. There were several nudes and one or two elaborate still lifes.

'So, you two are late and you bring with you what exactly?' the black woman said, looking at Doyle.

Hal was sitting on the edge of the chair. It looked as though it would swallow him whole if he were to sit back in it. 'This is Doyle. He is fresh from a bereavement.'

'Doyle?' The woman stared at him.

Hal nodded.

'Right, Doyle, take a seat,' she said.

His choice was one at the table or the remaining empty armchair. He crossed the room to the armchair. When he sat back all he could see was Hal with Rose by his side. Beyond them was a dark alcove.

'I suppose you want a drink now that you're here – keep everyone waiting even longer.' The woman's voice came from behind his chair.

Hal, who had been looking at the floor, glanced up at her. 'A brandy would be good.'

'Cameron, be a dear and get us all a brandy, would you?'

There was movement at the table followed by the sound of a cupboard door being opened, the tinkle of glasses and the gurgle of pouring liquid. Seconds later Cameron appeared with a tray containing several glasses. Hal and Rose took one, then Cameron turned to Doyle. He leaned forward to accept the brandy, then leant over the armrest to see the table. The black woman was staring at Hal. The thin man was looking down at his lap. The fat one with the hair was watching Cameron with obvious anticipation. Cameron went from one to another until they all held a glass.

'Well,' said the black woman, 'here's to good rains, good drains and a warm place to shit.'

As Doyle raised his glass he saw that Rose had downed hers in one and was now getting up. 'I'm going to get changed.' They watched her leave.

Doyle, feeling awkward where he was, stood and walked to the chair at the far end of the table. Just behind it, gathered in clumps beneath a pure white marble statue of a young, naked girl, bunches of blue and red hyacinths were interspersed with tiger lilies. As he took the seat he became aware of the sweet, heavy scent of the flowers.

The woman at the end of the table was looking at him. 'My name is Charlotte,' she said, 'and I do apologise if I seemed a little rude when you came in but our dear friend Hal does tend to stretch things. This, by the way . . .' she pointed with her glass to the thin man on her left '. . . is Sean Connelly.' She continued around the table: 'Slava,' he was the one in the leather jacket and the T-shirt, 'Rupert,' the one with the hair, 'and Cameron.'

'Nice to meet you all.'

Darting looks shot about the table. Doyle counted six wine bottles, of which most were empty. A wooden board with cheese sat before an overflowing fruit bowl. The rest of the table was empty but for glasses and discarded napkins that floated like icebergs among the crumbs.

Hal spoke from his chair: 'We met Doyle in a bar in the centre less than an hour ago.'

'Fresh from a bereavement?' Sean Connelly asked.

Doyle nodded.

'Sorry to hear that,' Charlotte said

'Life, death, comings and goings, always a lot of emotion

attached, what say you, Doyle?' Rupert said. His forehead glistened with sweat, some of which had trickled down by his temples. His smile looked as though it was powered by an intermittent electrical current.

'I don't know much about emotions. And I know even less about death, but together I know they make for a very unpleasant combination.'

Cameron passed the brandy bottle to Rupert. He grabbed it and immediately refilled Doyle's glass, then his own. Doyle lifted the glass and took a long draught. He waited for the kickback but it didn't come. Instead his insides seemed to rekindle, as though each cell had suddenly been pumped with a new jet of life. When he put the glass down he saw that he had emptied it in one. Rupert refilled it.

'I really am at a loss as to why we need to drag before us a self-confessed ignoramus,' Connelly said to Charlotte.

Rose entered, wearing a long white and pale blue gown that plunged at the neckline to reveal the fullness of her breasts. Behind her came an older couple, dressed in the black and white costumes of domestic service. Rose walked towards Hal, who vacated his seat to make way for her. Once she had sat down, she whispered instructions to the old couple. The woman went to the table and began to clear it – when she came to Rupert he wouldn't allow her remove his glass or his cutlery. The man dragged the flowers that were behind Doyle so that they clustered around the arms of his chair. Then he went to a cupboard at the far end of the room, opened it and pulled out some cardboard boxes.

'Sean, you are jumping the gun in taking a throwaway remark as evidence,' Charlotte said, to Connelly. She directed herself to Doyle: 'I'm quite sure you are well acquainted with death, and as for emotions, well, they are everywhere. They are the air we breathe.'

The scent of the flowers now curled in long fingers about his face, exploring him. He felt weak and was sure that food would allay this. He sank back in his chair and decided he would view what was going on in front of him as a spectator. He would not reply to Charlotte's remark – in fact, he would have nothing to do with any of it. He lifted his glass and swallowed. His head wanted to drop forward. To stop it, he leant it against the back of the chair. Then all he had to do was open his eyes to observe. The old servant man was lifting a string of Christmas lights from a cardboard box. Behind him, in the alcove, Doyle noticed seats arranged in rows. People were sitting on them. It was too dark to see who, but they were there, they were moving, an audience anticipating a show.

'Who died, Mr Doyle?' Connelly was asking.

'My girlfriend.' The words were out before he remembered that he had promised himself he would take no further part in this. Rupert refilled Doyle's glass but he doubted now that he had the strength to lift it. The smell of the flowers was growing more intense.

'And how did she die, Mr Doyle?' Connelly asked.

There was something in Connelly's tone that made Doyle feel compelled to answer. But his tongue was weighted to the floor of his mouth. 'Cut herself. In the bath.'

'Cut herself?' Connelly questioned.

Doyle looked at him. He was aware that Slava was trying to say something but he needed to get to Connelly, to straighten out the confusion that was inevitable if the tone of his last comment was allowed to stand. Doyle had the sensation of falling, falling when he should have been standing to face Connelly and whatever he was saying.

'We'll see,' Connelly said.

Slava was talking now. But Doyle did not want to know what he was saying. He wanted to reach Connelly, tell him he was wrong, but nothing inside him was functioning. Doyle turned to Slava and told him to shut up. Slava reacted by pulling back and raising both hands.

'I wouldn't be rude to Slava. Between him and Rupert they are all you have,' Charlotte said from the far end.

The old man was trailing the Christmas lights over an arced frame at the back of Rose's chair. He knelt then and plugged them in. A halo of white shone above her in triplicate. She sat beneath it like an erotic version of the Virgin Mary.

The servant woman was leading a figure by the arm to one of the seats in the alcove. Hal, who was standing by the fireplace, was arguing with two men about the contents of a piece of paper one was holding. Doyle turned back to Charlotte. 'I'm sorry, what did you say?'

'I said you shouldn't be so rude to Slava or Rupert. They are all you have. They are your defence.'

'What do you mean, my defence?'

'Well, it's obvious you did the nasty on poor old Daphne and we're going to put you on trial for that.'

Then Doyle caught sight of the old man. He was still in his rain gear and was still wearing sandals. Doyle felt a surge of relief at the sight of him. Here was someone from the outside world. But the feeling did not last long. The old woman was leading him towards the seats in the alcove. He turned back to Charlotte. 'I don't understand.'

'I'm not surprised,' Charlotte said. Then she smiled. 'We know everything.'

'Say nothing.' Rupert was wiping his brow. Then he looked at Slava. 'Come on, old boy, get into character. We need you!'

Slava shook his head. 'Why should I bother? He told me to shut up.'

Rupert looked at Doyle. 'Apologise!' he said.

'No.'

Rupert picked up the fork in front of him and plunged it into the skin at the base of Doyle's thumb. Blood gushed from it onto the polished table. Rupert lifted the fork and stared at Doyle.

Pain seared up Doyle's arm. Anger pumped through him.

'Rupert!' Charlotte shouted. 'Rupert, was that absolutely necessary?'

''Fraid so, Charlotte. He's not taking it seriously.'

'Get him a bandage,' she barked. Cameron stood and left the room.

Doyle gripped his hand. He could not believe that this overstuffed, pompous ass had just stabbed him. He looked at the wound: it was a ragged cut and it was bleeding, but he didn't think it was deep. He looked back at Rupert. 'You ...'

'Listen to me, old boy. You need to pay attention and follow our instructions. If you don't, there's worse than that to come.'

'Who the fuck do you think you are?'

'If you know what's good for you, you'll pay attention to my friend here,' Slava said, indicating Rupert. 'If anyone can get you out of this it's him.'

Rupert smiled. 'Why, thank you, Slava.'

Cameron entered, carrying a roll of gauze, some tape and a pair of scissors. He lifted Doyle's injured hand by the wrist and wrapped it in the gauze, then taped it tightly. 'There,' he said.

The old servant man was struggling with the armchair that Doyle had first sat in to get it across the rug to the centre of the room. People watched but no one offered to help. When finally he had it placed so it was facing the table, Hal hobbled across the room and sat in it.

'Has everyone got a drink?' Charlotte asked.

A murmur of voices arose. As far as Doyle could see, only those at the table had one.

'Good. Well, in that case it's high time we began. Sean, you're first, I believe.'

'Thank you, madam. My witness is already in the chair.'

Rupert swung around to Hal. The servant woman was placing a red velvet stool under Rose's feet.

'Then, if you will …' Charlotte smiled.

Connelly left his seat and walked towards the chair.

'Could you tell the court your name?'

'Hal.'

'And what do you do for a living, Hal?'

'I'm a witch.'

'I see. Now, tell me, does being a witch give you an advantage over other mere mortals – myself, for example?' Hal and Connelly smiled.

'I, too, am mortal.'

'Indeed you are, but does being a witch give you any insight into, say, a character?'

'I see everything.'

'And what did you see when you met the accused?'

'Objection!' roared Rupert. 'The witness's claim is completely unsubstantiated and therefore inadmissible.'

'Nonsense, Rupert,' Charlotte said. 'We all know Hal. Carry on, please.'

'Thank you,' Connelly said. 'If you'd like to answer my question?'

'I saw a guilty man,' Hal said.

A ripple ran through the alcove.

'Explain, if you would?'

'Guilt is common. We all have it, some, however, more than others. Another thing, it's blue. Sometimes sky blue, but in extreme cases cobalt.'

'You can see it – actually see it?'

'Oh, yes!'

'Enlightening! Continue.'

'Doyle's is navy.'

'Well, I never ... Thank you, Hal, you've been most helpful.' He turned to Rupert. 'Your witness.'

Rupert stood and drummed for a moment with the fork, then dropped it and turned to Hal.

'Have you any other name besides "Hal"?'

'Yes, yes, I do.'

'Would you care to share it with the court?'

'My witch name is Dubh Sidh.'

'Which means?'

'Dark Lord.'

'Quite a title!'

'Objection!' Connelly shouted.

'Indeed, Rupert, if you have a point, get to it.'

'Does the darkness of the name reflect a darkness in character, a negativity, a propensity for seeing ill in others?'

'Objection!' Connelly was now on his feet. 'Complete bollox as well as pure poppycock!'

'I agree,' Charlotte said. 'Rupert, if you don't have anything then don't waste the court's time.'

'Madam, I am trying to establish that the witness's attitude towards the defendant was negative from the start and as such he is unfit to be called as a witness in this case.'

'What cheek!' Charlotte whispered, her eyes widening. 'What an unmitigated cheek. Strike that from the record. Be very careful, Rupert. Take this as a warning.'

'I have no further questions.'

'Thank God for that. Next witness.'

'I've got one,' Connelly said, raising himself from his seat.

'Very well,' Charlotte said.

'Just a minor point, Hal, but you said you could see the guilt surrounding the accused, so I was wondering, is his guilt noted by any of your other senses?'

'Indeed, very much so. First and foremost there was the smell – nothing quite like the smell of guilt, a heavy, pungent odour that tends to sink so it trails along the floor behind the guilty like snail slime. The defendant, for example, has difficulty closing doors behind him since his girlfriend's demise, such is the sludge he drags in his wake. If you observe him now you will see he cannot move simply because the odour from his guilt is mixing with that from the flowers, creating an atmosphere around him that is literally too heavy for him to move. He looks as if he is sitting there, but he's not. He's nailed to the chair by the weight of his own inner recrimination.'

Doyle was aware that every person in the room was scrutinising him. He was tempted to make some casual movement, scratch his nose, something mundane, just to show them that he could. He did nothing. A feeling of sadness had passed through him, leaving him with an intense spoon-shaped weight in his chest and stomach. He did not move simply because he did not want to move.

'Anything else?' Connelly asked.

'There's the sound of guilt. It's like the screams of a small child coming from the depths of a dark cave, except that in this particular case the weight of the guilt was such that those screams have stopped. All I can hear now is their absence. A more chilling sound I have yet to witness.'

'Thank you, Hal. You bring poetry to squalor,' Connelly said, in subdued admiration, then made his way back to his chair.

Hal stood, made a slight bow towards Charlotte's end of the table, then turned and went into the confessional. He entered it through the main door, the one a priest would use.

When Connelly got to his place at the table he did not sit. He looked out into the room, as though gathering himself, then addressed Charlotte: 'For my next witness I would like to call a Mr Terrence Martin Hassler.'

Heads in the alcove turned as people sought to glimpse the new witness. The servant woman, who was feeding the fire with more logs, stood and walked towards the assembly. The old man was sitting at the front. She guided him to his feet and together they made their way to the chair.

Connelly again stood and approached. 'Terrence Martin Hassler?'

'That is my name.'

'Good. Now, can you tell us, do you know the accused?'

'I can.' There was a silence during which Connelly waited. 'I can tell you if I know the accused. It is knowledge within my possession.'

'In that case if you would be so kind . . .'

'The accused and I became familiar with one another in the course of a polite, but somewhat peripheral, conversation, so the only thing I can say with accuracy is I am familiar with several of the characteristics he displayed on that occasion and I am sure I would recognise him from them if I were to see him again. But to say I know him would be a lie, a distortion.'

Connelly was silent for a moment. 'How many times did you two meet?'

'Once.'

'And on that occasion did the accused mention his recently deceased girlfriend.'

'Oh, yes, he did indeed.'

'What did he say about her?'

'He said he killed her.'

Cries of 'Oh, yes!' came from Cameron. A chorus of murmurs came from the alcove.

'Objection!' Rupert was repeating, banging his hand on the table.

'What is it, Rupert?'

'The witness is bats. My client is innocent, and anyone can see that.'

'You may cross-examine the witness when Sean has finished.'

'My work here is done,' Sean said, and walked to the table slapping his open palm off Cameron's as he passed.

'Oh, Christ!' Rupert said, wiping his brow and getting to his feet. He shot Doyle a glance. 'I can't pretend this won't be tough.' He then walked in slow, contemplative steps to the chair, stood beside it, holding the uprights at the back, with the old man in his shadow. He looked as though he might burst into song. He took his time, smiled at the table, then turned to observe the alcove. When he felt he had the attention of the court he walked in front of the witness and said, in tones of theatrical bewilderment, 'Perhaps you'd like to reconsider that last remark.'

The old man shook his head.

Rupert began to walk away. He looked bereft.

'In what context was the remark made?' Slava said, from his seat.

'Is that allowed?' Connelly asked Charlotte.

She nodded.

'He was saying that he was unsure she ever existed, mentioned that he might have invented her. He was rambling, and my attention was elsewhere.'

'Why, may I ask?' Rupert said, spinning on his heels in instant recovery.

'I was wondering what species he belonged to.'

'I see,' Rupert said.

'Can I ask,' Charlotte interrupted. 'What did you conclude?'

'Couldn't satisfy myself on that one, but there was definitely something lupine,' the old man said.

Doyle could feel all eyes on him again. Rupert looked at Charlotte, then at the witness. 'You think my client is a wolf?'

'There is more wolf in him than anything else.'

'This may change the course of the entire trial!' Rupert said to Charlotte.

'Why would it?' Sean asked.

'Well, if it's true and he's a wolf we can hardly try him for murder. I mean, wolves don't murder people, they kill them, sure, but it's their instinct, their livelihood. Only people murder people.'

'Most profound,' Connelly said from his chair. 'But anyone can see plain as day that the accused is a man. This is ridiculous!' He directed his attention to Charlotte. 'Madam?'

She laughed. 'Like I give a shit. Just get on with it.'

Rupert looked as if he was about to say something to those at the table but instead his shoulders fell and he turned to the witness. 'Rambling, you said. You said my client was rambling.'

'He had just come from seeing paintings that featured his girlfriend's death.'

'Can you elaborate?'

'He said he was visiting an artist and in her studio there were two pictures starring his recently deceased.'

'Starring?'

'Depicting, then.'

The side door to the confessional opened and a tall woman came out. She crossed to the fireplace, genuflected in front of Rose and knelt. Slowly she parted the skirts of Rose's robe to reveal her feet and ankles. She bent forward and it looked, from where Doyle sat, as if she was licking Rose's toes. A figure came out from the darkness of the alcove, a young man, and entered the confessional.

The tiredness Doyle felt now came out of boredom. A headache settled in his skull like fog. He listened to the drone of the questions and answers between the old man and Rupert, but couldn't concentrate.

He looked about the room. The woman who had come from the confessional was still at Rose's feet. Her tongue curled between the toes as she massaged the soles with her thumbs.

Rupert approached the table. 'No further questions. You are free to go unless …' He looked at Connelly, who shook his head.

The old woman was there in case the witness required assistance, but the old man rose from the seat with vigour and made his own way back to the alcove.

'If it may please the court I would like a word with my client,' Rupert declared.

'Be our guest,' Charlotte said. They seemed to be drinking tea at the far end of the table.

Rupert sat. Slava leant over the table.

'Look, sorry, I've done the best I can but I'm afraid this is one we'll just have to put down to experience,' Rupert said.

Slava was shaking his head in sorrowful agreement.

'What are you talking about?' Doyle asked.

'The fat lady is singing,' Slava said.

'Would you like to explain to me what the fuck you're talking about?'

'We just didn't have the material,' Rupert said.

'It wasn't your fault,' Slava said, and sat back.

Rupert flashed a look at Doyle. 'Only chance now is what we call an F and F.'

Doyle stared at him.

'A full and frank. A confession!'

'A confession? Are you mad? I didn't do anything.'

Slava and Rupert smiled. 'If that is what you believe, you are the only one in this entire room to do so. Please, listen to the advice of my friend. If there is anyone who can get you out of this it is him,' Slava said.

Rupert gave a modest smile. 'Why, thank you, Slava.'

'I'm not confessing to something I didn't do.'

Slava was about to say something when Rupert interrupted: 'Can I ask you something, Doyle? Are you sure about that? Are you one hundred per cent certain that you had nothing to do with Daphne's death?'

Doyle was suddenly robbed of what he wanted to say, and the sadness he had felt earlier flushed through him. It was so complete it left him motionless. He saw the image of her still and dead, lying amid the chaos of red and neon.

'Right, good. Now, this is what you do. Go into the confessional and make the full and frank to Hal. He'll give you absolution – he has to if you're sincere. There'll be penance too, of course.'

'This is fucking ridiculous!' Doyle said.

Rupert shook his head. 'Bad attitude, is what I'm hearing. An attitude like that will lead to a very severe penance, capital even. Don't think it wouldn't.'

Doyle sat back. Whatever this theatre was about, his role was predetermined. He would simply run through the motions of it and then go.

Rupert was standing. 'The accused would like to make an F and F.'

Charlotte looked up from her conversation with the other two and smiled. 'Well, that is splendid!' Then, in more formal tones, she said loudly, 'Clear the confessional for the accused.'

The servant man left his position at the back of the chair and walked to the confessional. He opened the same door Hal had entered through and mumbled something. He then closed the door and stood still. Moments later the young man stepped out and went to the fireplace.

By now Doyle was standing. Slava had helped him up, cleared the flowers from his path and was escorting him across the room. He felt so weak he had to lean on Slava's arm. The servant man held the door open for him. Doyle looked into the booth. It was tiny and, except for a small platform to kneel on, empty. He had to stoop to enter. When the door shut behind him he was in complete blackness. Then a hatch slid open revealing a wire mesh, through which he could make out the line of Hal's profile.

'You want to confess?' Hal whispered.

'Apparently.'

'I'll give you a bit of advice here, Doyle, old man. Don't fuck about. If you do we can kill you. It's that simple.'

Anger flared, then receded. He was to play his part, that was all, play it and get out. That was all that was required.

'Right, fine, I confess.'

'To what?'

'To Daphne's death.'

'So you killed her?'

Play the part: 'Yes.'

'How?'

All he could see was the outline of the profile in front of him.

'I came into the bathroom. I had gone to get the blade she'd forgotten. I sat on the toilet seat. She was looking at me, which was odd, hadn't done that for a while. Lying there looking at me sitting on the loo seat holding the blade. She said, "Well?" and I leaned over to hand it to her and she didn't move. I think I said something like "What the fuck?" and next thing her hand just comes up out of the water, you know, like it's independent of her and it's just there, the wrist facing me, and I could see all the little veins running across it, like it was marble, and the sinews, and that's all I could look at and I knew what she was asking. We had talked about it, but in a theoretical way, and now it was there in front of me, and I was holding the blade and she didn't flinch. I looked at her eyes while I was cutting her and she was just staring at me as though this was it. All the sex and all the games didn't matter a fuck now because this was the greatest fucking game anyone could play with anyone else and I was doing it to her and she was lying there looking at me like I was a fucking hero. For the first time in her life, my life, something amazing was happening. And then the other wrist emerged and this time when I put the blade in it wouldn't cut because it was all slippery, and there was blood everywhere, it was coming out of her in jets, so when the second one started I just couldn't do it, and all the time she never took her eyes off me. Not once. It was like panic and calm at the same time, and that's the way it was because she put her arms under the water and I washed myself with the flannel, then threw it into the bath and walked out and got dressed and went off to work just as we'd said – except one thing. I never said goodbye. I forgot to fucking say it.'

There was silence. Doyle was on the verge of saying more but became aware that his heart was racing and his breathing had become rapid. Hal waited. Then, when he was sure there was no more to come, he cleared his throat and said, 'You feel better after that, I'm sure.'

Doyle didn't reply.

'Under the circumstances there will be no penance. You will provide that adequately for yourself. You are free to go.'

Doyle felt for the door, pushed it open and climbed out. The room had changed. The seats and people in the alcove had gone. The big armchair was back by the fireplace. Rose still sat but the halo was gone. Charlotte, Cameron and Connelly were grouped at their end of the table, talking and drinking from a bottle of red wine. Rupert and Slava were gone. The servant woman was wiping the table and the man was sweeping the floor. No one seemed to notice Doyle. He walked to the door of the room, opened it and slipped into the hallway. He made his way through the clutter to the front door, expecting a voice or even a body to present itself and try to stop him. It didn't come. When he got to the door he opened it and was surprised to find daylight. In front of him were the steps he had descended only a few hours ago. He climbed them now and crunched over the gravel to the gate.

He crossed the road to a stretch of grass and looked back. It was one long, low house with circular steps leading up to a door in the centre. Two gateways led into it. It was time to get home, perhaps pick up some food on the way, something crisp.

Eleven

Doyle woke with sunlight streaming through the window. He had forgotten to drop the blind when he got in. He lay waiting for the bell but that might, in theory, be anything up to an hour away and he needed to piss.

He turned in the bed. A week dead today. That was how it would be now: time measuring the distance between the event and the present. Time stretching that distance, time the healer, time the thief. And this time next month she'll still be dead, and the month after that and the month after that. And when I'm an old man, a muddle of memories, she'll still be dead. And when I go and all the people I'll see today have gone too, we'll all be no more than she is now. It's just a matter of timing. Nothing wrong with slipping off sooner rather than later, if the going gets tough.

There was a pain in his hand. When he lifted it above the duvet he saw that it was covered with a bandage. Rupert's face came to mind and, with it, a flood of images from last night: Charlotte, the mad giant rose at the end of the table, Connelly in his primness, the crowd in the alcove. The smell of the flowers had been so strong it had nailed him to a chair.

He sat on the side of the bed and stared at his feet. He curled his long toes: the nails needed cutting. He would have to find socks.

What was happening to him? Was this what losing your mind meant? He unfurled the bandage and saw clearly four separate punctures in a neat line. If last night was some kind of hallucination he would not have had these wounds. They meant that someone had stabbed him with a fork – but he could have done it himself. But the bar had been real. He knew where it was. Or maybe it wasn't – maybe the entire city of Bristol was an elaborate practical joke his imagination was playing on him.

It had happened first when he was walking to the police car with Geoff. There were magpies squawking in the trees and cold on his face and he had had to remind himself that there was to much detail for this to be a dream. But why was he even thinking like that? Was his mind aware, then, that it had slipped between the folds into a place saved for when reality was too much too swallow? Perhaps reality was nothing more than a spectrum, and where you pitched yourself depended on how you perceived it. Like money, it had value only as long as people agreed it had value.

Of course, there were different realities. There had to be – there had to be as many as there were people. And he, Desmond Edward Doyle, who until now had only ever witnessed one, had had the arrogance to imagine that everyone shared it. That was as crazy as thinking everyone lived in exactly the same kind of house as you did. People leave the scene of accidents giving different accounts of the same event. They all see the same thing but what their brains do with the information is different in every case. Of course there are different realities.

But if he were to retrace his steps, through the underpass where the drunk had called him a wanker and emerge at the bar, and if there was a barman called Gerard – that was the name Hal had used – who worked there, he would know that his sense of reality was somewhat in tune with that of the masses. But what if the bar was not there? If that were the case he would retrace his steps home, and if it was still there, he would go into it and not leave again. One thing at a time. All he had to do now was find some socks.

The bell of the Polish church sounded. Eleven times in all, perfect. Outside the sunshine was bright, and as soon as he started walking he realised that he was tired and weak. How long had it been since he had eaten?

The underpass was empty of the bruised gang of last night. Daytime reality didn't fit with their rhythms. Instead it was filled with people who, for the most part, walked with purpose and dressed with care.

The bar was there and it was a lot busier than it had been last night. Its daytime reality took much from the underpass, but now the clientele was dressed more smartly and an air of certainty hung about them that could occasionally flare into impatience. These were people who had business to go about. They had briefcases and read newspapers or sheets of printed paper in folders. They drank coffee. There were, however, two older men sitting at the bar nursing half-pints.

Doyle stood close to them, waiting to catch the barman's eye. When he did he ordered coffee and asked if they served food.

The barman looked at his watch and said he could do a sandwich. Doyle took the stool in front of him. The two old boys were observing him. He was aware of it and wished he didn't care but he did. He wished also that he had bought a newspaper.

By the time the coffee arrived the old men had taken all they could from his presence and had fallen back into the low drone of their talk. Doyle paid and, as the barman was giving him change, he said, 'Does Gerard still work here?'

'Gerard?' the barman said. 'Don't know any Gerards.'

'He was working last night.'

The barman backed away. 'Was he?'

'Yeah, he's a big guy, plays with his mobile phone?' Doyle was aware that there was a streak of desperation in his tone.

The barman shook his head and walked away.

The old man nearest Doyle moved a little on his stool. 'Bald, is he?' he said to Doyle.

'No, I don't think so. He was a big guy, tall and broad.'

'Gerard, you say his name is?'

'Yeah.'

The other man leant over from behind the first. 'Short-changed you, did he?'

Doyle was going to reply but thought better of it. Instead he said, 'You don't happen to know a …' he hesitated '. . . a little crippled guy who drinks here, uses a stick?'

They both stared at him now. 'Are you all right?' the one nearest to him said, his small eyes blinking.

'I'm fine,' Doyle said, and slid from the stool with his sandwich. He found a seat at the back of the bar. The sandwich had to be stock left over from yesterday: the filling was soft and it tasted of salt. The fact that the barman didn't know of a Gerard meant nothing. Barmen came and went all the time. He could be new – Gerard could be new. He would walk up to the house in Clifton and knock on the door. If Cameron opened it then everything was in order – well, order of a sort. It was a nice day – a good day for a walk.

He climbed Park Street and went up into Clifton Village, aware that the season had now properly changed. Buds, blue skies and buildings that looked clean in the sunlight.

He sat on the small patch of grass facing the house. Now, in proper daylight, he could see it was an elaborate two-storey structure made from sandstone. The two cars in there were parked facing the far gate. Some sort of vine grew from a thick pot by the front door. It had been trained to climb between the top of the door and the window-sills of the second storey and it was just now threatening to burst into purple flower.

He walked up to the entrance. A hand-painted sign attached to the pillar said 'Riversleigh'. The drive was gravel and over to the far left he could see the entrance to the flight of steps that would lead down to the door they had entered through last night. He felt the gravel crunch underfoot as he made his way to the steps. From the top he could see the porch and the door. Glass panels ran down either side of it and potted plants had been placed along the side walls. He had no memory of potted plants.

Just as he was about to descend, a thought struck him: What would he say if it wasn't Cameron or Charlotte who answered? He should have some story ready, a name at hand he could ask for.

The door to the main house opened and a small brown terrier ran out. The dog seemed to be heading for the low wall that skirted the garden when it caught Doyle's scent. It faced him and began to bark. An elderly woman appeared at the door. 'Phoebe! Stop that racket!' Then she saw Doyle. 'Can I help you?' She had raised her voice an octave to ask the question.

'Well, I don't know. I was here last night and I left something ...'

'Here? Last night? I very much doubt it.'

'I was in the flat, the basement flat.'

'There is no flat in the basement.'

The dog was approaching Doyle, growling. It seemed almost theatrical, as if it had sensed an opportunity to display its guarding qualities to its owner.

'Are you sure?'

'I don't like people snooping around my property.'

'I'm sorry. I might be making a mistake but I'm certain I was here last night.'

'Nobody lives down there. Now, please, get off my property.'

The dog had stopped advancing. It stood there now with teeth bared. Doyle nodded to the woman. 'My mistake,' he said, and turned for the gate. The dog resumed barking at increased volume. The woman watched him. At the gate Doyle thought of asking if any of her neighbours rented out their basements but knew there was little point.

Kneebone left his car in the public car park at Frenchay Hospital and entered through the main door. He wanted to get a cup of tea and a sandwich in the cafeteria before he went in to see the pathologist. It had been another unsuccessful morning on the domestic front. Jenny had phoned soon after he had got in last night, saying she would not be home. He hadn't even asked how her mother was. He was beyond that. He had spent the next hour cleaning the kitchen. Being stuck with such a long and mindless task had given him time to think. He was curious as to how, at this time of their lives, he and his wife had come to the point at which they spoke to each other in nothing but clipped sentences. Why was he so unwilling or incapable of being there for her while her mother was dying? It was almost as though he didn't care. But he knew this was not the case.

He also wanted to think about the Daphne Palmer case without the hum of the station in his ears. But his mind couldn't focus on anything for very long. And when he had finished he had sat on the sofa with a cup of tea and realised that all he'd done for the last hour was daydream. At least the kitchen was clean. If she came back in now she'd die of fright.

He was being stupid and childish. Jenny's mother was dying and all he could do was sit at home indulging himself in feeling abandoned. Had he really reduced himself to the point where all he wanted out of his marriage was an ironed shirt, food in the fridge and a fresh tube of toothpaste? He was pathetic. Why couldn't he supply them himself? Was that why he was angry – his inability to provide for himself? Because if a man wasn't capable of doing that what else was he not capable of?

He closed his eyes and listened to the clatter of cups and the steaming hiss of coffee machines in the cafeteria and knew it was a whole lot bigger than that. Maybe he was working too hard – maybe he had always worked too hard. He had put nothing into the marriage so it had, in real terms, ceased to exist. And the only evidence that it had survived was that there were clean, ironed shirts in his wardrobe and food in the fridge or on the table whenever he decided to return to the house to eat it. He didn't want to think about any of it. When things settled down again after Jenny's mother's funeral, he would make some changes. He knew he should have made changes long ago but even now he had a couple of things to sort out first. And one was the bloody Daphne Palmer case.

He smiled inwardly: when you find yourself running to murders and suicides to avoid facing the mess of your own life you're in serious trouble. But other people's messes were always easier to sort out than your own.

He wiped his mouth with the paper napkin and stood. He had to go in to see the pathologist now to be told that Daphne Palmer had committed suicide. And his problem was that he didn't believe it. Thirty years of dealing with this shit might have caused him to lose the ability to communicate with his wife and, Christ knows, what friends he used to have, but it had honed his instincts. No sooner had he established this than it collapsed. All he was sure of was the first part of the assessment: about his wife and friends.

As he slotted his tray into the trolley with other dirty trays, he reminded himself not to pre-empt what the pathologist would say or, for that matter, the state of his marriage and his social life. He was only fifty-three – there was time to rectify any failings that had come to light. He hoped.

John Milburn was one of those people Harry Kneebone had been dealing with now for a very long time, someone he had regular meetings with year in and year out, yet he had never got to know the man. When he saw him now the matter of John's age crossed his mind once again. He had a beard that was greying but the skin around his eyes was smooth and youthful. Kneebone could always come out and ask him, but John Milburn was not the kind of man to whom you could direct a personal question. Kneebone was sure that if he met him outside the realm of work, he'd have no idea where he knew him from.

'Hello, Harry,' Milburn said now, from his desk.

'John.'

'Daphne Palmer, I presume.'

'That's right.'

'I'll take you through in a minute.' With that Milburn sneezed, then ferreted about the pockets of his white coat for a tissue. Kneebone was amazed to see he was not in possession of one. He wished he had one to offer him. Milburn gave up pretending to look and stared at a report in front of him. After several moments he stood and said again, 'I'll take you through.'

They walked to the door that led into the morgue. 'You mentioned in the provisional report that there were some complications, albeit minor, you were worried about,' Kneebone said.

'Yes, yes, indeed. I'll show you.'

He opened the door and walked to the far wall where lines of vertical panels were divided into sections, each with a metal handle in the centre and a slot for a label above it. Many of the slots were empty. He went straight to the one marked 'Palmer'. When he slid it open, Kneebone felt the cold air rise up past him. The corpse it contained was covered with an off-white sheet that Milburn peeled back to reveal the sallow, peaceful face of the young woman. The skin was curiously flawless, as though what they were looking at was a wax model of the girl instead of her corpse. Kneebone looked at the rest of the body. The palms were face down but around the wrists there were marks and bruises of faded purple – it put him in mind of a petal from a withered violet.

Milburn lifted the arm that was next to him and turned the hand to reveal a deep opening that ran for almost two inches in a straight line down to the wrist.

'She was left-handed,' Milburn said.

'Why?'

'This cut on her right wrist is deeper than the one on her left. It's deep enough to do the job but right-handed people cutting their own wrists will cut the left arm first, which, normally speaking, will lead to a much deeper incision than when they turn their attention to their other arm. See, by then they're in shock, and they're holding a blade in a hand that has been injured so the resulting cut will be slight by comparison.'

'First cut is the deepest?' Kneebone said.

'Yes, that's correct.'

'It's a song.'

'Is it?' Milburn looked at Kneebone, then back at the arm he was holding.

'So what you're saying, John, is that she cut her right arm first?'

'All I'm saying is that there are two injuries on the girl's body that combined to cause her to bleed to death, one on the left wrist, one on the right, and that the one on the right wrist is deeper than the one on the left.'

'Which would be the case if she was left-handed?'

'Yes.'

'And that's always the case?'

'Always is a big word, Inspector.'

'Well, what other explanations could there be?'

'That someone other than the victim cut her wrists.'

'Given what you've seen, how likely or unlikely is that?'

'Hard to say. If this was all the evidence you had that it was murder rather than suicide, your case would be so thin it would be non-existent, but from a pathology point of view it's interesting – that is, if she was right-handed, which I believe she was.'

'Why do you say that?'

'You can tell from muscle formations in the arm, fingers, shoulder, lots of things.'

'Thank you for that. One other thing, the bruising around the wrists, any thoughts?'

'Well, naturally it got my attention but it's fairly low grade and it's irrelevant to her death. Bruising of that kind is built up from some repeated activity that went on, I'd say, for weeks, months maybe, before her death.'

'As if she had been repeatedly tied up, say?'

'Yes.'

'A willing participant in a sex game?'

'Inspector, I would have no idea about anything like that. They were not the injuries that caused her death is all I can tell you.'

'Right.'

John Milburn replaced the sheet and slid the drawer closed. They walked back into the office.

'Can I be so bold as to ask what the conclusion for your report will be?'

'That as far as I'm concerned it was death through self-harm.'

'Suicide?'

'Well, apart from that slight question mark around the right-hand/left-hand business, there's nothing here to suggest anything else.'

'What about drugs, tranquillisers, anything like that?'

'There were traces of THC in her blood, nothing more than the usual build-up you get in any casual marijuana smoker, and there was evidence she had been drinking alcohol the night before, but nothing substantial.'

'All that's going to do is give the defence the opportunity to claim it was a psychotic episode brought on by an indulgence in the mixture of marijuana and alcohol.'

'I take it from all this that you don't think it was suicide.'

'I don't know. There's something here I'm missing.'

'Well, I'm sorry I can't do more to help you. The girl's father seems to be a man with some clout – the coroner, apparently, is coming under a fair bit of pressure to have the body released.'

'When is that due to happen?'

'Well, I have no reason to detain it further here. I was waiting for this chat with you, Inspector, but if you have nothing concrete, I'll release it today.'

'For cremation, I presume.'

'These days, it usually is.'

'Do me a favour, John. Twenty-four hours?'

'I'm sure I can hold them off that long. Anything else?'

'No, thank you, you've been most helpful.'

Kneebone walked to the door, Milburn back towards his desk.

'Yes, actually, there was something else. Do you ever go to football?'

Milburn had just taken his seat. 'I'm a Bristol Rovers supporter – why?'

Kneebone smiled. 'Well, there you go, I didn't know that. Good day and thanks.'

He smiled, walking to the car. In a city where there were two football teams, neither of them major league, it took courage to support the lesser one. Finally he knew something about John Milburn.

As he drove back into town he tried to concentrate on Doyle. If he had slit his girlfriend's wrists while she was in the bath, there would have been a struggle. Yet Forensics had come up with nothing. He had read reports on the analysis of the bath water, samples from the floor of the bathroom, all clothing, both his and hers, and there was nothing anywhere in any of the hundreds of pages that could have connected Doyle with his girlfriend's death. Something was missing.

Geoff came to the conclusion that the best thing to do was come clean to Doyle about the notes. Daphne had either told him or she hadn't. If she had, he already knew and there would be no big surprise. If she hadn't, and Kneebone had found them, it was best Doyle heard it from him rather than that little slime-ball. Of course there was a third possibility, that she had destroyed the notes, and if that were the case it would be news to Doyle and how he would react was anyone's guess. But, all in all, it was better to get it out now. Christ! Geoff argued. They were only a couple of handwritten notes and while it might appear a little odd it wasn't against the law to write to someone.

As soon as he had a moment, which turned out to be around three in the afternoon, Geoff called Doyle. He sounded relatively normal, and when Geoff suggested that he might drop in later he thought Doyle met the suggestion with warmth.

He was full of apprehension climbing the stone steps to the red door. Doyle was a very difficult man to pre-empt. In fact, thinking about it now, Geoff had no idea how Doyle's mind worked. There was something impenetrable about him, something that denied you access. Geoff had never seen Doyle fall apart or even heard him badmouth a customer just to let off steam. And the events of the last week had seemed to drive him further into his warren of apathy.

Geoff was surprised by the inside of the flat. It was spotlessly tidy. The only odd thing was that Doyle had moved a chair so that it now stood in front of the sofa facing the window. This left nowhere to sit except the chair itself. But sitting there would make you feel like you were presiding over something. Maybe that was what he did all day now. Sat on the chair and presided over the view. Geoff stood in the doorway and leant against the frame. 'How have you been?' he asked.

Doyle was standing at the table by the window. 'Not bad, considering.' He was thinner. His eyes looked as if they were sinking into pools of shadow.

'Have you eaten anything lately? You look awful.'

'I'm not sleeping, which might explain it.'

'Were you offered anything? Counselling? Sleeping pills even?'

He shook his head.

'I can get you some pills, if you like.'

'I remember.' He smiled.

'I'll tell you what, I'll go and grab us a takeaway and a bottle of wine – OK?'

'If you like.'

Geoff was relieved to be out of the house: the air in it was still and stale and Doyle was becoming a ghost. How could he have slipped so quickly? He knew Doyle liked Indian so he ordered much more than two people could eat – then at least there'd be something in the fridge. While he was getting wine he bought a couple of six-packs of beer. He didn't know why but he didn't want to go back in to see Doyle unarmed with alcohol.

Geoff laid out the meal as appetisingly as he could, placing the wine in the centre of the table. Doyle raked at the food with his fork. Then Geoff noticed the marks at the base of his thumb. 'How'd you do that?' he asked.

'Fucked if I know.'

There was a silence.

'So, I take it your efforts to find an artist for the opening haven't been successful?'

'Why do you say that?'

'Look at you. You're half-dead, for Christ's sake. You need food but you're not eating, you need sleep but you're not sleeping, so I'm just presuming the other areas of your life are equally not happening.'

'Yeah, you're probably right.'

'About what?'

'About an artist.'

'So you haven't found anyone?'

Doyle threw down his fork. 'Just leave it, will you?' His brown eyes were trained on Geoff, who had never seen a reaction like this in him before. They stared at one another. Then Doyle reached for his fork.

'I'm sorry,' Geoff said. 'I have no right to come in here asking you shit like that, it's just …'

'You want me to jump into some kind of action, any kind of action, so as to stop me slipping under?'

'I wouldn't put it quite like that, but yeah.'

'It's really me you're thinking of?'

'Look, Doyle—'

'No,' he held up his hand, 'you look. Your concern is

misplaced, all right? I don't want it and I don't want any of the bullshit that goes with it. So if we're going to sit here for an hour or two eating and drinking I'd prefer if you didn't indulge in piety, pity or anything else plucked from the shelf of self-delusion because, right now, it would make me want to vomit. You understand?'

Geoff was silent. This was different. Finally he said, 'I'll do the best I can. So as long as we're talking straight, I came here to tell you something I didn't know if I should but seeing—'

'What?'

'I wrote to Daphne – notes, I mean. I wrote to her.'

Doyle was chewing now but he slowed as he focused on Geoff. His face displayed an expression that might have been amusement, Geoff couldn't tell.

'Explain,' Doyle said.

Geoff realised it was not a good time to go into this. How could he have been so stupid? Doyle was in the grip of a form of grief that made him appear lucid, rational, approachable even, yet he was anything but.

'What do you mean you wrote her notes, Geoff?'

Geoff sipped his wine to buy time. Fuck it, he thought, just say it. 'I saw her about a week after you and she came to that dinner party I had, remember? She walked into the shop with you, remember? And I just thought she looked kind of glum.'

'Glum?'

'Yeah, glum. So I sent her a note.'

'What did your note say?'

'That if she needed help I'd be there for her.'

Doyle looked to his right – he might have been staring out of the window. He had stopped chewing but he was breathing deeply and noisily. He then turned back to Geoff, smiling now. 'You're an arrogant fuck-wit, McAllister, do you know that? Where I come from they'd call you an interfering gobshite.'

'Maybe I should leave now.'

'And spineless to boot. Christ, but you're a gem.'

'What the fuck's got into you?'

'Oh, sorry, I'll revert back, shall I, into something you can walk on, wipe your feet on and then kick out of the way when it's inconvenient?'

'Look, man, you're taking this all wrong.'

'Fuck off – go on, fuck off out of here!'

Geoff stood. He had no clue as to what he could do or say to snap Doyle out of the state of mind he was in now. 'Look, it was just a note – but you're right and I'm sorry.'

Doyle stared at him. 'You said "notes".'

'Yes. She replied, and I replied to her. That's all.'

Doyle continued to stare, which Geoff found intensely uncomfortable yet he didn't feel he had enough control of the situation to turn and go. He was, for the first time, at Doyle's mercy.

'Why don't you sit down and finish your dinner? It's all immaterial now anyway.'

Geoff sat, aware only of Doyle chewing across the table from him. At least the fucker was eating. He looked down at his own food. He was still Doyle, he thought, despite the fact that grief had him transformed into a much more vile and aggressive version of himself.

'She had been talking about killing herself for a while, you know. Did she mention that in her reply?'

'No.'

'I had the usual reaction at first – you know, shock, horror, how can you think of such a thing, all that bollox.'

'Is it bollox?'

'Of course it is. We say it because someone taking their own life is an affront. We see it as an act of defiance but only because it punctures our illusion that we'll live for ever.'

'No one thinks that.'

'Don't we? When was the last time, Geoff, that you actually considered your own death?'

'It's not something I think about a great deal but that doesn't mean I think I'm never going to die. I am, everyone is. Otherwise it would be a very crowded fucking planet.'

'People who think about death are considered morbid, and "morbid" ain't attractive.'

As Geoff looked at him across the table, the thought crossed his mind that perhaps the grief had removed just enough of the layers for Doyle's real personality to show itself. 'So Daphne said she was going to do it?'

'I didn't say that.'

'Well, what, then?'

'Daphne said she wanted to do it.'

'Is there a difference?'

Doyle smiled. 'Oh, yes, a big difference.'

Geoff decided he didn't like what was going on here. He didn't like Doyle's mood, tone, anything that he was saying. 'Doyle, I think you should get out of here – this flat, I mean.'

'Why?'

'You need to be with people, not here on your own. It's doing you no good.'

'For fuck's sake, Geoff, stop this, will you? You sound like a bad play.'

'Can you just tell me what's going on with you?'

'I've done things now that I can't undo and it seems they're coming back to get me.'

'What do you mean?'

'It really doesn't matter.'

'But it does. Whatever you've done or think you've done, if you share it with someone else, it changes its perspective.'

'They used to teach us about perspective in Camberwell and maybe you're right, that what I need is a vanishing point.'

'Doyle, you don't. You just need some sleep.' Geoff stood. 'I'm going to get those pills. I'll be back in twenty minutes.'

'I'm going to stay awake tonight.'

'Why?'

'Night is a good time to get perspective.'

'Doyle, get off the bloody stage. You need sleep!'

'Do I?'

'Yes, you do. Please, Doyle, just do something for me. Go and lie down. When I get back you can knock yourself out for twelve hours.'

'And then what?'

'It'll be different then. Everything will be different.'

'I wish I lived in a world where twelve hours' sleep would change everything.'

Geoff stared at him. He needed to get away from Doyle, away from the poison that was leaking from him. He'd get him the pills, drop them off, and if the fucker was found dead in the morning, it would be a further extension of the tragedy. Whatever else, he, Geoff, couldn't stay. He wasn't any good in a situation like this. Surely to Christ there was family of some kind. 'Do you have any family?' he asked.

'No – well, I have two brothers but I haven't seen either of them for years.'

'Do you know where they are?'

'Last seen heading for the boat to England, but it could have sunk for all I know.'

Perhaps now, with Daphne gone, he was the only person in Doyle's life who gave a damn. He had never bargained for this. 'I'm going now,' Geoff said, 'and I'll be back with those sleepers, OK? Call me if you need anything.'

'Thanks for the dinner.'

Geoff was glad to be breathing fresh air once again. He knew the man inside that flat should not be left on his own – the thoughts his mind was throwing up were toxic. The best thing he could do for Doyle was get him help but from where?

He was surprised to find when he got home that it was still quite early. He sat at the kitchen table thinking about friends, acquaintances, ex-girlfriends, friends of his mother even, anyone who might be able to help or know someone who could. He was aware that as he sat there Doyle might be doing exactly what Daphne had done. But surely his mood was too lively for that. But moods, like winds, change.

He stood up and went to the bedroom where he found, in the third drawer of his bedside table, the small dark-brown bottle of pills his sister had given him. He spilt two into his hand, then went back into the kitchen to wrap them in clingfilm. The phone rang.

'Hello.'

'Hi.' The voice was hesitant, female. 'You don't know me, but my name is Gina Harding and I'm an artist. A guy came here, Desmond Doyle, to look at my work. He gave me a card. Your name was at the bottom. I got your number from Directory Enquiries – I hope you don't mind.'

'What is it?'

'It's hard to explain, really. He was here yesterday and, well, there's something going on that I don't understand and I need to talk to someone who knows him. This sounds mad. Look, I'm sorry, perhaps I shouldn't have called.'

'It's OK. What do you mean, "there's something going on"?'

'I've been trying to contact him but I can't. I need to get hold of him.'

'Well, as far as I know he's at home. I was just going round there now so maybe I can give him a message.'

'No, a message wouldn't work.' The woman sounded distraught.

'Well, maybe we could meet,' Geoff said, and immediately regretted it. He really didn't want to have to deal with some frantic artist.

'Now? Tonight?'

He couldn't tell if she was horrified by the prospect or relieved. 'Yes, if you like.'

'Where?'

'Where do you live?'

'Montpelier.'

Geoff had to rack his brains. 'There's a pub just up the hill from you, the Hillgrove – you know it?'

'I don't usually go into pubs ...'

'Well, you choose a place.'

'No, it's fine. Half an hour?'

'OK,' Geoff agreed.

'I've no idea what you look like.'

'I'm big, in my thirties, beard. I'll sit as close as I can to the door.'

'All right. Thank you.'

Geoff prided himself on being a capable man, someone who could negotiate his way around most problems, but he was beginning to see that there was a whole species of dilemma out there that he couldn't handle. And he was in the midst of one now: Doyle, with a frantic artist in tow. Christ! Health and Safety, Environmental Health, Town Planning, all of them would be a doddle compared with this.

He was just about to climb into the car when he realised he'd better cycle. He'd had two hefty glasses of wine at Doyle's and he couldn't imagine talking to Gina Harding in the Hillgrove without a drink. But this left his timing tight and he guessed that Miss Harding wouldn't be comfortable sitting in a pub on her own.

By the time he got back to Doyle's place there were only a few minutes to spare. He buzzed the door and waited. He buzzed again. He called the landline, then the mobile. Nothing. A minute later he climbed back on to his bike and pedalled off in the direction of the pub.

He recognised her as soon as he walked in. She was a neat-looking woman in her mid-thirties. Everything about her was crisp, delicate but agitated. 'Gina?'

She looked up. 'Yes.'

'Geoff McAllister.'

'Of course. Can I get you a drink?'

'No, you stay there. I'll get you one.'

She pointed to her glass. 'I'm OK, thanks.'

Geoff didn't recognise any of the beers on sale, but although the place was busy, the barman offered him a taste of anything he might like. He said he was happy to go with whatever he suggested. The beer he got was blond and his first sip told him it was good. He took another gulp and looked at Gina. She was sitting at the edge of her seat playing with a beer mat. He went over and sat beside her. 'So, what's this about?' he asked. If she were an animal she'd be a mouse, he thought.

She leant forward slightly. 'I don't know if this is all in my head but … Tell me, do you know Desmond Doyle very well?'

'He's been working for me for about four months so in a way I do and in a way I don't. Why? What has he done?'

'It's not him so much as his girlfriend, if that's who she is.'

'Daphne? But Daphne is …'

'Dead, I know, he told me, but the problem is she's trying to communicate something either to him or somebody else and she's using my painting to do it.'

This woman was off the scale. 'I'm afraid I don't follow.'

'I'm really busy at the moment – I have an exhibition coming up in September – but one day last week I had the sudden urge to stop and do some work with pastels. It was just I'd been working in oils so much I wanted a break, to do something a bit freer. Anyway, I ended up doing two really quick sketches. And when I looked at them I realised they were of a girl in a bath. In the first she's looking out of the picture at you and in the second she's under the water but she's smiling.'

Gina Harding was completely calm but he could see that what she had just told him was upsetting her. He had a thought. 'When you start a painting or a drawing do you not know what you're going to do before you do it?'

'Sometimes, and sometimes I haven't a clue.'

'I'm a chef. I couldn't imagine setting out to create a dish without knowing exactly what I was going to produce.'

'I can understand that.'

'So these sketches, did Doyle see them?'

She nodded. 'He actually threw up – or it sounded like it. I made him a cup of tea and that was when he told me about his girlfriend.'

'Jesus!'

'He came back the next day. I think he'd convinced himself that he'd imagined it. He was very quiet, didn't say a word, and when he saw the drawings again he ran.'

'When was this?

'Two days ago – Monday.'

'Look, I'm not very good with this kind of stuff.'

'You're not? Listen to me, neither am I. When I pick up a brush now I haven't a clue what's going to happen. It's messing me up.'

Geoff wondered for a moment if she was close to tears. 'I can imagine. Has anything like this ever happened to you before?'

'No! I've completely abandoned the work for the exhibition. All I do now is doodles, and I know they're all connected with this. I watch them happening and it's scaring me.'

Now it was clear that she was fighting back tears. Geoff had an urge to put an arm around her but somehow knew not to. 'What can I do to help?'

She flashed a brief smile. 'You have already. This is the first time I've been able to talk about it to anyone.'

'Do you think getting in touch with Doyle would be any use?'

'Yes, I do.'

'I was with him earlier and he was in a very strange mood, kind of aggressive. Now he's not answering his phone. Doyle is never aggressive.'

'I wouldn't say that.'

'He was aggressive to you?'

'Aggressive is a little too strong – and he had had a shock, I suppose . . .'

'This is a crazy bloody business – to tell you the truth, I'm worried. Just before you called I was sitting there wondering who I could call.'

'What do you mean?'

'Tonight his attitude was sort of like "Fuck you".' As soon as Geoff had said 'fuck' he realised Gina was one of those people who never used the word. He continued, 'After I left him I went home to get him some pills to help him sleep. When I dropped by to give them to him he wasn't in, or wasn't answering. I don't know.'

'Maybe he'd just gone out for milk or something.'

'Yeah, that's what I thought, but then I thought, Maybe he's in there but not in a condition to open the door.'

'I don't understand. You don't mean – like his girlfriend?'

'Well, it's just that he was so odd earlier and I had the feeling I shouldn't leave him – but I'm just not good in these situations. I didn't know what to do.'

'Is the flat far?'

'Two minutes.'

'We should go there.'

Geoff lifted his drink. 'Give me a problem that's tangible and I'm fine, but this ...'

'Come on.'

'I don't know what he'll make of us two appearing at his front door but you're right.'

They drained their glasses and left. It had turned blustery and cold. Geoff wheeled the bike as they walked up a side road and then to Doyle's flat.

When they rang the bell, there was no answer. Geoff looked at his watch: ten to eleven. He tried Doyle's mobile but there was still no reply.

'Is there another entrance?' Gina asked.

'Well, we could go around the back, see if there's any lights on.'

They walked down the side of the building and into the garden. The bottom half had been paved. They stood by the washing line and looked up at the back of the building. All four double windows, one above the other, were dark. Geoff took out his mobile again and called. Again it went to voicemail.

'Nothing.' He put the phone back into his pocket.

Twelve

It was Harry Kneebone's intention to go around to Doyle's flat early in the morning, subject him to a little in-depth questioning and, if necessary, pull him in. But the call he took on his mobile from Geoff McAllister at six thirty-seven changed that plan. Kneebone had to admit to a sense of smug satisfaction as he lay in bed listening to McAllister's troubled tones.

McAllister, apparently, hadn't slept much because he was worried about Doyle. It was his impression that Doyle was in his flat but not in a state to open the door.

'What do you mean?' Kneebone asked.

McAllister would not be drawn, just repeated his concerns.

'Right, I'll come down and bring a bit of muscle. We might have to force the door.'

'When will that be?'

'Well, I need to put my teeth in . . . forty-five minutes?'

'I'll be there.'

Harry Kneebone stepped from his house and looked at the sky. It was a day lifted straight out of November, cold and grey. When he had phoned ahead to the station to ask for some assistance in entering the premises of a man who was under suspicion of murder the duty officer had insisted on an armed unit.

'Look, I may need someone to break down the door, but that's all,' the inspector told him.

'I'm not sending my men into a murderer's flat unarmed.'

When Kneebone arrived they were waiting. After he had parked he went up to the window of the car they were in and told them to hang back until he had assessed the situation. He found McAllister waiting for him on the front steps.

'Hi,' Geoff said, getting up. He did look like a man who hadn't slept much. 'Still no answer.' His attention went to the gate. Kneebone turned to see that the two uniformed policemen had left their car and were standing there, one holding the red battering ram.

'The Big Red Key's arrived,' he said, 'but I think I'll try myself before we get Tom and Jerry there to knock the door off its hinges.' He climbed the steps and pressed Doyle's bell, then stood facing the grille. He waited a minute or so, then pressed another. It was answered by a woman. Kneebone spoke into the grille and the front door buzzed. He opened it, saying, 'Thank you, Jasmine, I'm in.' To the men at the gate, he said, 'We're halfway there.'

They took this as their instruction to move and walked past Geoff and up the steps. They were both clad in bulletproof vests with small packets of electronic equipment attached to the front. Geoff noticed handguns protruding from holsters strapped just above their knees. Everything, from their baseball caps to their boots, was black.

Inside, Kneebone had knocked on the door of Doyle's flat and was waiting for a reply. The man carrying the battering ram swung it off his shoulder and rested one end on the floor. Kneebone knocked again, this time shouting Doyle's name. He waited. Then, without warning, he did it again. All four listened.

After a minute Kneebone nodded to the officer with the battering ram. The man's upper body seemed to expand as he picked it up and approached the door. He held the handles in a grip that turned his knuckles white and had just begun his swing backwards when, behind them, Doyle's voice said, 'I do have a key.'

It took the man with the battering ram visible effort to stop, by which time Doyle was among them and fishing for his keys. 'Bit early for all this,' he said, acknowledging Geoff with a nod. He looked rested, bright and well.

'Thanks, chaps,' Kneebone said to his colleagues. 'I'll deal with it from here.'

They nodded and went out of the front door. Doyle, followed by Kneebone and Geoff, entered the flat. Geoff noted that it was exactly as he had left it last night: empty cartons and wrappers covered the table like withered vegetables.

Kneebone looked at the remains of the food while Doyle headed for the kitchen. 'I'm imagining everyone's for tea?' he called.

'Please,' said the inspector.

Geoff was taken aback by Doyle's apparent chirpiness. He had spent a night imagining every sort of horror and lain there cursing himself for his cowardice in leaving him alone. Now, as he stood there, he was aware of simultaneous relief and anger. Why couldn't he have just answered his bloody phone? It was almost as if the fucker had been punishing him.

Geoff dragged the armchair to the wall where it had been originally and then sat down. The inspector, who was now busying himself with the titles in Doyle's bookcase, noticed this. 'Make yourself at home, why don't you, Mr McAllister?'

Geoff didn't respond. The inspector to him had become a mosquito, irritating and irrelevant.

Doyle appeared at the kitchen doorway, enquiring as to how

the inspector took his tea. When it was ready Doyle brought the three mugs to the table. He began to scoop up the waste from last night and transport it to the kitchen.

When he returned he handed Geoff his mug and sat down on the sofa.

'So, your friend here was worried about you, Mr Doyle. On the phone first thing this morning he was in such a state,' the inspector said. He had moved to the table and parked part of his posterior on it.

Geoff looked from him to Doyle. He was perfectly entitled to leave, he thought. In fact, that was probably the best thing to do.

'You had no need to worry, Geoff.'

'You weren't answering your phone, your doorbell. And considering the mood you were in when I was leaving, of course I was worried.'

'Mood? What mood?' the inspector asked. When neither of them spoke he said, 'What mood are you talking about, Mr McAllister?'

'I don't know – he was aggressive.'

'I was angry.'

'Really! What were you angry about?'

Doyle and Geoff shared a look.

'Geoff told me last night that he'd been writing to Daphne.'

'Oh, for fuck's sake!' Geoff erupted. 'For a start it was totally inconsequential and, second, I told you that in confidence.'

'Mr McAllister, I'll be the judge of its inconsequentiality, and please bear in mind that in a murder investigation nothing is private.'

Geoff stared at Doyle now.

'So, what were you writing to Mr Doyle's girlfriend about, Mr McAllister?'

'Inspector, the reason you – and I, for that matter – are here is because I was worried about him.' He pointed at Doyle. 'If you want to interrogate me you'd better arrest me and I'll answer all questions in the company of my solicitor, but if you really think I had anything to do with Daphne's death, why would I be phoning you first thing in the morning concerned about him?'

Inwardly Kneebone was amused by McAllister's outburst. 'Keep your hair on, Mr McAllister. I think it would be best if we all had just a quiet, informal chat. And in that spirit, I'd like to ask you again, what were you writing to Daphne about?'

Geoff gave Doyle a long, hard look. 'I got the feeling there was something wrong with her. No, that's not strictly true. Maybe I fancied her, I don't know. What I said in the first note was simply that she looked a bit down and if there was anything I could do let me know.'

The inspector was staring at Doyle. 'Me, oh, my! Bit swift that, Doyle, the boss moving in on the little lady. Must have riled you to hear it?'

'It made no difference to me.'

'Did it not? How interesting! The man who pays your wages muscling in on your girlfriend, and especially during one of those times when you and she weren't exactly getting on?'

'He couldn't have muscled in on me and Daphne. He's not her type.'

'Well, if you'll forgive me for saying so, Mr Doyle, she didn't appear to be too fussy about "type" in her former days – at least, not if what you said in the interview was true.'

'That was then. She wouldn't have been interested in Geoff, or anyone else.'

'You sure about that?'

'Yes.'

'How can you be?'

'Oh, for God's sake, she was depressed. We talked a lot about it.'

'Really? At the station, as far as I recall, you said you and she had stopped talking some months back.'

'Well, we'd stopped communicating in any normal couple sort of way. We stopped chatting . . . but the big stuff, we talked about that.'

'The big stuff?'

'Yeah – life, death, her depression, all that kind of stuff.'

'And when did these talks take place?'

'In bed, mostly.'

'I presume you untied her first?'

'That's not funny,' Doyle said.

'Oh, sorry if I offended you. So, back to you, Mr McAllister. How often did you write to Daphne?'

'Three times. First one was as I told you. She replied to that in a curt sort of a way, you know, polite but distant, which is, I think, the way she was.'

'You don't know the first thing about how she was,' Doyle interrupted.

The inspector let the silence hang. It would be interesting, he thought, to see what came to the surface if these two had a go at one another. But the silence continued. 'Go on, Mr McAllister.'

'So in the second one – these were just notes, really – I said what I'd said in the first, about being of help and that, but I suggested she might like to meet for a drink. When she didn't reply to that I wrote again, saying I was sorry if I was bothering her and I wouldn't do it again. She didn't answer that one either.'

'So you found Daphne attractive?' the inspector said.

'Yes, I did. That's not against the law, is it?'

'Depends entirely on how you act upon your feelings.'

'Yeah, well, writing someone notes doesn't exactly constitute the crime of the century.'

'Crimes blossom, Mr McAllister, when people start acting

inappropriately towards one another. It's a case of one thing leading to another until, lo and behold, we're wheeling out another corpse.'

'I wrote to Daphne. I didn't kill her.'

'I never said you did.' The inspector slipped off the table and walked to a series of small framed prints that showed ocean currents and the ice limits for the Arctic and Antarctic. 'So, Mr Doyle, where did you sleep last night?'

'In Jasmine's flat.'

'In her bed?'

'I don't think that's any of your business.'

'Don't you?'

'No.'

Harry Kneebone moved towards the sofa. 'Eight days ago Daphne Palmer died in this flat of wounds that were almost certainly not self-inflicted.' He looked at Doyle. 'And one of you, or both, knows more than you have told me. I don't know what you're trying to hide but you're wasting your time. Whatever it is, I'll find it.' He walked to the door. 'Good morning to you both. I'll see myself out.'

They stayed silent until they heard the outer door close, then Doyle breathed a long sigh and got up. He walked to the table, sat and put his head into his hands. Geoff watched him, his anger now suspended. What had Kneebone meant 'not self-inflicted'? Doyle couldn't possibly have killed Daphne.

Doyle suddenly dropped his hands and turned to him. 'Fucking inspector – what does he think went on here? What right does he have accusing me – us?'

'He's a detective inspector, that's what he does.'

Doyle drove his fingers through his hair. It made him look deranged, Geoff thought. And then, almost to confirm it, he said, 'I think I'm going mad.'

'Why do you think that?'

Doyle rested his chin in his hands, covering his mouth with his fingers.

'Why did you say that?' Geoff said.

Doyle stared at him. 'What the fuck's going on with you?'

'What do you mean?'

'Writing to Daphne! What the fuck was all that about? And you said you didn't know Gina Harding and you did!'

'I didn't.'

'You were in the fucking garden with her last night! The fucking garden, Geoff!'

'The first time I met her was last night. She called me.'

'You're a fucking liar!'

'I'm not lying. She called me because she was trying to get in contact with you and you weren't responding.'

'I don't want to see her – she's a fucking nutcase.'

'You're welcome to your opinion but I'm not lying. She did phone me. I was on my way here to deliver these.' He fished from his pocket the two pills he had wrapped in clingfilm and threw them towards the table. They landed on the floor several feet from Doyle. He glanced at them.

'She phoned me. She was upset so I offered to meet her. After a drink we came here to try to find you.'

'Is this knight-in-shining-armour shit something new or did I just not pick up on it before?'

'What are you talking about?'

'You see Daphne and you think she looks sad so you write her a little "buddy-up" note. Gina fucking Nutcase calls so you run to comfort her. That's what I'm talking about. I had you down more as a find-'em-fuck-'em-and-forget-'em kind of guy.'

'I wasn't trying to muscle in on Daphne. I wasn't. That's the fucking inspector's take on it and he's wrong. Daphne was beautiful, for fuck's sake! The first time I saw her walk into the shop I couldn't believe you'd pulled someone like her.'

'Thanks.'

'Well, I couldn't. And I just got the feeling from her that she was out on a limb somewhere and I thought, Fuck, Doyle will never handle this. I know – it was arrogant and stupid but it's what I thought, so I wrote the note. I really wasn't trying to move in there.'

'You didn't think I could handle her?'

'No.'

'Jesus, Geoff, she wasn't a motorbike on a wet road, for Christ's sake!'

'Everyone has to be handled to some degree.'

'No, Geoff, they don't. Daphne decided what she wanted, depressed or not. She'd decide and then I'd fall in behind her, or not. She left me room to get out if I wanted.'

'You mean, out of the relationship?'

'Out of whatever – the relationship, her plans, decisions, anything and everything. It was up to me.'

'What are you talking about? What was up to you?'

'Whether to be involved or not.'

'Involved in what?'

'Plans, Geoff, plans. Any plans she could muster.'

'Like her plan to kill herself.'

'I'm not too sure how involved I was with that one.'

It was still early when Kneebone got back to his desk. He had been reinvigorated by the morning's work. For openers he had never been more certain that Doyle was involved. He was equally certain now that McAllister was not. He just did not act like a guilty man. But the most interesting thing to come to light this morning was the relationship between Doyle and his upstairs neighbour, the lovely Jasmine. That might yet throw up something.

He checked his watch and decided to see if John Milburn was at his desk yet. He was in luck, but what Milburn told him was not good news. Milburn was planning to release the body by midday if there were no further developments. Daphne Palmer's father had been using some very weighty connections to put the pressure on.

'Don't these people realise we have a job to do?'

'Harry, you suspect something's amiss here and maybe you're right but I don't have enough to detain the body, you know that. So you've got a couple of hours or I'm going to release it. I don't have any choice.'

'And you've found nothing since?'

'I've been all over her, Harry, and I told you what I found. I've no reason to go back unless you give me one. Sorry.'

'Right, thanks.' He put down the phone. Normally, when the truth was ready, it dropped into your hand like a ripe fruit. Sometimes, though, the tree needed a good shake. Maybe this was one of those times.

He phoned the sergeant on duty and told him he now needed an arrest attempt made on this morning's suspect, plus a woman who lived in the flat above him, a Jasmine Kennington. He reaffirmed that neither had previous so he doubted they'd cause trouble. 'I'd appreciate it if you let me know, Ray, as soon as you have them in custody.'

An hour later Ray phoned back. 'They're here, all suited up and ready for you. She's a feisty little thing.'

'Trouble?'

'Nothing major.'

'I'll give them a little while to cool off, then have a word. Her first, I think – better organise a brief.'

'Hers is on standby.'

'What about Doyle?'

'He's in a cell but he's gone very quiet. We're keeping an eye on him. I'll get Midwinter – that's who he had before.'

Jasmine came into the interview in her white paper boiler-suit looking ready to spit fire. The hour or so she had spent in the cell had neither calmed nor frightened her. She appeared so undaunted by what was happening to her that Kneebone wondered if she might have experienced this under a different name. He made a mental note to do a thorough background search on her.

She and her solicitor, a woman by the name of Badham whom Kneebone had never seen before, took their seats, Jasmine opposite him. Beside him was Bowls, a young detective sergeant.

Kneebone turned on the tape and went through the formalities, during which he noted that Jasmine did not take her eyes off him.

'So, Miss Kennington, can you tell me please the nature of your relationship with Desmond Doyle?'

'There is none.'

'But you slept with him last night.'

'So?'

'So there has to be some kind of relationship.'

'Go fuck yourself!'

'Look, Jasmine—'

'Don't fucking "Look, Jasmine" me, you bastard. You woke me up this morning and I fucking let you in! Next minute I'm dragged to this fucking hell-hole to be told to strip. Strip! For fuck's sake! And for what? Sleeping with the guy from downstairs! I've been working shifts for the last two weeks and I can tell you I don't need this fucking shit. I just don't need it.'

'Let me ask you again, what is your relationship with Desmond Doyle?'

'Fuck off!'

'Right, suspending interview at,' Kneebone looked at his watch, 'ten forty-three. Suspect will remain in custody. Thank you all.' He turned off the tape and began to get up.

'You can't do that!' Jasmine roared.

'Can't do what?'

'Keep me locked up here. I have fucking rights!'

'Miss Kennington, we are conducting a murder inquiry. It has recently come to our attention that you are having an intimate relationship with the main suspect in that inquiry so I am going to keep you here for as long as it takes for you to co-operate.'

'But I've done nothing.'

'Cells are full of people who did nothing.'

'Mr Kneebone, if you could be specific as to the exact nature of the charge against my client it might help,' Miss Badham said.

'All I'm trying to do is ascertain the nature of the relationship between your client and the main suspect in the case.'

'My client was arrested on suspicion of aiding and abetting in a crime. Has that charge been changed?'

'No.'

'This is fucking ridiculous! What do you want to know?' Jasmine was still speaking with volume but her tone had lost its edge.

'Do you want to resume the interview, Miss Kennington?'

'I just want to get out of here, so if that means answering your stupid fucking questions, then yes.'

Kneebone stared at her for a moment, then sat and turned on the tape. 'Interview resumed at Miss Kennington's request. Miss Kennington, please tell me the nature of the relationship you've had with Desmond Doyle.'

'I really didn't have any.'

'Did he sleep in your bed last night?'

'Yes.'

'Did you have sex?'

'Yes.'

'I'll ask you yet again. What is the nature of the relationship you have with Desmond Doyle?'

Jasmine exhaled in a long, low sigh. 'Jesus fucking Christ, I don't believe this, I really don't. I felt sorry for the guy.'

'You're obviously a very compassionate woman, Miss Kennington,' Bowls said. When she didn't reply he added, 'A lot of nurses are.' She glanced at him with irritation. 'But you must be kept very busy if you sleep with everyone you feel sorry for.'

Kneebone suppressed a smile.

'That remark is beneath contempt!' Badham barked.

'May I apologise on behalf of my colleague?' Kneebone said quickly, before Badham took off on some long tangent.

'Be warned, Inspector, I will not tolerate such attitudes.'

Kneebone looked at her. He did not know how much she knew about the process they were involved in but suspected he would have to play very closely by the rules if he did not want this interview scrapped. 'We've apologised, OK?' He turned his attention to Jasmine.

'The day before yesterday he knocked at my door. I'd only met him a couple of times in the hall and I told him I understood how he felt because I'd lost a brother so, if he was feeling lonely or low, he should drop up, and he did.'

'What happened?'

'I opened the door and he was standing there, looking like he hadn't slept for days. I'd been on shifts and I was sleeping so it seemed the most sensible thing just to put him into the bed beside me and when I did he fell asleep straight away.

'That was the first time he came to visit you?'

'Yep.'

'And last night?' Kneebone asked.

'I didn't have to go in today, so on my way home last night I called by to see how he was doing. He had some wine on the go and I had a glass and we ended up in my bed together, only this time we did have sex. Happy?'

Kneebone flashed Bowls a quick look to make sure he was not tempted into making an unwise reply. 'May I ask if he suggested anything unusual?' Kneebone asked.

'I'm sorry?'

'Did he suggest any unusual sex games, bondage, slapping, anything like that?'

She hesitated. 'No!' she said, as though slightly disgusted by the idea.

She's lying, Kneebone thought. He stayed silent, observing her until she was showing visible signs of discomfort. 'Are you sure, Miss Kennington?'

Another moment of hesitation. 'I'm absolutely certain,' she said.

She lied well, he'd give her that. 'What if I tell you I don't believe you and what if I said we could hold you here while we apply for a warrant to search your flat for evidence?'

'On what grounds?' Badham said icily.

'That such evidence exists.'

'Inspector, you sound to me like a man grabbing at straws. I will fight any warrant application vigorously so you'd better be on very firm ground.' She smiled.

He stared at the two women in front of him. He had played his card and played it badly. But all was not lost. Jasmine had given him something: Doyle was not quite the sweet innocent he had made himself out to be. Kneebone could now be almost certain that he had instigated sex games with Jasmine last night.

'Thank you, Miss Kennington. Just one more thing, may I look at your wrists?'

'My wrists?'

Kneebone nodded.

Reluctantly Jasmine pulled up the sleeves of the paper suit, first the left, then the right, and brought both hands forward. There was a clear mark encircling each wrist but it had been made by the elastic in the suit's sleeves.

'Could you turn your hands so I can see your palms?' Kneebone asked.

Jasmine looked at her solicitor, who nodded, then turned her hands over. As well as the indentation from the elastic Kneebone thought he could make out redness just above them. 'Are those bruises on your wrists?'

'No.'

'There are definite marks there, Miss Kennington.'

'When I'm not in a cell, Inspector, I like to wear bracelets.'

'Thank you for your co-operation, Miss Kennington, you're free to go.'

Doyle sat on a thin mattress covered with blue plastic. In front of him was a wall of white, rectangular tiles that went from floor to ceiling. The cell door was open and in the doorway, seated in a plastic chair, a policeman was reading a tattered magazine. Every so often the man would look at him but neither had spoken since they had taken up their positions more than an hour ago. Doyle would have liked to get up and walk about – he felt as if his buttocks had gone flat – but he didn't want to disturb the status quo.

He was noticing things this time that he had missed on his first visit. There was a spy-hole in the wall in front of the toilet bowl and a CCTV camera in the corner on the ceiling. Someone had thrown shit at it so now it resembled a disintegrated wasp's nest. He heard voices calling from other cells along the corridor. So people were here in cells with the doors locked. Why, he wondered, did he warrant such special treatment? There could only be one reason: self-harm. He thought about the expression. It should be preceded by 'excessive' or 'unacceptable' because all those people lowering pints and lighting cigarettes or joints were self-harming but they weren't being watched doing it.

He came to a compromise – he lay down. The policeman watched him until he settled. Doyle felt a ripple in his bowels and knew that if he had been alone he would have released a long, loud fart. He began to wonder about the man in the doorway. How much did he get paid? Was he married? Did he have kids? Anything was possible. He might be a martial-arts expert who still wet the bed. Doyle wondered what his name was. He opened his eyes and looked at the face again. It was pudgy, with a dark, heavy beard. Doyle decided that the man's name was James and that he lived at home with his parents; he had two brothers and went out with a girl called Karen who worked in a shop. He then looked up at the white ceiling, wondering why they hadn't cleaned the shit away from the camera.

An hour or so after Geoff had left this morning, Doyle heard a knock on his door. When he opened it, all Doyle could see was uniformed policemen. Two entered his flat, read him his rights and told him he was being arrested for Daphne's murder. He hadn't been expecting this but somehow it hadn't surprised him. As an event, it fell in alongside everything else that had happened. He heard Jasmine's voice coming from upstairs and realised that was where the rest of the police had gone. But what would they want with her? As he was being escorted through the hallway he heard her shouting. It sounded as if she was putting up a fight. It made his insides wither. This thing kept twisting into something increasingly nasty. Outside there were two cars. He was put into one and driven off.

At the station it was the same as before. He was taken to a room and told to remove his clothes. The two policemen who had driven him there watched him strip and get into his paper suit. There was no finger-printing, DNA-swabbing or photographing this time and he was taken straight to a cell. He realised when he got there that he hadn't spoken a word since the police had entered his flat.

Someone up the hall was shouting for a cigarette. The voice had gone from anger to pleading and now it was working itself back to anger.

Last night Jasmine's voice had done the same. But it was fine now, she wasn't angry with him any more – or, at least, she hadn't been before they'd arrested her. This morning she had inadvertently put her hand on him while she slept. He opened his eyes and, in the muted light, gazed at her profile: she really was very pretty. He slid his hand to her breast and squeezed gently. Her eyes opened and she looked confused for a moment, then smiled a sleepy, lazy smile that made him want to see her face contort in pleasure as it had last night.

He heard the clip of heels outside and watched the policeman turn. He was almost out of his seat when Martin Midwinter came into view. He flashed Doyle a smile and nodded to the policeman, who folded the magazine in half and sauntered out of view, taking the chair with him. Doyle sat up to make room for the solicitor.

'Hi,' Midwinter said. 'Are you all right?'

Doyle shrugged. 'I'm OK. Why am I here?'

'Beats me. There's no new evidence unless they plan to spring something on us out of the blue. You haven't made a statement, have you?'

'No.'

'Good.' He smiled and looked about. His eyes rested on the shit-smeared camera. He sighed and turned back to Doyle. 'Have they offered you anything, tea, coffee?'

'No.'

'Wait a second.' He was about to get up.

'It's OK, I don't want anything.'

'You sure?'

'I'm fine.'

'It's my guess they've just brought you here in a desperate attempt to get you to cough up to something, so it's really important that you don't say anything you don't strictly have to. I'll be with you so if you're unsure about anything stay quiet and I'll deal with them. You sure about a coffee?'

'Yeah.'

I wouldn't blame you. It tastes like what's hanging out of the camera there.'

'There's a question I want to ask you.'

'Yeah?'

'Is suicide, by legal definition, an act you have to commit on your own?'

'I don't quite follow.'

'For example, if you saw someone attempting to commit suicide and you didn't do anything to prevent it or try to stop them, are you guilty of anything?'

'I don't know, I'd have to look that up, but I'd guess it would depend on the circumstances. The law is based on reasonability. Why do you ask?'

'You hear stories all the time, parents taking a child immobilised after an accident to Switzerland so they can have an assisted suicide, things like that, and sometimes they get away with it and sometimes they don't.'

'Assisting someone to kill themselves is against the law – even killing yourself is against the law – but there are certain grey areas within it and attitudes are changing.'

Doyle was silent. Eventually Midwinter said, 'Is there anything you want to tell me?'

'No.'

'Because if something like that has gone on you should tell it to me so we can plan how to show it in its best light.'

'No, there's nothing.'

'You're absolutely certain?'

Doyle didn't answer. Once the silence had established itself Midwinter busied himself with papers he pulled from his briefcase and then began asking questions about Jasmine. When the tone and brevity of Doyle's answers informed him that there was little mileage in the attempted conversation he abandoned it and settled into the long wait for the call to the interview room.

Kneebone noticed that the ease and friendliness Doyle had shown this morning were now gone. He entered the interview room and sat, arms folded, looking blankly at a point on the table in front of him. Midwinter sat beside him, as crisp as a biscuit fresh from its pack. They waited for Bowls to join them, then Kneebone went through his tape routine after which he did nothing but observe Doyle. It was Bowls who spoke first.

'We have evidence that Ms Palmer was murdered.'

Midwinter moved in his chair. 'Why was I not informed of this?'

'We have our reasons, Mr Midwinter,' Kneebone said, wondering if his entire project, tentative as it was, was going to be blown out of the water by objecting solicitors.

'I am in this room to make sure that the rights of my client are not abused. If you do have information, we want to hear it. Your methods here are unacceptable.'

'Daphne was right-handed, Mr Doyle, wasn't she?' Kneebone asked.

Doyle looked up from the table. He stared at Kneebone, then allowed his gaze to find the table once again.

'A right-handed person cutting their wrists will cut the left one first and then the right. As a result the second wound will not be as deep. This, however, was not the case with Daphne, Mr Doyle, was it?'

Doyle did not lift his gaze.

Kneebone continued, 'The incision made in Daphne's right wrist was deeper than the one in her left, which would suggest that someone was kind enough to cut her wrists for her. Who, I wonder, would be unselfish enough to do that?'

But for his index finger sliding back and forth over the edge of the desk Doyle sat motionless.

'Daphne didn't cut her own wrists, did she, Doyle?' The inspector's tone was calm.

In the silence that followed Doyle looked up at him as though he was unaware of the question.

'You slit them for her, didn't you?' Kneebone asked, and waited for the man opposite him to lift his head and say yes. The head did not move.

'You probably thought you were helping her and – who knows? – in a way, maybe you were.'

'It wasn't like that,' Doyle said, sounding utterly bored.

'Then tell me, what was it like?'

'You're just completely wrong, Inspector. I didn't kill Daphne.'

Kneebone and Doyle stared at one another. 'Who did, then?'

'She killed herself.'

Kneebone sat back on his chair. There had to be a way through this wall in front of him. No one was that hermetically sealed. And the way in was usually revealed in what the suspect showed was important to him or her. But the man in front of him now was so disengaged from the proceedings it was like interviewing a corpse. He would have to try a different tack – but what?

'Inspector, may I enquire if that is the extent of your evidence against my client?'

Kneebone looked at Midwinter. He wanted to say, Please, not now, I know all about rights and safeguards and all the other paraphernalia at play here but this man beside you is a killer so let me do my job. But he didn't.

'Because if it is,' Midwinter continued, 'it's circumstantial. You know that, I know that.'

He gave it one last shot: 'What did she say to convince you that it would be OK? You're not a stupid man and I know you loved her so why – why – did you allow yourself be talked into it?' He was watching Doyle closely. 'You've allowed yourself to be used as an instrument in her suicide. That was a very selfish thing for her to do.'

'She didn't use me as an instrument,' Doyle said, without looking up.

'But you were there when she did it?' Kneebone said.

'I was in the shop.'

'You may have been in the shop when she died but where were you when her wrists were opened?'

Doyle shook his head and mumbled something. Kneebone leant forward, asking him to repeat it. Doyle met his eye. 'I've done nothing to be ashamed of!' He lowered his head again.

'I'm quite sure you haven't but, with respect, Mr Doyle, that's not the point. We need to know what happened in the bathroom on that morning.'

'I'll tell you what happened. Daphne died. There – you happy?' Doyle said.

This wasn't working. 'Of course,' Kneebone said, 'it's probably convenient to have her out of the way.'

Doyle looked up.

'You and Jasmine.'

Doyle smiled. 'There is no me and Jasmine.'

'There was last night.'

Doyle was silent.

'The girl you lived with, the woman you loved, is not a mile away, lying in the morgue, and you're having sex with the girl upstairs? You're a real romantic, Doyle, you know that?'

Doyle smiled. 'Thank you, Inspector.'

Kneebone felt a stab of intense anger. 'The games you said Daphne instigated. She didn't – it was you. It was you who liked the bondage and the pain.'

'You don't have to answer that,' Midwinter said.

'You know nothing,' Doyle told the detective. 'You haven't got a clue what went on between me and Daphne. No one does.'

'I'll tell you one thing I do know. Guilt is a burden which, when borne alone, will cripple you, slowly but surely, and twist you till you yield.'

'Well, in that case it's lucky I'm not guilty of anything,' Doyle said.

Harry Kneebone's insides were on fire. It was as if every over-spiced takeaway he'd eaten in the last two weeks had decided to haunt his bowels.

'Do you have any other evidence against my client?' Midwinter was asking, knowing full well that the interview was all but over.

Kneebone's answer was silence.

'Well, that being so, I presume my client will now be released.'

'Your client is free to go,' Kneebone said, as evenly as he could.

*

Driving back to his office, Kneebone tried not to think, but he couldn't ignore how he felt. He had either completely misread the entire situation and Daphne Palmer had killed herself or Doyle was a murderer of unusual heartlessness and temerity. Either way, it didn't matter now: he would have to phone Milburn to tell him he had come up with nothing. 'Christ!' he said aloud. 'How could I not have landed that piece of shit?'

Thirteen

Doyle was aware that Jasmine was back too. A muted form of Bob Dylan's 'Tangled Up In Blue'. He thought about putting on music himself, something to drown the sound, but knew he had to go up to her. He was reluctant.

His hesitation was based on how she'd see what had happened to her this morning and the likelihood that she would blame him. But there was no point in putting it off – she lived on the next floor. Dylan was getting into another track when the phone rang. It was Ruth. She sounded almost excited. 'They're releasing the body – did you know that?'

'No,' he said. He felt a weight within him lift. 'That's good.'

'It's fantastic – I can't tell you. Mum's gone right down in the last few days. I've been so worried about her.'

'When will the funeral be, do you know?'

'Soon as possible. Dad will sort it.'

'Right.'

'When will you come down?'

'I don't know.'

'I think Mum was a little disappointed that you left so fast the last time.'

'I'll see what's happening here and get there tomorrow or the day after.'

Standing in front of Jasmine's door, he wondered would she have heard the knock over the music. Then it opened. 'What do you want?' She radiated anger.

'To say I'm sorry.'

She opened the door a little further. 'About what exactly?'

'Getting you arrested.'

She disappeared and, seconds later, the volume dropped. When she didn't return to the door he stepped inside. She was standing by the window. 'Who are you?' she said, without turning around. 'You come over all gentle and damaged but you're not. You're a fucking animal.'

The top half of her body was framed by light that streamed in past her. She turned and faced him. 'I don't think you know the difference between what a game is and what it's not. Do you know what crossed my mind when I was in that fucking interview this morning? I just couldn't think of one single reason not to say how deranged you really are because if they're looking for a weirdo they have one in you.'

'I don't know what you mean!'

'You tied me to my fucking bed and then stuck your dick into me.'

'Jasmine, you asked me up here, we were kissing on the sofa and you were feeling my crotch.'

'I didn't want to be tied up like some farmyard beast!'

'I don't understand – you were laughing …'

'When I thought you weren't serious I was laughing. I thought we were both having a laugh but we weren't – you weren't. You frightened me. You frighten me now.'

'Jasmine, I didn't mean to frighten you, I thought you wanted—'

'I want you to leave!'

'Jasmine, please, I'd never want to hurt you …'

'Look at my fucking wrist.' She held up her hand.

'But what about this morning?'

'I had to figure some way to get you out of my bed – out of my flat.'

'Jasmine, this doesn't make sense. You just opened the door to me now, let me in.'

'Look, Doyle, I don't know you but I know you're not what you seem. I could have told the police all sorts of things this morning but I didn't. I just want shut of you. You understand?'

'Why didn't you?'

'Tell the police?'

'Yeah.'

'Because I don't want to get tangled up in your sordid life and if I made a complaint or confirmed their suspicions I'd be up to my tonsils in you. What you did or didn't do to your girlfriend is for you to deal with. I just don't want any part of it, or you, or those fucking bastards at the station – I want none of it. I want you to leave now, just go – get out!'

'I'm sorry.'

'Fuck off!'

Back in his flat, Doyle moved the armchair so it faced the window, then sat looking out at a low sky. It was a ploughed field of grey, tumbling and rolling itself into different shapes. Was she right? Was he an animal? He heard her footsteps thunder on the stairs and then the front door slammed, leaving a silence that was broken by the repeated cry of a seagull hanging motionless in the moving air. She had been wearing stockings. That was what had done it. Maybe he'd got mixed up. When Daphne had worn stockings they usually ended up around her wrists and she'd be lying there, pleading with him to fuck her hard and he was to call her a slut, and that was the game, or the start of so many games. And, Christ, Jasmine had seemed to like it too.

What was happening to him? His world had turned to cloud that he fell through into other people's. And because theirs was not as solid or stable as they presumed, he kept falling. Or maybe this is madness, he thought. Jasmine's take on last night and this morning was so different from his it begged the question, which interpretation was right? Neither, both, one? And if one was right, which? And whichever was wrong, was that person mad?

If it was him, if he was now mad, was he alone? Foolish question: whatever his mental state, he was alone with it. Laughing lovers, wrapped in each other's arms, are alone in their joy.

Would Daphne have felt alone in her last minutes in the bath? And if she did, was it a joyous feeling or terrifying? Why, he wondered, had it to be either? He needed a wind to blow through this flat, to lift the curtains and quietly slam doors.

The telephone rang. He stood and thought of opening a window before he picked it up, but its demand was urgent.

'Oh, good, you're back. How was it?' Geoff said.

'You mean my trip to the police station?'

'Yes.'

'How did you know about that?'

'I called you earlier, and when there was no answer I called Kneebone's office and eventually found out he'd gone to the station to interview you.'

'Yeah?'

'Can I drop in? I'm just down the road.'

'If you must.'

'I need to see you for a minute.'

Doyle resumed sitting, but could not slide back into the state where his thoughts crawled like insects over the dead. Big Geoff was on his way and he, too, was a separate bundle of reality that had to be negotiated around. Part of his reality was cooking so perhaps, Doyle thought, I'll have him bake a cake. Maybe that would work, steer people to where they feel most comfortable and let them linger there, immersed in what they believe is their own usefulness. And while they're entertained you can go about the business of living.

The buzzer startled him. Doyle pressed the button that opened the front door and when he opened his own door Geoff was standing in the middle of the hall. Doyle went back to his seat. Geoff entered and sat at one of the chairs by the table. 'How did it go at the station?' he asked.

'It hasn't changed much since we were last there.'

'What did Kneebone want?'

'I think for me to say I killed Daphne. I don't know. I don't know what anybody wants. I don't care.'

'I'm sorry about writing those notes.'

'It doesn't matter.'

'No, it does. I feel I betrayed you. I didn't mean to do that.'

'You want absolution?'

'Look, I care about you – I care about what's happening to you.'

Doyle watched him for a moment, then said, 'They've released the body.'

'Have they? When's the funeral?'

'Soon as it can be, I suppose.'

'When will you go? I'll go with you – I'll drive.'

'No, thanks, I'm better on my own.'

Geoff placed both elbows on the table and sank his fingers into his hair. 'Jesus Christ, some fucking palaver this.'

'Some fucking palaver is right.'

'Will you do me a favour? Will you contact Gina Harding? She's really keen to talk to you.'

'Why?'

'I know it's hard for you to see things from other people's point of view right now but this whole thing for her is a total nightmare that she had nothing at all to do with. Whether those paintings she did are Daphne in the fucking bath or not I don't know, I don't care. Just see her and put her mind at rest.'

'Putting minds at rest is not a particular talent of mine at the moment.'

'She says she's got some drawing she wants you to see.'

'She's an eighteen-carat fucking nutter – you know that, don't you?'

'She's just a person, a little strange, maybe.'

'When did you get all sensitive?'

'I didn't.'

'Fancy her, do you?'

'Look, there's nothing wrong with her.'

'Nothing that a frontal lobotomy wouldn't fix.'

Geoff was showing signs of despair so Doyle said, yes, he'd phone the woman.

'Thanks. Listen, you don't want a job for the rest of the afternoon, do you?'

'Not really.'

'The labourer didn't turn up and I need the render taken off the back wall. If you bull into it it'll be done in a couple of hours.'

'I'm not in the mood to bull into anything, Geoff.'

'What else are you going to do? It's a quarter past three now – I'll give you fifty quid for the rest of the day and fix you up with something to eat. It'll only take a couple of hours.'

Doyle sighed. A characteristic of Geoff's reality was that work was the solution to all of life's problems. It was his avoidance therapy. 'Right, I'll do it, but just to shut you up,' Doyle said.

The wall Geoff had referred to turned out to be the entire back of the three-storey building. There were several non-rendered spaces where the windows were, a new one on the ground floor that looked into the kitchen, and a gap for the double doors at the side. But no matter how many windows or doors there might be, he knew he couldn't clear all of the render in what remained of the day. He said this as Geoff was showing him a pair of 'ear-defenders', plastic spectacles, a chisel with a broad, blunt blade, and a lump hammer.

'Just whack the fuck out of it, see how you get on, and I'll rustle you up the best carbonara you've ever tasted.'

The wall was pebble-dashed so Doyle placed the chisel's blade between a series of pebbles, then hit the top with the hammer. The chisel slid across the surface causing his knuckles to grind against pebbles as it went. When he looked at his fingers he saw torn white flesh that quickly reddened. Straightening his fingers was painful. He held the chisel at less of an angle this time and hit it again. It barely made a dent. He altered the angle and hit again. This time a lump of render fell from the wall. He had to belt the scar it left several times with the chisel to get down to the brickwork beneath. There, he placed the blade against the cliff-face he had created and hit again. More shot off. After a good five minutes he had cleared an area about the size of a crisps packet. He continued to smack the top of the chisel and, once a rhythm was established, found that he could clear strips several feet long and about six inches wide revealing the meticulous work of bricklayers long since gone to their graves.

*

The sound of his work penetrated the kitchen. At first Geoff was very aware of its staggered progress but when the blows began to fall with even regularity he stopped hearing it. If he stood in one corner and looked out of the window he could catch a glimpse of Doyle. He was all elbows and wrists and the hammer passed dangerously close to the side of his head with every swing.

When the food was ready he went out to get him and saw an area of raw brickwork about the dimensions of a double bed. He had gone about the task with diligence.

As Doyle began to eat, Geoff noticed the mess of his knuckles. Grey dust had settled into the wounds so that they appeared to have been cemented up. 'I should have given you gloves,' he commented.

Doyle didn't reply: he was eating. Before he went back outside, he said, 'I think I'll go to Dartmouth tomorrow.'

'Contact Gina before you leave, would you?'

Doyle shook his head and smiled.

'You sure you don't want me to drive you?'

'Positive.'

When he got in, Doyle ran the bath. His neck and shoulders were aching and the skin on his knuckles had swollen around the cuts. They stung when he lowered them below the surface of the water. When he eased himself into the bath a flood of relief enveloped him and the pain in his muscles leaked away.

He wondered had she felt the same sensation of ease. Resting his head on the rim, he knew he could slip into sleep. His fatigue was so complete he doubted he had the strength to lift himself out of the bath. But sleeping in it was not a good thing: it led to death and, if not that, to cold and shrivelling. As he lay there the story of Shackleton came back to him. The explorer had sailed away from Elephant Island with two colleagues in a lifeboat to cross the

Southern Ocean and bring back help to the rest of the crew. Five sleepless, freezing days later, they beached the boat at the foot of a cliff on snow-covered mountainous South Georgia. They had not been able to sail around the island to the settlement at the far side because the strength of the prevailing wind would have blown them to oblivion. They climbed to the top of the cliff, then began the long haul over the mountains and glaciers. During the second day his two colleagues demanded that they stop to rest. Shackleton knew that if they fell asleep in those conditions they would not wake, which would mean death not only for themselves but for all those left on Elephant Island.

But rest was a pure and simple demand. So Shackleton let his men sleep and woke them two minutes later, telling them they had been asleep for an hour. This they accepted, got up and found the settlement they were looking for later that day.

Doyle would have to employ an effort no less heroic. He dragged himself, dripping, to the floor, found then there was no towel and walked to the cupboard in the bedroom to see if there was one there. There wasn't. He dragged one from the laundry basket but it was damp and stale-smelling. He sat on the bed and, when he thought he was dry enough, got in. He lay there balanced on the edge between wakefulness and sleep, aware that his fingers were sore, his shoulders and arms ached. His thoughts were laid out on the pebbles of a beach to dry.

When he woke he lay there listening to the sounds. Cars, an aeroplane far off making its approach, schoolchildren. It was morning. The Polish church bell rang and he counted eight.

In the muted light he examined his fingers. Each cut had a different degree of severity. The deepest was on his middle finger. The index had escaped with a scratch and the two beyond the middle one were ripped. The cuts had become craters so from a certain angle his knuckles resembled a ridge of volcanic mountains.

But enough of cuts and long, fruitless monologues: he had things to do. Daphne had been released from her cold drawer and might, at this very moment, be hurtling down the M5 on her way to her funeral. And he should hurtle after her. He needed to pack – for how long? Two, no, three days. He'd have to find out about bus times. And he'd promised Geoff he'd contact Gina Harding. A feeling of dread sank into him at the thought of it. He pictured her face, the concern, the anguish. What was it about her that brought on this feeling of hostility? Was it because she had revealed all those things he so effortlessly hid?

He felt better after his night's sleep. He had tea and toast listening to the radio thinking that this, just a few weeks ago, was what it had been like, except that Daphne had been in bed in the room down the corridor and he'd been daydreaming about this and that, thinking maybe in the shop they should order in some mung beans, or change the display at the front. Now it was the same, just different things to daydream about. That and the fact that there was no one in the bed in the room down the corridor.

He brought his cup and plate into the kitchen and looked at the time – a quarter to nine. Was that too early to phone Gina? He didn't know. He could pack first, find out the times of buses and trains and then call her. By the time he did so an hour had gone by.

'Hello, Gina, this is Doyle, I believe you were looking for me.'

'I'm so glad you called. How are you?'

Already he felt resistance towards her. 'Fine, yeah, you wanted to see me?'

'Yes, that would be good. I wonder if you wouldn't mind coming here? I'm in for the rest of the day so any time is fine.'

'This morning, round now, would be good.'

'I'll put the kettle on.'

What was the implication of that remark? That hospitality was assured? That a warming cup awaited him and the person who made it would, in the same spirit of conviviality, ensure that his visit was awash with comfort and pleasure?

Why was he doing this, reducing her remarks to something cheesy, setting up a platform on which she could take her place and he could sit, observe and criticise?

Twenty minutes later he let the brass knocker fall on her front door, listened to the echoes and waited. Without warning it opened. She looked younger and smiled. 'Hello,' she said. 'Thanks for coming.'

When he stepped inside she said she'd just made some tea, then turned and walked upstairs. 'You go ahead and I'll bring it in,' she said, opening the door to the kitchen. He went on into the living room and once again he found himself among the tiny furniture with the unevenly painted walls and, once again, had the feeling that nothing there was real. At least today the sun was not screaming through the net curtains: the day outside was dull and damp; low cloud would escort Daphne down the M5.

Gina came in with a tray and placed it on the narrow table by the window. 'There you are.'

'Should we take these to the studio?' Doyle asked.

'We could, but maybe let it draw first.' She glanced at the teapot as she spoke. Did she expect a pencil to sprout from the spout and start making rough impressions of the room?

He sat on the chair he had squeezed into before and she on the edge of the sofa opposite him. 'Geoff found you, then?'

'Yes, he told me you two were looking for me.'

She smiled and looked away.

'Can I ask you about something I've been wondering about?' He tried to keep his tone friendly.

'Please do.'

'Is all the furniture in this room a shade smaller than normal?'

She looked at the various pieces around the room, as though they had just popped up from the floor. 'No!'

'But that piano, that's small – smaller, isn't it?'

'That's because it's not a piano. It's a clavichord, a kind of miniature harpsichord.'

'Oh!'

She went to it and opened the lid, revealing a keyboard that was intricately inlaid with different-coloured woods. She spread her fingers across the keys and pressed downwards. The sound was a delightful collection of delicacies that sprang into the air and then were gone. She pressed down again, striking the same chord, and with her other hand hit a series of individual notes. The melody was simple and repeating but the chords she played behind it carried it through different moods, different landscapes. It had a sweetness that dispersed before the listener had fully realised it, as if she were making sculptures from smoke in a room full of draughts. Suddenly she stopped. 'The tea will be tar.' She picked up the pot and poured. Doyle watched the amber fill the white porcelain.

'Was that Mozart?'

'Mozart!' She almost laughed. 'Gosh, no, that was me, something I wrote ages ago.'

'Really? It was lovely.'

Her eyes shone. She added milk, changing the amber into an opaque orangey-brown. She's clouded it, he thought. He felt calmer now. Was she a different person than his impressions of her had led him to believe? Maybe, maybe not. Maybe now his impressions were just creating something different, different but equally wrong.

'You wanted to see me?' he said.

'Yes.' She was suddenly hesitant and nervous, the old Gina back. 'Yes – something's come up in one of the pictures.'

He felt his insides tighten. 'What do you mean?'

'Well, you'll see when I show you. There's just something else.'

'Do you mean you've been working on it some more or is this just something you've noticed?'

'I haven't touched them. I've done other drawings. This was something I saw yesterday.'

'Other drawings?'

'Sketches I think might be relevant.'

If he could have sat back he would have, but the chair did not allow it. What was he doing in a room full of undersized furniture with a woman who was on so different a wavelength that he could never hope to communicate with her? 'We'd better take a look.'

'Can I say, before we do, that I know you must think me mad. Sometimes I feel I am, or at least I'm rapidly heading towards it. But I haven't called you here to torture you. I just really want you to see what she's trying to tell us.'

Doyle sighed.

The two large pastels were in exactly the same place as they had been before. And, from what he could tell, nothing about them had changed. But he wasn't surprised by that. If he was surprised at anything it was his own innate stupidity in having allowed Geoff talk him into being there.

They stood in front of the easel and Gina began to speak: 'You see on the wall above the bath? I thought it was a picture until I realised it's a mirror.' There was a mirror in that position above the bath in the flat but he couldn't recall if he had told her.

Probably not. Doyle looked at that area of the picture and saw a collection of haphazardly drawn lines that could have fitted into almost any shape the imagination suggested. 'If you look at it you'll see another set of mirrors reflected in it.'

In the bathroom in the flat there was a small cabinet above the washbasin that had a mirrored door. Left open at a certain angle it bounced a reflection onto the mirror above the bath. It was this she was talking about because in the reflected reflection there was a face. But it appeared and disappeared, depending on how you chose to see the marks on the paper. And they were that, incidental marks left by the pastel as it had been drawn over the coarse paper, or where lines crossed over one another. But once you'd seen it you couldn't quite unsee it. And if it was a face it was a man's face: he was bald and with a beard.

He didn't want her to speak and she must have sensed it. He had to try to think. He looked again at the figure in the bath, dark hair flowing in waves from a pale face that itself looked hollow. And looking at that face he was aware of the face in the mirror looking at it too. With one movement he could raise his hand and just rip the picture from its easel and tear it to shreds. He stepped back from it. Destroying it would at least prove that it existed. You can't wreck something that's not there. But it was there: he was as sure of it as he was sure that he himself was there. And if it was there and it contained what it clearly appeared to contain, then nothing was normal or could be normal or correct or valid. Was this a situation that existed only in this room, its presence brought about by some consensus he was unaware of yet one he shared with the woman standing next to him? But, fuck it, reality was not consensual. A thing either existed or it didn't. Here, in this room, nothing made sense.

He turned from the picture and sat on a paint-splattered wooden chair by the far wall. He was ignoring the sick feeling in his stomach. Everything in the room that he could see, hear and smell conspired to create within him the desire to run.

After several minutes she turned to him. 'You see it too, don't you?'

He was not sure what she was asking him and he felt anger at the question. If he said yes, would she presume he believed what she believed – that they were two adventurers together in the throes of some cosmic adventure? That this was a puzzle to be solved? He was clear that, whatever was going on here, his interpretation of it was going to be a lot different from hers. But if he said no, he would be isolating her, leaving her alone to face something she couldn't understand. He didn't want to side with her or her with him. But sitting there, with her waiting for a reply and that picture behind her, all of it, it was beyond his ability to conceive.

The words he was tempted to use were: It's just a collection of fucking lines, it could be anything. But to do that would be nothing more than using arrogance in an attempt to ignore the obvious, it would fool no one.

'Who do you think it is?' she asked.

He couldn't bring himself to look at it, yet he was compelled to. The face was even clearer from this distance. It was a man in his late thirties, forties maybe. A voice in his head kept screaming at him that it was just a collection of incidental lines on a piece of paper. But when he ignored the volume of that protest he could plainly see the man's face. He looked from it to Gina. 'I don't know,' he said.

They were only three words, but Gina Harding reacted as if she had been airlifted from the deck of a sinking ship. She was walking towards him, smiling yet again. 'But you do see it?'

'Yes, yes, I see a face.'

'Whose, and why is he there?'

Gina was talking with the kind of breathlessness that Doyle associated with actors in old musicals. 'I don't know,' he said again.

'I'll get the sketches.'

'I've got to get some air.'

'Sure – go through the kitchen, there's a garden at the back, I'll be down in a minute.'

Doyle sat in a deck-chair in the small, walled garden surrounded by potted plants. A pear tree had had its branches straightened and stapled to the grey stone of the back wall. Above him the clouds were loosening to allow the light to become strong enough to form shadows. A blackbird, perched on the highest part of the gable, let out a sudden burst of high-pitched notes. Gina came out, carrying loose sheets of paper under her arm. She put them on a small square pine table and dragged up a chair.

Her voice was full of a terrible enthusiasm: 'Here's one I did yesterday – just bushes and stuff but, look, if you see here, there's a window. Like a building that's been allowed to become overgrown. And, look, here's another, a chest of drawers, and this one ...' her hands were trembling, '... I mean it's some kind of a child's chair.' It was a pencil sketch of a small wicker chair that stood between an abandoned rag doll and a teddy bear that had fallen on its side.

'Gina, you drew these, right?'

'Yes, I did.'

'Well, if you drew them, then you put these things in them, right? So why are we treating them as though they've been faxed from outer space?'

'Because in a way I think that's exactly what is happening.'

Doyle had to stop himself from standing up and walking. 'I'm having a lot of trouble with this.'

'What do you think it's like for me?'

'I don't want to seem rude here, Gina, but will you explain to me why I should have to take what comes out of your imagination as something relevant to me in my situation now?'

'These drawings, the pastels upstairs – none of it is mine. You saw the kind of work I do. For a start it's in oils and meticulous – I work really slowly. But this is just a mess. Look at it! When it first happened I just thought I was unwinding, loosening some internal muscle. But it was really fast, you know – the drawings just happened. They were completely unconsidered, totally random. But with these it's a totally different experience. I find myself sketching and don't know what or why ...' she was spreading more drawings over the table '... and I don't want to be doing them. It feels like I'm being borrowed.' Her eyes had watered.

For the first time Doyle caught a glimpse of the depth of her upset. 'I'm sorry you've been put through this.'

'I want it to stop!' She was shaking now, her mouth open and tears rolling down her face. 'I just want it to stop.'

'It will, Gina, it will.'

'But how?' She was trying desperately to regain herself. 'How will it?'

'I don't know, but it will. I'm going to Dartmouth today for the funeral. When I get back I'll do whatever you suggest, visit whoever you want.'

'I've been so frightened and so angry and I don't know where to turn.'

Doyle reached across and took her hand. As she gripped his, the knuckles stung. She looked with alarm at his expression and, when he released his hand, and she saw the wounds, she said, 'Oh! I'm so sorry.'

Doyle smiled. 'Gina, stop worrying, it'll all be OK, I know it will.'

Fourteen

Walking back from Gina's, Doyle felt that something inside him had eased. Maybe because now things would start to happen. Daphne was going home. While she was in Bristol nothing moved but the sludge of Kneebone's accusations and the long haul into a borderless world.

The easing might have had something to do with Gina. They were not friends, they never would be, but during that exchange in the garden she had shown a vulnerability that had made her more approachable. Oddly, it had made her seem younger too.

The mood survived the conversation he had with Ruth. He had called, expecting to speak to Margaret, to say he had decided to come down that afternoon. In a voice spiked with irritation, Ruth explained that her mother was sleeping.

'The train gets in to Totnes a little after two,' he said.

'Well, I can't pick you up. I'm alone here with Mum and she can't be left.'

'I can get a bus.'

'I'm sorry. If Garry gets back I'll let you know and come and get you, but I doubt he'll be here by then.'

'I'll get the bus to Kingswear, take the ferry and walk up – it's not a problem.'

'Mum can't be left on her own.'

'You said.'

As the train pulled out of Temple Meads station the sun shone through the breaking cloud and lit the river as far as the suspension bridge. The buildings of Hotwells and Clifton seemed to glow in it. It was a view that had the intricacy and delicacy of a highly complex model.

As he watched it pass he wondered if what he was looking at now was his home. It seemed odd to think it might be. He would never have regarded Wexford, the place where he had grown up, where he could trace his earliest memories, where he had learnt to swim and had his first kiss, as home, so why here? He had singularly failed to register the concept of home in any of the places he had lived. Doyle had known people from college who suffered from homesickness and had been unable to understand how a connection between material objects and a person could develop to the point where the person became ill if they were not surrounded by them. 'But it has nothing to do with the bricks and the wallpaper, you prat,' he could hear Daphne saying. 'It's the emotional connection between you and your family, you and your friends, that somehow gets woven into your material surroundings as you grow and develop.' Yes, well, maybe, Daphne, my darling, but that didn't happen in my case and I don't know why. 'Because your dad was dead?'

Maybe.

'Because you're emotionally malformed?'

Maybe.

'And you have the gall to call that poor Gina Harding a nutter?'

Well, she gets images faxed to her from outer space, I only talk to the dead.

Gall, a very Daphne word that. And why was she talking to me then? The answer was she wasn't. You were in daydream dialogue. Yes, but why now – because I'm on my way to her funeral? No, because you're falling into the trap that the tired and emotionally stretched sometimes do. Oh, yeah? And who the fuck are you? Just another daydream cruising.

Ruth was not on the platform at Totnes so Doyle transferred to a bus that rolled the rambling hills through the countryside and villages until it dropped him close to the river at Kingswear. There he boarded the ferry to cross the river to Dartmouth, a three-minute trip. It was a ferry but what that word conjured for most people was nothing like what he was on now. It was a flat stage, with room for half a dozen cars, and a cabin, only a little bigger than a telephone box, wedged into one side of it. At the far side the cars drove down a ramp and onto a road that immediately wound around corners and uphill.

Doyle walked through the narrow streets, whose shops would soon be heaving under the weight of the tourism the town attracted, and began to make his way towards the house. He was breathing hard as he climbed Crowther's Hill but he was aware that something other than shortness of breath was wrong with him. His heart was pounding and his arms and legs felt weightless, as though they had suddenly become polystyrene. He put his bag down and sat on a low-brick garden wall. When he put his head into his hands he realised his forehead was damp and cold.

Perhaps he should have eaten. That might be it. He was eating so irregularly now that his system must be in revolt. He waited for a minute or two, until he could feel that his legs and hands had been given back to him and his breathing was steadying. Then he stood and noticed the curtain move at a front-room window.

He continued uphill. When Ruth opened the door to him she

immediately looked concerned. 'Jesus, Doyle, you look awful. What's wrong?'

'I came over a bit weird walking here,' he said, as he went into the hallway. He caught a glimpse of Margaret looking at him from the kitchen. She was standing, holding the counter. She smiled at him. At least, Doyle thought she did, but she was a long way from him.

'Come and sit down. Mum's up. I'll make you something to eat – sandwich OK? There's beef.'

'I'll just use the toilet.'

In the downstairs loo he was struck that everything in it was in variations of the same colour, probably referred to as 'stone'. Why did people feel the need to do that? It was something he could remember from his childhood. But perhaps that was more to do with the nature of memory: when it fades, colour leaks away first.

What he released from his bowels told him that his interior was not in good order. His heart was still fluttering and the damp had reappeared on his forehead. He splashed his face and tried some deep, controlled breathing but it made little difference. He walked into the living room and sat down, hoping Ruth would come in with a sandwich, place it before him and then leave him alone.

Instead Margaret appeared. Today she seemed quite agile. She came over and sat close. 'You don't look well,' she said. 'You've not being looking after yourself. I can see that.'

He could think of nothing to say.

'Go over to the cabinet,' she said. Doyle did not want to move. He looked at her and saw that she was expecting to be obeyed. He stood and walked towards a tall beech cabinet. 'In the drawer on the left you'll find brown-paper bags. Take one and come here.'

He did as instructed and when he was seated she told him to open it and breathe into it. The bag opened and closed like a crinkled old lung. After several minutes his breathing began to slow and his heart stopped racing. He took the bag away from his face and looked at her in search of an explanation.

'I know a panic attack when I see one,' she said.

'A panic attack?'

'Yes, that's what you've just had. A massive release of adrenalin for no apparent reason. Rapid beating of the heart, short, gasping breaths, loosening of the bowels, the body getting ready for fight or flight.'

'You're serious?'

'You've never had one before?'

'No.'

'Well, don't make a habit of them. They're very annoying.'

He could feel his body begin to calm. 'But why the bag?'

'The rapid breathing over-oxygenates the blood. Reinhaling your own breath counteracts that and you start to recover.'

'You've had them?'

'Mine began with the menopause. They happen less often now.'

'I thought I was having a heart attack.'

Ruth arrived with a huge sandwich on a plate. 'You thought you were having a heart attack?'

'Desmond had a panic attack,' Margaret told her.

'Christ almighty! I thought that only happened to menopausal women.'

'Don't be ridiculous, darling.'

The bread was fresh and between the slices Ruth had put slabs of roast beef, mustard and rocket, a strong mixture of flavours. He ate and listened to them tell him of the arrangements, which they had been happy to leave to Theo. They were upbeat. This surprised Doyle, pleased him too. He had been expecting a subdued and silent household, echoing regret, recrimination and remorse, but they, like him, had had enough of that and now there was joy that they could finally get on and bury their child and sister.

There were to be prayers tomorrow night at St Luke's church and the funeral would take place at eleven the following day. Afterwards there would be drinks here at the house. They began to discuss the caterers. Doyle could see that Margaret wished for everything to be homemade but Ruth was insistent that that would be impossible. There was a moment when Margaret's eyes suddenly filled with tears – pure frustration at not being able to do the thing in the way she felt it should be done. But Ruth sounded well practised at diverting her mother's good but impractical intentions.

Doyle could not say for certain whether it was listening to this discussion or the aftermath of his panic attack, but either way he was overcome with exhaustion. The beef became too tiresome to chew, so he rested his chin in his palm as the two women went around the well-rutted course of their conversation. Margaret suddenly broke from it and looked at him. 'What's happened to your hands? They're a mess.'

Doyle looked at them. The knuckles of his left hand were raw and beneath the thumb of the right one the fork wound had reddened. 'I cut them, accidents.'

'You should go upstairs and get an hour's shut-eye. You look drained.'

'Mum's right.'

As he stood, Margaret said, 'You're in Daphne's room as before. I hope that's all right.'

There was something in her casual mention of Daphne that caused a wave of sadness to rebound within him. He was stunned by its weight and ferocity. Ruth stood. 'Come on.'

As they climbed the stairs she said, 'You can use my old room, if you prefer.'

'No, Daphne's is fine. Thank you.'

Ruth came with him into the room, propped herself against the dressing-table and folded her arms. 'Mum's really glad you're here.'

'She seems good.'

'She's remarkable, considering.' There was a silence. 'I've been staying here almost every night since,' she said, 'but I'd really appreciate a night off. If you're up to it, I'll take off when you get up. This place is suffocating me.'

'Of course, I'd be happy to. Take off now if you like. I'll be up in twenty minutes.'

'No!' The anger was out again. She took a minute to catch it, bring it back to its cage. 'No,' she said again. 'Mum cannot be left on her own, not over the next few days. She seems fine but, believe me, with all the medication she's on she's liable to set the house on fire. Don't leave her on her own.'

'OK.'

'Sorry, I didn't mean to get angry. Have a sleep, take as long as you need. I'm going to cook now and when you get up I'll go.'

Once alone, Doyle unlaced his shoes, kicked them into the corner of the room and lay on the bed. It was good that the funeral was set to happen and the grieving could begin. At the thought he felt a huge surge of emptiness. When all the ritual was over and the years slipped in and out and the decades passed, she would still be dead. She would always be dead.

He awoke to voices coming from the hall but could not make out who they belonged to. He looked at his watch: a quarter past seven, dusk outside. He arose and stood. He felt as though he had been dragged out of a sleep and needed more. Everything seemed wrong in this room now – the posters and paraphernalia with which Daphne had adorned her walls over the years. They were indicators of a childhood that should have ended with adulthood.

When he came into the living room Garry was sitting at the table with Ruth and her mother. So, too, was Theo. Doyle's arrival stopped their conversation.

'Ah! Up, I see,' Theo said, in his usual brisk tone. As Doyle took a seat, Ruth stood and went to the kitchen. He was joining them at the end of the meal.

'You look a little better,' Margaret said.

'Yeah – I must have been asleep for hours.' He acknowledged Garry with a nod.

'I hear you were looking a bit grim,' Garry said.

'Well, according to the doctor here I was having a panic attack.'

'Panic attack? Ridiculous! What has the boy to panic about? Never heard such rot,' Theo said.

Ruth returned and put a plate of what looked like beef curry in front of him. Garry passed him a glass of wine.

'So they've told you about the arrangements?' Theo said.

'Yes . . . eh, tomorrow St Luke's and the funeral the day after.'

'Had to pull out some bloody big guns to get Daph's body released, I can tell you.' He had finished his meal and was now sitting forward, his elbows on the table, holding his glass in both hands.

'You did well,' Doyle said, and wondered why he had allowed himself to be sucked into the back end of Theo's self-congratulation.

'Well, someone had to do something. Can't allow the police to dictate the pace or we'd be here till bloody Christmas.'

'Anyone for pudding?' Ruth asked. She sounded weary.

'Not for me. I'm off to the club. I'll wait for you, Doyle, if you'd care to join me.'

Ruth looked at Doyle, then at Garry.

'I won't, Theo,' Doyle said, 'thank you all the same. Perhaps tomorrow.'

'Thought I'd take the boat out tomorrow, clear the head with a bit of fresh air. Always use an extra hand.'

The thought of spending two or three hours on a boat with Theo was more than Doyle felt he could endure but now he had somehow cornered himself into it. And looking at the older man, square-shouldered and brisk, Doyle knew that for all his bluster he was a crumbling mess, most probably in need of a friend. 'Yes, that would be great.'

'It depends on the weather, of course.'

'If you're staying here, Doyle, I think perhaps Garry and I will take off,' Ruth said.

Margaret, who had been sitting in front of her full plate, looked over at her daughter. 'I don't need looking after, dear.'

'I'm not suggesting you do, Mum, but company's nice.'

'Well, company or no company, I'm off to the club,' Theo said, and stood. Once again Doyle was struck by the physicality of the man. He was tall, poised and impeccable, his blue eyes piercing and his jawline strong. He wiped his mouth with a napkin and nodded at Doyle. 'I'll see you all later.'

The room seemed to breathe easier in his absence. Margaret put her fork down and sat back in her chair. Ruth started clearing plates. Garry was about to join her when Doyle said, 'Leave them. I can do it.'

'It won't take a second,' Ruth said. She was like an aeroplane on a runway: all she wanted was to be gone.

'Finish your dinner, Desmond,' Margaret said, picking up the bottle of red wine from the table. 'This, of course, is the worst thing for me at the moment but …'

Ruth, who had gone to the kitchen, returned to collect more debris. 'Mum, I've stacked the dishwasher. There's pots and pans and stuff in the sink but, if you don't mind, Garry and I are going to go.'

'No, not at all, dear, run along. Doyle and I will get them done.'

Doyle nodded in agreement. 'Goodnight, Ruth, see you tomorrow.'

'Enjoy the boat trip,' she said, with a smile that might have been sarcastic, Doyle couldn't tell. 'I think Dad might have had enough of his yacht-club bores. Goodnight.'

'He's been driving me crazy recently,' Margaret said, when Ruth had disappeared.

'He's just like the rest of us,' Doyle said. 'He's confused and doesn't know what to do or say and feels it's getting worse by the day, by the hour.'

'That's you you're talking about.'

'It's us all, surely.'

'Is it?' She smiled. Then tears filled her eyes. Doyle wished he could access the stock that lay within him. 'I've always liked you,' she added.

'Goodnight,' Garry said, from the doorway. Ruth was behind him. They seemed not to want to enter the room for fear of getting trapped.

'Goodnight, you two,' Margaret said. Doyle smiled at them, and seconds later the front door closed.

'God, she couldn't wait to get out of here,' Margaret said.

Doyle thought it better not to say anything.

'The last time you were here you ran off too without so much as a by-your-leave.'

'Sorry, I was—'

'Oh, there's no accusation. I was just wondering if anything between you and him caused it?'

'No. Well, I can't remember, to be honest. I think it was because I felt everyone was looking at me as the one with the answers. And I didn't have any.'

'She disappeared to Bristol happy and hopeful and a few months later she's killed herself. And you were with her so it's natural we'd look to you. No?'

Doyle put down his knife and fork and picked up his glass. 'Did something happen to Daphne when she was younger?'

Margaret was staring at her glass. She picked it up as though she was going to drink from it but didn't. She sat still, holding it in front of her. Doyle wondered had she slipped into some temporary coma. Finally she said, 'I really don't know how to answer that.' Then she put down the glass, leant forward into the table and hoisted herself up using her arms. She was less agile now than when Doyle had arrived that afternoon. She took her stick, moved to the sofa and eased herself down.

If he stayed where he was he would be too far away from her to conduct a conversation. Perhaps that was why she'd moved. He sat for a moment, wondering what to do. But this was Margaret: out of all Daphne's family she was the one he felt most comfortable with. He stood, taking his glass, and sat in an armchair facing her.

She looked at him, eyes heavy with tears that seemed to gather but not fall. 'You live your life, do your best. Two girls, enough money and a husband who is ... well, I don't know what he is, or was. He was a provider, no one could argue with that.'

Doyle waited for her to continue. But she was sounding tired: perhaps she needed sleep.

'You asked if something happened to Daphne when she was little. Well, I've asked myself the same question. Not often and never in the light of day, if you know what I mean, but sometimes my thoughts wander that way.'

'Why?'

'Did she ever mention Alison?'

'I don't think so.'

'Well, that might be significant.'

'Why?'

'Because they were best friends. Since primary school they were Tweedledum and Tweedledee. Get my wine, would you, please, Desmond?'

Doyle fetched her glass and the bottle. He handed her the glass and put the bottle on a low table next to the sofa. 'I shouldn't do this. Bad for my complaint, the doctor said, especially red. Cheers!'

Doyle went back to his seat and picked up his glass. 'Your health,' he said.

She smiled. 'Alison disappeared when she was fifteen.'

'What do you mean, "disappeared"?'

'She ran away from home, turned up in London, pregnant. Still there as far as I know.'

'But friendships, especially between young girls, break up, don't they?'

'Yes, perhaps you're right. They were inseparable, though.' She repeated the word, then drank. 'The thing was, Daphne turned about that time.'

'Turned?'

'Yes, became a teenager, I suppose people would say, but there was more to it than that. As a mother you know these things. She was withdrawn and angry. She couldn't seem to stand being in the same room as any of us, wouldn't go out on the boat, anything like that. And the problem was that there was nothing about her behaviour that you couldn't put down to something else.'

'I don't follow.'

'Well, you think of drugs first, don't you? I searched her room a few times and found nothing – didn't even know what I was looking for. She and Alison spent most of their time in the garden shed anyway, a place she knew I found difficult to get to. Theo said it was all in my head. Maybe he was right. But there was something – I could feel it.'

'So what happened?'

'She became precocious – promiscuous, too, I don't doubt – and then it was away to university and London.'

'So it was a phase she went through?'

Margaret didn't reply. She was staring at her glass again. Then Doyle remembered what Ruth had said about the amount of medication she was on. Could that explain the pauses? But she was going to bury one of her two children the day after tomorrow. She was entitled to as much leeway as she wanted to take.

She looked at him. 'I did a terrible thing yesterday.'

'What?'

Suddenly she smiled. 'Your face,' she said. 'Sorry, it's just that your face dropped.'

'What did you do?'

'Dragged out some of the old photo albums.' She waved to the corner where the wheelchair lay folded against the wall and Doyle saw them on a table, covered with brown fake leather.

'Why was that terrible?'

'Because it was so lovely to look at her . . . so lovely and so painful.'

'I'd like to see them.'

'Bring them over.'

Immediately they'd opened the first page Doyle knew what she meant. Looking at Daphne's young, smiling face, he felt a sudden physical pain in the chest yet also, in some part of his mind, a flood of pleasure at seeing her preoccupied by something that had nothing to do with anything that was to come. It was followed by simple sadness.

There were lots of photos of the girls and their mother, in the Palm House at Kew Gardens, feeding pigeons in Trafalgar Square, all taken by Theo presumably. The colours had become slightly distorted – the lighter ones bleached, the darker ones running to reddish-brown. Margaret looked so young – she'd been pretty too. Later the girls were pictured with their friends – there was one of Daphne staring defiantly at the camera, her legs crossed at the ankles. Beside her stood a blonde girl, taller and very pretty with an expression that mixed innocence with self-assurance.

As the pages turned Doyle witnessed Daphne's progression from child to teenager and then to young woman. He saw how time and genetics had sculpted her into the person he had first seen in the pub three and a half years ago. The photographs that caused the worst pain were those where she looked genuinely happy. In most of those she was with the taller blonde girl. He and Margaret were fixed by a repulsive fascination, Margaret, beside him, licking her fingers to turn the pages, dribbling a continuous monologue of names, anchoring each image in a time and a place.

'This one was after the move from London . . . The first boat . . . we got her soon after we moved here. Theo used to say, "What's the point in living by the sea and not having a boat?"'

There were lots of pictures of the whole family, as well as other adults in or around the boat. She turned another page. 'Ah, there's *Malaise*.' It was a dark green yacht, much sleeker than the first.

'Is that the one you have now?'

'Yes, though this is more Theo's than ours. I don't know why. Well, I do. The girls don't like to sail now and I can't any more.'

'Is it getting any better?'

'The ME? It does for a while but then it comes back. You've got to learn to listen to your body. The doctor I see here is better than the one before but, really, they're all pretty useless. I don't get as tired as I used to and I'm much better with sound now, light too.'

'It sounds dreadful.'

'I used to think it was the fly in the ointment. Now I'm not so sure there is any bloody ointment.' She turned another page. The girls were older. She turned again. A picture of *Malaise* charging through the swell, sails full. Beneath it was a picture of a bare-chested bald man leaning against a mast. He had a beard and was smiling but with a slightly quizzical expression, as though he doubted the person holding the camera could use it properly. Doyle felt himself turn cold. The image he was looking at, the expression on the face of the bearded man, was what had been reflected in the mirror in Gina Harding's drawing. He put his finger on the photograph with such force that Margaret turned to him.

'Who is that man?' Doyle said.

'Don't you recognise him? That's Theo. I liked him with the beard but he didn't keep it long.'

'How long?'

'What?'

'How long did he have the beard?'

'I don't know – a year, less maybe. What on earth's got into you?'

Doyle stood up. 'Sorry – look, I'm going to do that washing-up now.'

'It's not easy looking at these photographs. It's poisonous, really, but once you start you can't stop.'

'I'll just be a few minutes. I'll make some coffee when I'm finished.'

'None for me, thanks.'

*

He emptied the sink of the pots and pans and filled it with clean hot water. He sank his hand into it, magnifying it, watching the wrinkles and the line of punctures from the fork exaggerated under the glossy seal of the surface. If blood were to start funnelling through the wound it would soon be lost to view: the blood would cloud the water as milk did tea or coffee.

The face in the photograph was the same as the one in Gina Harding's picture. Doyle was back there again, his brain desperately seeking an explanation. Without one he was looking into the wilderness. What circumstances could possibly exist that had Gina Harding doing drawings she didn't want to do about subjects about which she knew nothing? It was a question without an answer, but it was still a question. Questions without answers were powerful things. If they fuelled religions, who was he to battle with them?

Regardless of how or why, Gina Harding had drawn a picture of Daphne's death and in that picture was her father. But take one step beyond that and you were into a place where nothing made sense, nothing was real and nothing could be relied upon.

When he had finished he went back into the living room and saw that Margaret had fallen asleep. She had closed the photo album and put her glass on the table. It was only nine thirty but he too felt tired. He rubbed her shoulder. Her eyelids lifted and her head turned as though she were an automated doll. 'Yes,' she said. 'I'm on my way.' She focused on him then and suddenly became flustered. 'What – what is it?'

'Nothing, Margaret, you fell asleep. It's time to go to bed.'

'Oh, Christ, I'm always bloody doing that.'

'It's OK. Would you like anything?'

For a moment she looked lost. 'Yes, please, a glass of warm water.'

'Do you need a hand up?'

'No, I'll manage.'

Doyle went back to the kitchen and plugged in the kettle. When it was ready he brought the glass of warm water into the living room. She was gone. He looked up the hallway towards her room. The door was ajar. He decided to give her time to organise herself. He opened the album and scanned the pages until he was looking again at the man with the beard. Who had taken it, and when? He looked at other pictures on the pages before and after it for another of the bearded Theo. There were none, bearded or otherwise. He turned back to it. It told him nothing other than the obvious: that this was a man in his late forties leaning against a mast. He tried to conjure the image in Gina Harding's drawing again but couldn't. He closed the book, brought the glass of cooling water down the hall to Margaret's door and knocked.

She was sitting up in a single bed. Everything in the room was impeccably neat and everything matched.

'Here's your water.'

'Thank you, Desmond. Are you going to bed now?'

'Yes, I think I will.'

'I'm tired.'

'Tell me, Margaret, you mentioned that Daphne and her friend used the garden shed a lot. Is it still there?'

'Gardeners come now – I can't do the work that's needed and Theo has no time. I know they let the hedge grow up around it but I can't tell you if they pulled it down or not.'

'I'll take a look in the morning.'

'Why? What's in it?'

'I just wanted to see where she hung out, that was all.'

She stared at him, then said, 'Goodnight. I hope you sleep.'

Fifteen

Doyle awoke to the chatter of birds. Their antics in the rafters outside filtered through the gaps in the old window-frames. He lay, his head deep in soft pillows, thinking she must have done this too. All through her late childhood and teens, on mornings when those photographs he had seen last night were to be taken. What would she have thought about? It would have depended on the season, on the day of the week, if she'd done her homework or not, if she'd met a boy, fought with her best friend. As an adolescent did, she'd have lain here, allowing her thoughts to be conducted by dark songs sung by young men whose later suicides would make that form of exit seem romantic, acceptable, poetic even. Or had she just lain here drinking in the monotony of the moments, allowing time to escape its confines on the clock-face and wander in the permanent present? And were her thoughts ever arrested, as his were now, by the smells of cooking coming from downstairs?

The light entering the room was made pale grey by the long, dark curtains. It illuminated ridges that ran lengthways across the ceiling, places where, in former days, beams had been. Or perhaps they were still, but buried now beneath another ceiling.

He got out of bed and opened the curtains. The sky was coated with a layer of white cloud that was lit from behind by a sun Doyle doubted would be seen today. The view was of little other than the trees opposite. They were coming into leaf. Beyond them, a house stood on a lawn. He caught glimpses of it through the branches. Back on the bed he stared around the room, feeling that if ever he should be able to drift into her mind it was now. But he could not. He was sealed in his own.

He dressed and made his way down the first flight of narrow stairs onto the creaking wooden floor of the landing below. Here he was faced with three doors, the nearest of which he knew was the bathroom. As he stood over the toilet, he looked at the bathtub. Empty, white and rounded, it told him nothing. This mood, this quiet, contemplative meandering into the past, using your imagination like a white stick, was not good. Its destination was depression and it might not even stop there. He washed his face, studied his image in the mirror. He told himself that he could choose whatever road he wished for his thoughts, then wondered if that was true.

In the kitchen Garry was at the stove. 'Good morning,' he said. 'Sleep well?' He was holding the frying pan above the Aga, rolling its contents from one side to the other. 'Just doing some sausages. They're local, very good.'

A copy of the *Daily Telegraph* was open on the table in front of him. If Doyle were to answer the question that Garry had asked, he would have had to say no, that sometimes he had drifted into sleep and at others he had shot down rapids of it at speeds so terrifying he had been wrenched awake. Sleep, real sleep, was now for him like wealth or enthusiasm, a condition other people enjoyed.

Doyle scanned the headlines, turned a page and realised that Garry was asking him another question. 'Sorry, what did you say?'

'Will you have some breakfast?'

'I'll try a sausage.'

'They're not vegetarian.'

'Neither am I.'

'I thought you were.'

'No.'

They were good. Garry ate his swamped in ketchup as he read the sports section. Doyle was aware that the two of them had never been alone together in a room before and felt that perhaps this was a good time to become acquainted with the man who would, most probably, have become his brother-in-law. All he knew of him was that he smiled a lot, seemed kind, loved Ruth and sport. It was odd, that. Doyle would never have matched them. Ruth had no interest in sport – she was too fragile, too ambitious – and she smoked. But they had been together longer than Daphne and he had. And would go on being together long after Doyle had drifted away from them all.

'The early birds!' Margaret said, from the doorway. Doyle turned towards her. She was wearing a floral dressing-gown and seemed to be moving well. She went to the fridge and took out a bowl containing a white substance. She brought this to the table and then got honey from a cupboard. Garry watched her, and Doyle thought he could read in his face an internal debate: should he get up and offer to help her or stay put? It was difficult with Margaret: at times she was independent to the point of stupidity and at others she was content to be waited on and fussed over. This morning she had an air of determination.

'Do you think you will go out with Theo today?' she said, watching honey leave the spoon and fall into the white.

'Might do. What time is he leaving?'

'Oh, he's gone already, left an hour ago.'

'Well, if he's gone, it's too late.'

'No, no. He'll be pottering down there all morning. He said he was going to go out after lunch if you want to join him.'

'That's what I'll do, then.'

Garry glanced at him as though he wanted to make sure he had heard correctly. Doyle wondered was there some ordeal connected with going out on the boat that he was unaware of.

'The service is at five so don't be late, and also, I'd appreciate a certain degree of sobriety.'

'Of course,' said Doyle, trying to figure out the implication of her words.

'Well, you say that but I know bloody well that Theo will have the gin bottle out as soon as it strikes twelve. You can count on it. I'll not have you two turning up drunk.'

Garry gave him another look, this time with a smile attached.

'Margaret, the last thing I'll do on a boat is drink.'

She stared at him, then said to Garry, 'Where's Ruth?'

'Outside.'

'Has she had breakfast?'

'Toast earlier.'

Margaret sighed and began to stir the contents of her bowl. Doyle took his plate to the sink.

'I'll do that,' Garry said. 'Why don't you ...?' With his eyes he indicated the door leading to the garden. The suggestion was that Doyle should go and see if Ruth was all right. Doyle nodded and went out into the light.

She was sitting on flagstones just outside the back door. Her arms were wrapped around her knees and smoke streamed upwards from a cigarette she held in her fingers. In front of her the garden sloped downwards, a collection of pathways and hedges. In the middle there was a lawn, an oasis of uncomplicated greenery. Beyond the garden the slated roofs of their neighbours' homes stood at odd angles, descending to the town and the river beyond. The boats moored in long lines looked like necklaces laid out in a box. On the opposite bank the town of Kingswear rose in a red-brick confusion of shapes and shades that indicated roads and rows of houses. Like Dartmouth, the buildings became more elaborate but fewer as the hill climbed.

'Amazing view,' Doyle said, sitting beside Ruth.

'Kind of immune to it.'

Doyle felt the hollow sensation in his lungs that could only be satisfactorily filled with cigarette smoke. It was a long time since he'd had it and he knew it would pass, but this morning he wanted to indulge it. When he asked her for one she didn't comment, just handed him the pack and a lighter.

It felt both peculiar and comforting in his mouth. He removed it, held it in his fingers and examined it: a simple bar of sweet poison, white with a brown section at the top. Behind it cultures clashed and debates raged; it filled hospitals and graveyards and the coffers of the Treasury. Millions had been made and millions had been spent and all for this little stick of nicotine.

He lit it and inhaled. His lungs instantly kicked back, forcing him to cough. The yearning didn't ease. He would probably have to smoke four or five before it did. His head felt light and his stomach suddenly swollen with sausage. He stubbed the cigarette out on the paving stone.

Ruth hadn't noticed. She lifted hers to her mouth at regular intervals and sucked at it with such intensity Doyle thought he could hear it burn. When she exhaled, a thin stream of bluish smoke came out.

'As a drug, nicotine has nothing going for it,' he said.

She turned to him. 'Since when did you get so high and mighty?'

'It's true! It's a crap drug.'

She inhaled again. 'Are you going out with Daddy today?'

'Why is everyone asking me that? Is there something I should know?'

'No, it's just a bit unusual, that's all.'

'Because I've never done it before?'

'No, that he asked you in the first place.' She inhaled again. 'He knows none of us wants to go so why would he ask us?'

Was there a hint of bitterness about that last remark, Doyle wondered. He thought it best not to pursue it. 'Did you know Alison?'

'Why are you asking about her?'

'Margaret was talking about her last night.'

'Christ! That was scraping the barrel.'

'How do you mean?'

'Well, if she was dragging out Alison, who else was she parading from the long list of Palmer ghosts? Aunt Alice and her affairs?'

'She said Alison and Daphne were friends since primary school but Daphne never mentioned her to me – I mean never, not once.'

'Well, why would she?'

'Because things get aired – just seems strange.'

'Alison was a local girl and I think Mum and Dad were a bit sniffy about the locals when we first moved here. They're such snobs.'

'Who did they expect you to hang out with?'

'Better-class kids. But Alison was a problem. She had an awful upbringing and she was kind of . . . I don't know . . . It was like part of her was already an adult. I never liked her. But she was my kid sister's best friend. To me they were both dross.'

'Your mum says she disappeared.'

'I can't remember, really. There was a rumour that she got pregnant and went to London.'

'Daphne didn't talk to you about it?'

'No. I wasn't interested. So, why are you going sailing?'

'Because the man asked me – you were there. He asked me so I thought maybe he needs to chat, or the company.'

'Never realised you were so facilitating.'

'Ruth, what's wrong?'

'Tomorrow I'm burying my sister who was fine and fun-loving and a laugh and now she's dead because ... because—' She stopped. Doyle was watching her profile. She was staring into the distance. He looked at the garden. There were shadows now – the sun must be burning through the cloud.

'Because of me?'

'Maybe. Who knows? I'm sorry, I'm not a good person to be talking to right now.' She got up and walked in front of him. She was wearing denim shorts and flip-flops. Her legs were long and very white. 'Look, I'm sorry but I just can't deal with anyone else's emotions. I actually don't care about anyone right now.' She walked inside.

Looking at his feet, he realised he didn't have the right shoes for a boat. In fact, he didn't have the right clothes for it either, or for the funeral. It didn't matter. If the worst came to the worst he'd ask Margaret for some money and buy what was appropriate.

He stood and took the path to the right; it skirted the lawn and led to the hedges beyond. Looking up at the sky now he could see that that layer of white was dispersing, it was almost blue in places.

Beyond the hedge there was undergrowth that spring was thickening with fresh greenery. He studied it, wondering where, within this untamed wilderness, a garden shed might have been. A line of tall pine trees stood in the far corner. He decided to make his way through the grass to them. Beneath the trees, the ground was covered with brown pine needles and at the edge there were swathes of almost purple bluebells. He strolled over and sat with his back to a tree, breathing in the silence. When he closed his eyes he became aware of the bird twitter. It was broken by the clumsy caw of a jackdaw or a rook close by. In the distance a dog barked. Above him a blackbird pierced the air with a series of notes that rolled together in a long chord of sweetness.

Despite the peace he felt compelled to move. When he stood he saw that a row of rhododendron bushes behind the trees sealed off access into the garden beyond. He made his way along the almost solid wall of plastic-looking leaves, searching for a way through, but it was unyielding. Finally, as the ground became rocky and steepened, a gap appeared.

On the other side it was obvious that no one had been into this section of the garden for years. Stalks as thick as a man's wrist grew higher than his head. Between them young growth flourished. At his feet the earth oozed a brackish slime. He could make out the perimeter of the garden. It was formed by a line of overgrown hedges and tall trees. But there was nothing anywhere that might hint at where a garden shed would have stood. Then he noticed a section of greenery among the bushes that was not moving. It was slanted – possibly a mossy roof? It was beneath a cluster of bushes and overhanging trees. He began to work his way towards it.

When he got close he could see that it was, or had been, a shed. Now it stood, dark and damp, as if it was about to be swallowed by the growth all about it. He guessed that in better days the garden tools had been stored there. Now its planks were warped, pulling away from each other, and the thick branch of a buddleia pushed through an empty window-frame.

The door was shut. When Doyle pushed it open, he heard a sharp crack overhead. Instinctively he stepped back. The door had probably been playing a pivotal role in the shed's survival. Looking inside was like looking into a cave. There was nothing but the dangling threads of old cobwebs. As his eyes got used to it he saw thin, almost colourless blades of grass that grew from the floor and wove their way around a cupboard that was standing by a wall.

He stepped closer and peered in. By the back wall there was a child's chair. It was so laden with dust that it looked swollen but he could see from the legs that it was made of wicker work. On either side of it, slumped on the floor, lay two forms that might have been taken for dead children. The one to the left was fat, and although it was misshapen now, Doyle could see it was a teddy bear. On the other side of the chair he could see the thin legs of a rag doll emerged from its collapsed, deformed body. The face, fallen forward, was smiling into the space on the floor in front of it.

As he became aware that he had arrived at a decayed version of the drawing Gina had shown him yesterday he also realised that his breathing was fast and shallow and his heart was racing. He turned away, looked at the sky above the shimmering green and tried to breathe evenly and slowly. When he felt himself calming he turned back and knew he had to go inside. Everything had led him here.

There was a step up to the floor. Holding on to the door-frame he took it and entered. Straight away long cobwebs wrapped themselves around his face. He pulled them off and the floor creaked. He waited for signs of collapse. When it didn't happen he thought it best to sit – it would distribute his weight more evenly and get him out of the way of the webs. It would also put him level with the cupboard's drawers. As he lowered himself to the floor he felt it give under his weight. Suddenly his knee broke through the board under it. But it did so almost silently. The floor was rotten with damp – it had disintegrated rather than splintered. Peering into the hole he had made, he saw another layer of planks.

The cupboard was to his right. He lifted a hand and pulled

open the door. The top hinge split and it swung forward. He had to move his head fast to avoid it. His breathing was quickening again. He had to stay in control. He told himself that nothing here could harm him. Finally, he reached out and pulled the cupboard door free of its remaining hinge. It fell to the floor with a dull thud.

Gently he opened the other door. There were just two shelves. On the bottom one there was a framed photograph of a young man with a quiff, clad in tight jeans, high-heeled boots. The frame was tarnished a chalky white but the picture beneath the glass was undamaged. Beside it were the stumps of three green candles and a piece of paper that had been tied with a green ribbon. Doyle tried to pick it up. It was wallet-sized and covered with mould. It disintegrated into dust in his hand. Next to it was a plastic comb, then a purple cigarette lighter, a mirror and a small mound of mould that might have been anything from a dead bird to a sandwich.

The upper shelf was empty but for a crinkled transparent plastic bag. Doyle picked it up, then slid to the door to examine it in the sunlight. He held it in one hand and placed the other on the floor behind him. As soon as he put pressure on it to push himself, the floor gave way and his hand dropped to the boards beneath it. He was seized by pain – it was his left hand and it had landed on the bruised knuckles. He raised it. The knuckle of his middle finger had begun to bleed slightly. He looked at the floor. His hand had not broken through it, as his knee had, but had dislodged a short board that must have been loose. When he looked into the gap he saw another plastic bag. This one was white, from one of the local supermarkets. Inside he found several small bound notebooks.

He was tempted to see what else lay in the space between the floor and the boards but he decided it was best to get out. He tried to shut the door but it no longer fitted its frame.

He held the two plastic bags and retraced his steps to the gap in the rhododendrons, then headed for his oasis under the pine tree. There he sat and put the bags down beside him. He was in no rush to open them. He lay back and let the weak sun bathe his face. If Gina's drawings were about the shed, which clearly they were, and this was the fruit of the search, he was not sure he wanted to see what was inside them. It was possible that there would be nothing of interest. It was, after all, a young girls' den, a place where ghost stories had been told, where schemes of how to get rich and famous were hatched while stolen cigarettes were smoked.

He lifted the bag he had found on the shelf and, through the crinkled plastic, he saw sheets of paper and a bound notebook. There was also a packet of photographs. He took out the loose pages. The paper was thick and perforated at the top as though it had been ripped from a pad. There were half a dozen pages covered with drawings and the handwriting of someone young. It was a story about a character called 'Odd Sock Bob'. The pencil marks had become very light and many of the words had faded. He slid them back into the bag. The notebook had a red cover. The writing inside was by the same hand but it had matured and become legible. The first two pages bore the title, in large, almost Gothic script, 'The fashion designs of Daphne Palmer and Alison Gordon' and underneath, in smaller script, 'The '97 Collection'.

There were drawings of dresses, skirts, blouses, tops, hats, scarves and shoes. There were even hairstyles. Halfway through the book the drawings stopped. Doyle looked at them again. They had been meticulously coloured. Some of the designs were startling with their stripes and choice of colour. Doyle tried to recall had Daphne ever talked about clothes design. He knew she had sketched but not while she was with him. It was something they had talked about doing together. He replaced the book and lifted out the photographs. The damp had stuck them together into a solid block. The one facing out was of Daphne standing by a tree, holding what might have been the rag doll in the shed, but it was so discoloured that the detail was lost. He tried to prise the photographs apart but succeeded only in tearing them. These, too, he put back into the bag.

He unravelled the white supermarket bag and peered inside. There were two light blue books, small but bulky. He took out the first. A Paisley pattern was embossed into the cover. He opened it at the front page. It was a mass of names, mostly boys', and doodles. Some of the names were surrounded by hearts, others had been crossed out. In the centre were the words 'Daphne F. Palmer. Top secret. Keep out!!!' On the next page it said, 'Diary 1998', in dark brown print, beneath which there were spaces for personal details. Daphne had filled in every line. He leafed through the pages of conversion tables to Thursday 1 January.

In handwriting that was clear and neat, she had begun with the resolution to fill in the pages every day. She went on to say how bored she was: 'Christmas has to be the most boring day ever invented. Sat around all day watching the adults stuff themselves with drink and food. Mum was bad and Dad just sat there. Lucky Aunt Alice came or R. and me would have to do everything.'

The first day back at school was 5 January. Although she said she hated and deplored school there was an excitement about the entries. 'A. got this amazing top and skirt that she's wearing on Saturday.' It ended, 'Greg Butterworth is a dickhead, I hate him.' Other pages were filled with details that were difficult to follow without background knowledge. Most people were referred to only by a letter and others popped up encased in either heart shapes or in big letters backed in shadow. They would then disappear without trace. Greg Butterworth never got a second mention.

In February blank pages started to appear. Mondays, however, always seemed to be full. 'A fancies T. So do I but they would be amazing together. I love her hair, love his too. What to do???' There were frequent references to Mum: 'I feel so guilty, she's lying there most of the time and I hate it. I just want a Mum like anyone else's.' Then later, on 19 February, 'Got home and Mum had baked bread. R. was in a good mood too. Daddy's in London – good riddance!'

Doyle jumped ahead to the early summer and was caught by a sentence on Monday 6 July: 'Daddy says he'll buy us something nice, I don't care what he buys us, I know why he's doing it.' He read on: 'A. says she's going to get the dress from the catalogue.' He looked back to Sunday 5 July: 'Went to the boat with A. Mum stayed and Ruth did as well. Dad went below with A. He told me to look for boats. I know what they were doing. I feel sick. I hate A.' Then Doyle read through that week. Except for Monday's reference, Daddy wasn't mentioned again. July 28 was the first day of the holidays and the entries became sparser. But 'breasts' caught his attention on 4 August: 'A. says her breasts are sore after Daddy's game. I asked her if she was sore down there. She says that that doesn't matter but she's lying. I know. I hate this.' On Friday 28 August: 'On the boat with A. Daddy anchored in Coleman's and gave us our presents. A. got a skirt and top. Skirt was sooo short! My dress was slinky and purple. When we put them on Daddy wanted to cuddle and all that. I went up top. I hate him. I hate A. And I hate Mum.'

Doyle closed it. This was the diary of a twelve-year-old. The other was a diary for the following year, 1999. She had not bothered to fill in her personal details but other than that it started almost word for word as the first: a promise to fill in each day followed by a short diatribe on how much she hated Christmas. He scanned the pages searching for the distinctive way in which Daphne had formed her Ds, with a large loop at the back. Daddy was hardly mentioned at all in the first few months. On 16 June she mentioned that 'Daddy's gone for his cruise in Scotland.' Then nothing until 11 July: 'Daddy's come back with a beard. A. says that's it for her – like she has a choice, stupid bitch!' On 10 August: 'Stayed in my room all day – so sore. Mum was on at me. A. says she's going to tell. She says he should be in prison. I'm so scared.'

On 13 September: 'Got a postcard from A. She put it in an envelope so Daddy wouldn't see. It's awful in London. I don't know what to do. He doesn't even talk to me now. I don't care. I hate him. I hate him so much!'

Doyle put it down and leant against the tree, aware that his stomach was swelling. Theo Palmer was a solicitor; he sat on the local council; he had a disabled wife, two daughters, a yacht. Everything about the man, his physical presence, his demeanour, spoke of someone solid, someone sorted, yet here was evidence that he had had sex with his daughter and her friend.

He picked it up, found the entries again, read and reread them. The feeling in his stomach was twisting into anger and revulsion. He had bought them off with dresses. Doubtless chosen for his own titillation. Doyle put it down. This sleazeball had manipulated his own daughter and her friend, isolated them and forced them to have sex? Doyle saw him at the bar surrounded by friends. His suaveness, his elegance, all a sham, a curtain to hide that he was a man who liked to fuck little girls? It just didn't fit. He was the kind of man who made you think he was in control of every detail of his life. He was a disciplinarian, he ridiculed human weakness. He was a total and complete hypocrite, a vile and dangerous degenerate.

Doyle stood. All the sexual weirdness that had come from Daphne was because of this: 'Treat me like a bitch because I am one.' He felt weak now, recalling her words. He sat down again and put his head into his hands. Her father had abused her and distorted all those natural, healthy instincts into something she had decided she could not live with . . .

Tears flowed from Doyle now but they were tears of anger, of frustration. He had to see him. He had to make the sordid wretch realise what he had done. When Doyle showed him what he had just read, the bastard would have nowhere to run. He reminded himself that Theo was clever. If he was going to confront him he would have to think it out, take a copy to the boat. He could make copies on the printer in the study.

Doyle started back to the house. Perhaps the boat wasn't the best place for this. Theo would be cornered – they both would. But it was either that or tonight after the service. Anyway, it was academic: Doyle wouldn't be able to stop himself confronting the fucker as soon as he saw him. The boat would be as good a place as any, better than many, in fact, because Theo wouldn't be able to escape. Doyle's heart began to pound and his breathing became shallow. He had to stay calm now and do what he planned.

When he walked in Margaret was sitting at the table making a list. Doyle hesitated in the doorway.

'Where have you been?' she asked.

'Just in the garden.'

'You've been gone a good hour!' She focused on the plastic bag he was holding. 'Is that a Williams's bag?'

Doyle looked at it. Blue writing in a curve above a sketch of a shop read 'T.W. Williams and Son'.

'Yeah, just some rubbish I found at the back of the garden, going to bin it.'

'That place closed down years ago. Imagine!'

'I'll be back in a minute.' Doyle left the kitchen and went into the hall. He waited outside the study until he was certain that no one was about, then went in. He was about to close the door when he heard Margaret: 'Desmond, if you want to go to the boat you'd better set off soon – it's nearly twelve.'

'I'll just be a minute,' he said.

Sixteen

Doyle watched a figure bent in some task at the front of the boat. He called and waited. When there was no response he called again. This time Theo waved, then stood and walked to the back of the boat where he untied a small grey dinghy. He climbed into it and rowed to the jetty.

'Didn't think you were coming,' he said, as he neared.

Doyle's shoes were black leather with thick soles, far too substantial for the flimsiness of the rubber boat. Theo noticed them too. 'Just take them off for now, plenty of kit aboard.'

He removed them, then his socks, and stepped into the dinghy. Cold water raced around his bare ankles.

'Sit in the back,' Theo said, with authority, pushed off from the jetty and began to row. 'Turned out quite nice,' he said. 'Bit of wind from the south-west – feel it when we get out, dare say. Just trying to fix the lead to the genny. It has a God-awful habit of snagging. You don't sail, do you?'

'No,' Doyle said.

'Not going to be sick, are you?'

Doyle thought the only honest answer to the question was yes. 'No,' he said.

Theo smiled. 'Good.'

When they got to the big boat Theo climbed aboard with surprising agility. He then held the dinghy so that Doyle could do the same. 'Here – hand me your shoes and the oars, then hold on to the rails and pull yourself up.'

Doyle hoisted himself upwards and clambered aboard. On deck Theo handed him back his shoes. 'Never know, might make a sailor of you yet.' He walked the dinghy to the back of the boat where he tied it off. A little uncertain as to what he should do, Doyle followed him. He had the four photocopies he had taken from the diaries in the inside pocket of his jacket. He stepped into the varnished cockpit.

'Not a bad day at all. Should get a fair romp out of the old girl,' Theo said, making his way past Doyle. He lifted up one of the seats to reveal a large storage area. He placed the oars in it, closed it and stood beside Doyle. 'Now why don't you go below, find yourself some kit up forward – boots and all sorts there. Get yourself a jacket too. Give me a shout if you need to.' With that he stepped on to the deck and walked up to the mast.

Should he do this now? Put his hand into his pocket and pluck out the evidence that proved the man bouncing around on the deck of his yacht was a paedophile? Or should he wait until the fucker was calm and relaxed, then hit him with it? There was something almost enjoyable in watching him. The man who had no time for human failings would, very soon, have to face his own.

Doyle peered into what Theo described as 'below'. To one side there was a small desk and to the other a cooker. Beyond that, separated by a wooden panel, he could see a dining table and seats. Above them, bookcases had been slotted into the sides. Doyle approached the entrance, still carrying his shoes, to begin his descent.

'Go down backwards – save you falling on your face,' Theo said, from the deck.

Doyle followed the instruction and found himself in a large, comfortable space. Up on the far wall was a bell and beside it a painting. There was also a door that Doyle presumed led to the forward area Theo had mentioned. When he went through it he saw a toilet to the left. Beyond that was a cupboard, which he opened. Several brightly coloured jackets hung on hooks and on the floor there were pairs of boots and leather shoes. He put his own shoes down, put on his socks and chose a pair of boots. He swapped his jacket for a deep red one, then placed the photocopies in the front pocket of his trousers.

Ahead, he found another cabin, which tapered into a V at the top presumably because it was near the front of the boat. Doyle stared around the saloon. Was it here that Theo had handed out the slinky dress and the short skirt? Was this where he had penetrated his daughter and her friend?

As he was making his way back through the saloon there was a sudden, deafening burst of sound. It took him a moment to realise it was the engine. Doyle climbed the ladder to the cockpit. Here the sound was muted. Theo was up at the front again. He threw off a line that was attached to a small yellow buoy, then walked back.

'Just the job,' he said, looking at Doyle. 'Here, better put this on.' He handed him a red horseshoe-shaped harness. 'Pop it over your head and adjust the straps to make it comfortable.'

Doyle noticed that Theo was wearing one too. 'It's a life-jacket,' Theo told him. 'Confounded things, but it's the law. In my day the stupid drowned.'

It was awkward to fit. Theo had moved to the tiller. He pushed a lever at his feet and the boat began to move forward. By the time Doyle had figured out how to do up the various straps they were clear of the little cove and heading out into the mouth of the Dart river. The boat swayed and lurched in the swell. Doyle's stomach rose and fell, and he began to feel light-headed.

With the tiller wedged between his legs, Theo zipped up his jacket. 'This time of year there's always a bite to it,' he said.

Doyle sat down. He knew he would have to get used to the motion.

'She'll be a little steadier as soon as we get some canvas up. You'll have to take her while I do that.'

Did Theo really expect him to take control of the boat while he worked on deck? They were now out in the middle of the river with the open sea just ahead. The water here was a deep green, slapping the sides of the boat and sending up splashes of spray.

Doyle tried to zip up his jacket under the straps of the life-jacket: he was getting cold. He gave up. The land either side of them was diminishing quickly. As time passed the motion seemed to become more regular and less pronounced. He looked at Theo. The wind was whipping the silver curls on the sides of his head and the tiller poked out between his legs.

'Soon,' Theo said, 'we'll throttle back, you hold her into the wind and I'll get some sail up.'

'I've never steered a boat before,' Doyle told him.

'Nothing to it, old man. You just point it where you want it to go and that's about bloody that.' Several minutes later, he said, 'Here, take it – get the feel of it.'

Doyle stood up and peered ahead. The boat narrowed into the sharp point of the bow, and beyond that the blue-grey of the sea, which stopped at the long line of the horizon. He made his way to the tiller. Theo let go and Doyle took it. It was warm and vibrated with the engine.

'Swing it about, get the feel of it,' Theo told him, as he began sorting out a mess of coloured ropes in front of him.

The fumes drifting up from the exhaust at the back of the boat made Doyle think he would retch at any second. 'I'm not feeling well,' he said to Theo.

'Look at the horizon and you'll be fine.'

Doyle stared at the broad, straight line in front of the boat. With everything else in motion it was the only thing that remained still. Staring at it did settle him.

'Move the thing about, Doyle. This is a boat – you don't have to be afraid of it.'

Doyle swung the tiller away from him and, oddly, the boat went off in the opposite direction from the way he had pushed it. He immediately brought it straight but the boat continued its slow turn. He pulled it the other way gently, and the boat straightened. He tried the manoeuvre once more, this time exaggerating it a bit. The boat responded but there was a delay. It was much slower than a car. Playing with the tiller was taking his mind off his guts.

'Right,' Theo said. 'Can you throttle back?'

'Sorry?'

'Throttle back!' Theo leant across him, put his hand on the lever he had pushed forward with his feet earlier and straightened it. The sound of the engine died to a hum and the boat seemed to lurch more slowly into the next wave. 'Now head her up into the wind.' Theo was pointing at one of three dials on a panel by the entranceway to 'below'.

'Theo, that doesn't make any sense to me.'

'What the hell? It tells you exactly where the wind is coming from – just feel it in your face, then.'

The boat was slowing and rocking more deliberately in the waves. Theo was standing with a rope in his hand. After several minutes he turned to Doyle. 'What are you waiting for?'

'I don't know what to do'

'Here, give me that.' He discarded the rope and took the tiller. Doyle stepped aside. 'There, you see. You point her into the wind, couldn't be simpler. ' Theo walked back to his rope, leaving Doyle once again to take the tiller. Theo began to haul on the rope and as he did the sail began to climb the mast. At first it shot up, but soon he was getting less than a foot at a time and the effort was greater. He wrapped the rope around a small silver drum in front of him, which he then began to turn with a handle.

When the sail caught the wind the boat heeled a little and the tiller felt as though it wanted it push against Doyle.

'Keep it head to wind!' Theo called, as he turned the rope on the drum. This appeared to take a great deal of effort. Occasionally Theo cast him a look. 'Pull it towards you, man – you're sailing her off.'

Doyle now had no idea which way to push the tiller but with Theo's hostile glare bearing down on him he pulled it towards him. Nothing seemed to happen. Theo left the drum and came back to the tiller. He pushed the throttle forward, increasing the revs, and steered with the big sail flapping out of the mast like some giant one-winged butterfly.

'Got to keep her head-to-wind. If you don't, the sail fills and I can't get it up. Hold her on that point there.' Theo was pointing to the compass that was on the other side of the entrance to below from the three dials.

How can you just presume I'll know how to read a fucking compass, you stupid pompous wanker? Doyle said to himself, as he took the tiller.

Theo began to wind the rope onto the drum again and the sail slipped up the mast, the racket of its flapping cutting out all other sound. When he had finished, he hauled on another rope that dangled from the end of the boom and the sail was quiet. 'Steer off a bit now,' he said, then added, 'Point the boat down that way.' He was indicating to his left.

Doyle managed to get it heading in that direction but it was more difficult to manoeuvre the tiller now. It wanted to pull away from him.

'Don't worry about the bit of lee-helm. It'll go as soon as we get the genny out.' The man was talking a nautical form of Greek. 'I'm going to unfurl it, then I'll take the helm and I want you to grind. I'll start it off for you – just continue what I do when I take the tiller.'

Doyle's heart sank. He hadn't understood a word of what Theo had said – couldn't even guess at the sense of it.

Suddenly a huge sail in front began to unravel. It whipped and slapped at itself with a cracking sound. As Theo worked one of the ropes that came from it around another drum this sail too began to silence. He stood panting, then came to the tiller. 'You take over, old boy, younger, fitter.' Hesitantly Doyle moved to the drum. He tried to turn it, but it didn't move. Then he tried it the other way. He got some movement but not much.

'I'll point her up, then you give her a good grind,' Theo said.

Suddenly the sail and the ropes that came from it were slapping violently, with a horrible noise. Behind him Theo was shouting but fortunately Doyle couldn't hear. He wound the handle in the drum and slowly the sail quietened but as it did resistance mounted.

'Go the other way.'

Doyle began turning in the opposite direction. That, too, quickly became difficult. But the sail had stopped flapping and finally he heard Theo say, 'That'll do.'

Doyle sat down, his back pressing into the cockpit panelling.

'Take the handle out, old boy. Rule aboard is, lose a winch handle you replace it with two, and they're not cheap.'

Doyle turned back to the winch but the handle wouldn't come out.

'Push the trigger at the top,' Theo instructed.

There was a small lever at the end of the handle, which he pressed. The handle popped out easily.

'At your feet,' Theo said.

Doyle found a white plastic pocket in which another handle was already resting. He put his alongside it.

'Good job,' Theo said. 'We're looking very smart.' He bent down and pulled the throttle handle up straight. The engine sound, which Doyle had forgotten about, disappeared almost completely. Then Theo pushed a button in a panel just behind the throttle and suddenly all noise ceased. All that was left was the sound of water splashing at the front of the boat and the hiss as the water rushed passed them.

'Now, when you've fully recovered I want you to take her while I nip below and fix us a drink.'

The thought of taking the tiller again filled Doyle with dread. Theo was holding it with just the tip of his forefinger and thumb. The boat was heeling over and charging through the water. Doyle felt that if he took it everything would become chaotic and Theo would be barking nautical gibberish at him from below.

He crossed to the other side of the cockpit. That way, he could put his feet up on the corner of the seat opposite and watch the passing water. It was mesmerising. It funnelled past the boat so rapidly, yet just a few metres out its flow seemed leisurely and further away it was still.

The boat's movement was gentler too: it rocked slowly and evenly as it plunged through the furrows and crests of the waves. The sun was strong enough to sprinkle the surface with dazzling dots of light that came and went in an instant. Looking upwards, Doyle saw the vast curve of white that was spread out in front of him. Tiny blue ribbons flew from the back of the sail and everywhere he looked there were ropes. The cockpit floor was covered with them. But there was peace now in the plunging, a rhythm that was soothing.

He looked at Theo who, for once, seemed content not to be doing something, or planning the next stage in moving his boat through the water. The curled white hair at his temples fluttered and his sharp dark eyes stared ahead. He was the picture of detached contentment. And yet he had had sex with his daughter and her friend on this very boat. Doyle wondered how he would react when he showed him the photocopies. The question that plagued him was not how Theo could do that to his daughter but why a man like him would risk so much. He was busy, successful, wealthy: he stood to lose everything by indulging in such a dangerous activity. The question of how he could have damaged his own daughter in that way was unanswerable. It had probably not entered Theo Palmer's head.

'Think you can handle her now?' Theo asked. 'I believe the sun's over the yardarm – well over, in fact.'

'I'm not sure I can.'

'Nonsense. I'll show you what to do.'

Doyle got up and Theo moved out of the way. Doyle took the tiller and looked ahead. The boat seemed different now, as though it was comfortable in its task of rising and falling through the water. The deck up front was wet and every time they plunged into another wave a new shower of glistening spray coated it with a fresh layer of shine.

'You're doing fine. See? She practically sails herself!'

'Yeah, but when you go downstairs it'll all go wrong.'

'The worst you could do is make the sails flap, and I'll be on standby. You can't do any harm.'

Theo's desire to fix himself a drink would seal off any objection from Doyle.

Strangely, what the man had just said was proving right: the boat did appear to be sailing itself. Doyle had his hand on the tiller but his fingers were loose. Sometimes the bow appeared to wander a little to the right but then would come back and steadily plough on towards the horizon.

The sun came clear of a cloud and dazzled him. Theo appeared at the hatchway and managed to climb up into the cockpit holding two glasses filled with a clear bubbling liquid and rattling with ice. 'Ah!' he said. 'Sun, just what we needed. Here.' He handed Doyle a glass.

'Sorry, I should have told you – I don't want one.'

'It's only a gin and tonic. It's not going to kill you.'

'I'm just about holding onto everything as it is.'

'Fine. You seem to be getting the hang of things.'

'Well, like you said, the boat's sailing herself.'

'Yes, she's a real beaut, wouldn't trade her for the world. You happy there?'

'Fine.'

Theo sat where Doyle had sat just five minutes before. He sipped and stared ahead. After a few minutes he turned and pointed to a headland that was far off to their right. 'That's Start Point,' he said, and fell back into silence.

Doyle suddenly noticed a fishing boat a few hundred yards to his left. It was small and there were two figures on deck. It had been hidden by the sail. The two men aboard temporarily halted their work to watch the yacht pass.

'Bloody lobstermen – always got to be on the lookout for them. Them and their bloody pots!'

Doyle bent low to see under the sail but it blocked out quite a large area of what was in front of them.

'Bloody awful business this, can't tell you.'

'You mean Daphne?'

'Of course – what else?'

When Doyle didn't reply, Theo said, 'Has us all on edge.'

Doyle looked at the folds of skin that gathered around the collar of Theo's jacket. The hand holding the glass seemed old, thin and feeble. What he had done, he had done. He was hardly likely to do it again. Suddenly Doyle was angry with himself: that was a ridiculous line of logic. The man in front of him could be fucking half the children of Dartmouth. He was a weak, wretched creature, whose actions had caused untold pain and, most probably, his daughter's death.

'Whatever happened Daphne's friend?' Doyle said. The question was out of his mouth before he had decided how to confront the man.

'Which friend? She had lots.'

'Alison – Margaret was talking about her last night, showed me pictures of her.'

Theo jolted. 'How the hell should I know?'

'You took them out on the boat a lot so you must have got close—'

'What the bloody hell are you talking about? Lots of Daphne's friends came down to the boat. Lots.'

'You didn't buy them all slinky dresses and short skirts, though, did you?'

Theo whipped around. 'What in Christ's name are you talking about?' The words were meant to be strong, dismissive, but the voice was edged with panic.

'You bought Alison and Daphne dresses. You got them to put them on down in the saloon there.'

'What the … what the hell are you suggesting?' He turned his head away quickly and drank, then turned back. 'What the bloody hell are you talking about?'

'You know what I'm talking about. I found diaries Daphne kept when she was twelve and thirteen, same as Alison.'

'Diaries? What fucking diaries?' A vein swelled in his temple. 'What diaries?' he shouted. He stood facing forward, putting his hands out either side of the hatchway to below. He stayed there, swaying with the motion, for perhaps a minute. When he turned he wore a mask, Doyle thought. It was smiling but the eyes were frightened. 'Young girls ...' he said. 'Young girls are full of fantasies, especially about their fathers ... never read Freud?'

'These were not fantasies.' Doyle took the four folded pages from his pocket. Theo stared at them. 'These are photocopies from the diaries, have a read.'

Theo drained his glass, took the pieces of paper and sat. He held them for a long time, then opened them, read them, folded them and handed them back to Doyle. After several minutes of complete silence, he said, 'We'd better tack.'

'Theo ...'

'If we don't bloody tack we'll be on the rocks. Is that what you want?'

'Fine, let's tack.'

'Right, two-man job. When I tell you, bring the tiller towards you. She'll go up into the wind. When that happens I'm going to release the sheet and take it in on the other side. All you have to do is keep the tiller over until I tell you to straighten it. Got that?'

'Yes.'

'Good. Go!'

Doyle moved the tiller towards him and the boat shot off to the right. Both the sails began to flap wildly. Doyle's instinct was to push the tiller back into the centre but he ignored it. Slowly the sails shifted to the other side of the boat and Theo hauled on a rope from the one at the front. He wrapped it around a drum, got out the handle and started to wind it, first one way, then the other.

'Here, you finish it off,' he said, panting, to Doyle, and went to take the tiller. Doyle had no choice but to comply. As he was turning the handle he realised that of all the places to confront Theo the boat was undoubtedly the worst. It was his ground, his medium, and Doyle was more than metaphorically out of his depth there. When, finally, the sail was silenced he sat, remembering to take the handle out. This is a weapon I have in my hand, he thought, then slipped it back into its holder.

He, too, now was out of breath. He looked behind. They had come very close to the shore. The sun shone on the cormorants that were standing on black rocks. They were holding their wings up to dry. He looked ahead then under the sail. There was nothing to hit now except France. Start Point was hidden behind the sail.

'So, what are you going to do?' Theo said.

'It's true, then?'

Theo winced. 'It's there in bloody black and white.'

'What I can't figure out is why a man like you would indulge in that ...'

'In that what? Depravity? You see, this is what I can't stand. The likes of you standing in judgement over me.'

He was angry now, but self-contained. His eyes narrowed on the horizon.

'When you heard that Daphne had killed herself, did you not think then that what you did had caused that?'

'Don't talk to me like you're a fucking lawyer, you prick!' He said it without looking at Doyle.

Once again Doyle became aware that he could not have been in a worse place. He was robbing Theo of his self-worth, stripping him down to the repulsive piece of scum that he was and he was doing it in an environment in which the man was completely at home but he, Doyle, was not.

After minutes of silent sailing, Theo cleared his throat. 'Could you hand me the other drink, please?'

It was wedged into the far corner of the cockpit. As Doyle leant over to get it he wondered how easy would it be for Theo to do something with the boat, make it heel violently so that Doyle would lose his balance and fall over the side. He clasped the glass – the ice was barely visible now – and handed it to Theo.

The sky had become cloudless but for a stretch of white above the horizon. The sea was a pure blue, the sort you saw in children's picture books. It was, probably, a perfect day for sailing.

'So,' Theo said, 'you've uncovered a secret. Feel good about that?'

'You don't want to know what I'm feeling.'

'Disgust you, do I?'

Doyle did not want to enter into conversation with him. He wanted to be off this boat, away from Theo Palmer and anything to do with him.

'You asked me why I indulged in—'

'Theo, I don't fucking care why.'

'Maybe not, but I'll bet you at about eleven or twelve you started realising that there was a whole new and exciting game that involved women, girls, and that the game was sex. But for me it was not like that. Thought there was something wrong – for a while I even considered I might be queer. Just no interest. I did a damn good job at pretending, but I wasn't, you know, keen.'

'Theo, I don't care!'

'The girls' mother wasn't that keen either, truth be told. We did it – well, I mean, obviously – but, Christ, there was little joy in it. Really couldn't figure out what the fuss was about. Then I saw two young girls playing in the lake. Hot day in the park, all that, girls stripped down to their knickers. When they got out you could see everything and I couldn't get it out of my mind . . . just couldn't stop thinking about it. That was when we moved. Hated to think what it meant, you see, thought the move would clear the air. Managed to keep it at bay, fight it off, you know. Hard, though, when the girls started bringing back their friends. Especially Daph – she was so much more vivacious than her sister, her friends, too, birds of a feather, all that. But I behaved. Took myself off as much as I could. No hanky-panky, I said, none. Then Alison appeared. Christ, that girl was like every fantasy I'd had come true. She knew, see, knew straight away what I was like, really like, and knew what I wanted. She wanted it too.'

'Stop this!'

'Trust me, she did want it.'

'You were an adult!'

'You've seen pictures of her – you know.'

'She was a child!'

'She did want it.' His tone was defiant now.

'And Daphne, your daughter?'

He gave a short laugh, 'Believe me, there were things about that girl *you* don't even know about, I dare say.'

Doyle stood. 'Shut up! Say another word and I'll burst your fucking head open.'

'Well, well, the righteous indignation of those without sin.'

'I don't fuck children.'

'Only because you never felt a desire to.'

Doyle sat again. His heart was hammering now and his breath was short. He had to remain calm. He couldn't afford to be drawn into the whirlpool that was in front of him. 'Theo, I want you to turn the boat around and go back.'

'So you can do what? Call the police, the press, see me publicly humiliated? Would that make it all right for you?'

'You can get help.'

'Yes – I'm sure I'd attract a delightful collection of visitors to my cell.'

'Was it you who made Alison pregnant?'

'You get sucked into the drama rather quickly, don't you?'

'Well, did you?'

'For your information, I never had vaginal intercourse with either of them.'

Words he had read this morning came back to him: 'I know how sore that is . . .' Suddenly an image came to Doyle that made him want to heave. 'Just stop! I don't want to know.'

'No, you don't, and neither will anyone else. But they'll be glad to see me hang.'

The boat sailed on. He had to get Theo to turn it around and head back. But Doyle's thinking was locked into the image Theo had just evoked. Moments of silence passed.

'Theo, I'm asking you, please, turn the boat around.'

'First you must do something for me.'

'What?'

'Below, in the locker above the bunk by the head – the lavatory – there's a small case. I want you to bring it to me.'

'Theo, just turn around and then I'll get you whatever you want.'

'This is important.'

'Then we'll turn back?'

'You have my word.'

'Where is it?'

'Past the lavatory there's the V berths. Above the one on the toilet side there is a locker. It's in there.'

Doyle stood. He looked at Theo. It was hard to define the man's expression. Everything about his face had been sculpted by perpetual arrogance, but now there was something else. It was in his eyes. Was it fear? Doyle couldn't tell. As he approached the entrance to below, remembering to go down backwards, he saw that Theo was still staring at him – it was as though he wanted to say something but couldn't. Doyle hesitated, but when Theo didn't speak he went down the steps.

The air was stilted and hot compared with outside and everything was at an angle. It was much more pronounced down here than it appeared up top. It made movement through the cabin difficult. But Doyle found handrails exactly where he needed them and, gripping them, made his way forward. The door to the toilet had shut: he had to push against it to get through. When it slammed behind him he realised the angle of heel had closed it. He had to kneel up on the bunk to get to the locker. It opened when he stuck his finger into a hole and released a catch inside. When it dropped down Doyle saw two shelves, both narrow. Neither contained anything that could be described as a small case. He riffled through what was there – some flags, what looked like ribbons made of thick nylon, a packet of batteries and that was it. He searched the locker forward of it, then those on the other side. There was nothing.

He looked back at the closed door. Had Theo sent him down there, knowing that the door would slam behind him, and locked him in? Doyle scrambled from the bunk and pulled on the door handle. It opened. His heart was pounding and he felt dizzy too, but that was from being down here, the airlessness, and the motion. Using the grab rails he worked his way back to the galley, then up the ladder. There was no one at the tiller.

Doyle got up into the cockpit. He looked up the deck. There was no one. He looked back. There was nothing. Then he saw, on the seat, the life-jacket that Theo had been wearing. It lay discarded, its black straps dangling, like entrails. Doyle looked out into the waves behind the boat. He saw, thought he saw, a small buoy bobbing. Theo's head? He blinked to clear his vision. It was gone. He shouted his name. With two hands cupped around his mouth he shouted it again. But the sea behind him was like the sea all around him, a collection of waves that revealed nothing.

Seventeen

Thoughts bombarded Doyle, creating a confusion from which he could take nothing but fear. And the fear was deep, born of the knowledge that he was in a situation where everything that surrounded him was alien. It could change at any moment and he would be powerless to stop it, alter it or control it. He was at the mercy of something he knew nothing about.

He stood and looked out behind. There was no sign of Theo. He looked up the deck: perhaps there was a locker or a hatch, some place from which Theo would suddenly appear. But the deck was clear and smooth, water splashing over the bow. The boat was sailing onwards. He was alone. He sat.

The first thing was to check if there were any other boats about. He stood and tried to scan the sea. It was the same everywhere he looked, hard to know if what he was looking at was the place he had just looked at. Under the forward sail was Start Point. It was small – it might be ten miles away or two. There were no boats anywhere. Even the lobstermen had disappeared.

He had to get the boat to turn around. And the way to do that would be by the tiller. That was what steered the boat. What had

Theo said? The worst he could do was make the sails flap. The tiller was steady, pointing ahead, jerky little movements making it tremble every few moments. If he were to pull it towards him, as he had done when they tacked, would he have to release the rope on the drum as Theo had done? And if he did, he would have to try to take it in on the other side too. What would happen to the tiller, or the boat, in the meanwhile?

He had to think. Doing the wrong thing now would be fatal. He looked up at the sail. It was huge, powerful and silent. At the top of the mast there were lights and metal objects, one of which looked as though it was an aerial, which meant there had to be a radio. There had to be a radio! He went to the stairway and looked down. Above the desk opposite the galley was a bank of gadgets and one, he could see, had a microphone attached to it. He clambered down and picked it up. He pressed the button on the side of it. Nothing. He pressed the switches on the box – there were three – but still the thing would not come to life. He looked at the rest of the equipment: there was a sat-nav, a sonar, even a small radar screen but no light or sound. None of it was receiving power. There had to be something to turn this lot on. Doyle stared into the mass of detail. There were buttons and switches attached to every bit of it – he flicked them, twisted knobs, but nothing came on.

Then, to his right, he saw a line of switches behind a Perspex panel. Each was identified with a small card beside it, indicating its purpose. There were switches for the fridge, the water-maker, the radar, sonar and there, at the bottom, he saw one that read 'SSB Radio', and underneath it another: 'VHF Radio'. He opened the panel and flicked both switches. He picked up the microphone and held in the button. Still nothing. He was missing something.

Suddenly the sounds from outside changed and the boat straightened. Doyle raced up into the cockpit. Both sails were slapping back and forth as air ripped through them. He went to the tiller. He pushed it to the left. The boat slowly shifted its heading but the momentum had gone. Above him the main sail was flapping like a flag. He pulled on the rope that came from the boom. The sail now rippled in tighter waves. All forward motion was gone.

There's an engine! He looked down at the throttle and saw the button Theo had pressed to turn it off. He pushed it now. Nothing. There had to be a major power switch somewhere on the boat that had been turned off.

He remembered that his mobile phone was in the pocket of his jacket downstairs. On his way down the steps one of the straps of his life-jacket got caught in the rail. He struggled out of the thing, then raced for his jacket. The phone showed no signal. He brought it up to the cockpit. Still nothing. He waved it about, then stood on the seat, but no bars appeared to tell him he had a signal.

He went onto the deck, careful to avoid the boom that was now throwing itself about at will. The safest place to be was up by the mast. Bending, to keep his centre of gravity low, he made his way forward. Then, grabbing hold of the lines that came down by the mast, he stood upright and looked at the phone. One of the bars came on. He pressed the number nine three times, then 'call'. No vibration came through his hand. The bar disappeared and a sign popped up, 'No Signal'. He held the phone away from him and the one bar appeared again. Then another. He had two bars! He pressed the 'call' button again. When nothing happened he brought the phone back. The 'No Signal' message was showing. He left the mast and walked a few steps up the deck. The forward sail flapped and cracked to his left. The two signal bars were back. He pressed 'call' and felt the phone vibrate in his hand.

At that moment the sail, in one movement, slapped backwards

into the centre of the deck with a power that knocked Doyle off balance. The phone flew from his grip. As he quickly regained balance he watched it land on the deck and slide by the foot of the rail. It came to a rest in a shallow pool of seawater that had been trapped by a rope that was curled around a cleat. When he got to it, it was sodden, its screen showing the colours of a pool of petrol.

He made his way back to the mast. He had been stupid, and the price of stupidity here would be death. He looked up at the sail. It draped down from the blue as placid now as a curtain. He slid backwards to the cockpit and went below. He sat by the table in front of the bank of electronic gadgetry. There was a way out of this and the answer was in front of him. Somewhere there was a switch, or a button or a lever that would make this lot come alive. He just had to be calm, rest for a minute, then find it. That was all that was needed.

But something new was gathering within him, a feeling of despair so utter it seemed to suck everything from him. He could not allow this emptiness attach itself to his thoughts because if it did he was dead. But suddenly all efforts to survive seemed futile. It no longer mattered if he got out of this alive or not. Daphne hadn't survived and neither, it seemed, had Theo. Why do people want to survive? What do they want to do? Because if it was just staying around until age moistened them up for death there really wasn't a lot of point.

He had to stop this. He would breathe gently, quieten his mind and then find this switch. He turned away from the board and looked towards the galley. He would breathe himself into a state of calm, and then he'd have a chance.

To the left of the stove he noticed a small indentation. It was in shadow but Doyle thought he saw a small, circular brass handle. He stood and walked towards it. It was a door. The sight filled him with fear. He turned the handle and it opened. The first thing he saw was a mirror and in it was Theo's reflection. He was in profile, watching the door as it opened. Doyle pushed it all the way and saw that Theo was sitting on the side of a bunk, holding a small handgun. 'You give a man no peace,' he said.

Doyle stared at him. 'I thought you'd jumped ...'

'Thought about it. Couldn't stand the thought of drowning, then remembered this.' He gestured with the gun. 'Thought I'd have no problems popping myself but don't seem to have my daughter's courage.' He stood up. 'Anyway, seems you're making a complete mess of sailing my boat.' He pointed the gun at Doyle. 'Unable to kill myself and not having the inclination to kill you, interfering so-and-so that you are, I've formed a plan. Go up on deck, please.'

Doyle stepped backwards. Theo was definitely pointing the gun at him. In the galley he turned and began to climb the steps to the cockpit. He thought of the winch handles. But even if he could get to one, what would he do with it? Theo was behind him, holding the gun a few feet from his back.

'Open the locker.' Theo indicated the seat in front of him. Doyle lifted it and saw the oars. 'Take them out and put them on the deck,' he said. 'And there's some water, too. Better take a bottle.'

At the back of the locker, among a debris of old sail bags, there was a case of bottled water sealed in plastic. Doyle broke the covering and took out a bottle.

'Now close the locker.' When Doyle had done this, Theo waved the gun towards the back of the boat. Doyle, followed at a little distance by Theo, made his way there. 'Undo the painter,' Theo said. 'The rope for the dinghy.'

Doyle had forgotten they were towing the little rubber boat. He bent down, undid the knot and then stood holding the line.

'Take it up to the middle of the boat, please.'

The dinghy moved easily though the water. Doyle bent low to avoid the boom as he made his way up the deck. Theo stayed by the cockpit.

'Now tie it to the railing.'

As he did this, Theo walked up the deck. Then, stepping on to the cabin roof, he walked around Doyle and stood three or four feet away, still aiming the gun at him. 'Get the oars and the water.'

Doyle went back to them. He looked at the winch handle. Then back at Theo.

'Bring them up here – come on!'

These, too, are weapons, Doyle thought, holding the oars. But Theo was standing well back, steadying himself against wires that went from the side of the boat to the top of the mast. 'Now, leave the oars on the deck and get in.'

Doyle looked down at the small grey rubber boat. It had one seat, a rubber cylindrical tube across its middle, and the bottom was full of water. 'Theo, I don't know how to row and it's miles to the shore. You don't have to do this, please.'

'You started it, you interfering piece of shit, so you have two choices now. Either get in or get shot.'

Doyle climbed over the side and, holding onto the rails, lowered himself into the boat. The rubber floor gave way under his weight. Once in, he sat.

'Here.' Theo was standing over him, the gun in one hand, an oar in the other. Doyle took it and Theo handed him the other. 'Don't lose them,' he said, and began untying the line to the dinghy. 'Christ, what kind of knot do you call this?' This might be my last chance, Doyle thought. Shall I reach up and hit him with an oar? What was he thinking? He could hardly even stand in this wobbly boat. He sat there watching, noticing that the waves were much bigger down here than they appeared from the deck of the big boat.

With the knot untied, Theo stood holding the line. 'It was a great misfortune that you found those diaries, but you did. This, however, gives us both a fighting chance.' He wrinkled his forehead. 'Good luck.' With that he threw the line down to Doyle and immediately the two boats separated. Theo walked down the deck keeping pace with the dinghy as it floated astern. 'Row steady. You're against the tide so make each stroke count. You may reach Dartmouth by nightfall. Oh!' He picked up the water. 'You almost forgot this.' He threw the bottle through the air, a silver missile gliding. It landed with a splash in the back of the boat.

Doyle watched him in the cockpit. 'Theo,' he shouted, 'please don't do this.'

Theo hauled on ropes in the cockpit and the sail at the front curled into itself. He pulled the main sail in tight, then bent down out of sight. A moment later a cloud of black smoke erupted from the back of the boat and the water just behind it churned. He didn't look back, just grew smaller as he motored away.

Doyle wanted to scream at him. He wanted just one more chance to be on the same deck as Theo and, no matter what, he would jump on him and grind his skull into the wood. He thought of what the sound and the feel of that winch handle breaking through the bone into the softness beneath would be like. He put his head into his hands. When he looked up the dark green yacht was already distant. Start Point was so far away now it was just a thin strip of darkness. Behind him he could see the headland that was the entrance into Dartmouth. It was light grey, with yellowy-brown stone and dark vegetation rimming the top. It was bathed in sunshine but it was a long way off. The mouth of this bay was vast. The sea and the sky seemed like a continuous, interchangeable bowl of blue.

The waves danced about him now even higher than they had

been when he was alongside the big boat. He picked up an oar and, as he had seen Theo do, slid it through the black rubber clasp that was mounted on the side panels of the dinghy. Once the first one was in he held on to it while he manoeuvred the other. He held the ends, put the blades into the water and started to pull. The left one jumped clear of the water, throwing him backwards. As he fell he let go of it and, to his horror, found it had slipped from its clasp and slid overboard. He leapt at it, leaning over the side of the dinghy as far as he dared and finally got his fingers to it as it bobbed in the waves. When he had it inboard he put it back into its hole, then started again to row. This time he would be much gentler. But the boat would not move forward as he imagined it should. It swivelled off to the right and, in trying to bring it back to a straight course, he managed to turn it in a complete circle. Again he stopped. He had to take control. It was possible to row this thing – he had seen it done. But that, he remembered, had been in the calm of a sheltered cove.

If ever he got the opportunity again he would kill Theo, no questions asked. Nothing mattered but his death. He was a shit, a coward. Doyle felt rage mount in him that he could almost taste.

He had to survive this. He had to get to the shore. It had to be possible. He placed both blades in the water and pulled. One popped out of the side of a wave and swung into the air, almost coming out of its hole again. He would just do small strokes. He managed one, then another. Then he looked over his shoulder to see which way he was facing. He was heading to Start Point. He had to turn the boat.

He noticed that his arm and his shirt, under the jacket, were wet. It must have happened when he was reaching for the oar. He noticed it now because it was cold. He would have to be careful. He looked at his watch. It was ten to three. It would be dark in four, four and a half hours. He needed to relax and concentrate. He could do this but he had to start getting clever. First learn to control the boat and then slowly but surely guide it into the shore – any shore would do.

He picked up the bottle and drank, he hadn't realised how thirsty he was, then began again. The waves rocked the boat so that it was hard to get an even amount of pressure on both oars at the same time. And the effect of uneven pressure made the boat shoot sideways. On lots of strokes the water that the oar blade was in would disappear as the wave collapsed, leaving him pulling through air, which made him fall backwards. But he did not lose the oar as he had when this had first happened.

He concentrated on small, even strokes and found that he could get the boat heading in the direction he wanted by leaving one oar in the water and rowing with the other. He was aiming for the land they had been close to when they tacked. He could see it clearly. It could only be a mile or two at most.

He rowed steadily, using short strokes with only the occasional fall backwards. He looked over his shoulder regularly to make sure he was heading in the right direction. His feet were soaked now as the water raced around them and the rowing was hard on his shoulder muscles.

He stopped and had another drink. As he did the boat turned sideways. Despite all the effort, he did not appear to be getting closer. Also, as soon as he stopped rowing, he felt cold.

It had been warm when he'd left the house so he had arrived on the boat in only his jacket and shirt. He had swapped his jacket for this red one he had found in the locker. It was probably waterproof but it had no bulk. He zipped it up, thought briefly about the life-jacket he'd left tangled on the rail, and started again.

Despair was gathering. If he let his guard down for a moment it would rush in and overwhelm him. He concentrated on his breathing and getting the oar blades to stay in the water as he pulled. Stroke after stroke after stroke he pulled, not stopping to look around or even think about it. He would become a rowing machine. He would get to the shore.

When the strip of land he was heading for began to appear over his right shoulder he stopped. He'd been rowing not for it but alongside it. He cursed, manoeuvred the boat so it faced the land and began again. This time he kept an eye on the headland. After what seemed like a half an hour, with his shoulders aching, he stopped and drank. Again the dinghy drifted sideways to the land. It was not getting closer. He put the bottle down and lifted the oars again. Blisters were appearing on his palms. He rowed again. This time he didn't concentrate on his breathing: his mind drifted from thought into daydream. Would the bastard have shot him? Impossible question to answer. He was callous, capable of anything. But cold-blooded murder? And where would he go now? France? Maybe he'd just keep sailing, out into the middle of the Atlantic, all the way to South America, hide out with the people of Peru. Lots of little girls and boys to play with there.

He had stopped rowing. He was bobbing back and forth, the oars clear of the water, being taken by the tide. If anything, the headland was further away. Maybe if he could have a rest . . . No, he thought, Shackleton wouldn't have rested: he'd have been over there by now, scaling the cliff, ready to race all the way to Dartmouth and alert the police to the runaway paedophile.

He had to row. It must be the tide, he thought. It's carrying me out to sea. But the tide will turn, and when it does, so will my fortunes. Dream on, drummer boy, and let your oars do the work. Daphne could help now, ask the powers-that-be – and she must be closer to them now than I am – to blow a little wind my way. Just a puff or two would do.

His oars were not working. They sat now in the water not moving. He needed to get them going again. He pulled and the ache in his shoulders joined the sharp pain in his hands to merge. Fuck the pain! He would row. He would become a Shackleton man and skim across the surface, like a landing swan.

When you are moving towards something its size will appear to grow; when you are going away its size will appear to diminish. But this headland would not obey the one simple rule. It was, if anything, shrinking. He concluded that he was drifting away from the land and all his work had counted for nothing. Maybe it had slowed the rate of drift but that was as good as it got. And two miles off was the same as ten miles off, as far as the sea, the waves and life expectancy were concerned.

Then, at the base of the headland, he thought he saw the red hull of the lobstermen's boat. There was definitely something red where the sea and the land met. It had a white bit at the front too – might that be the wave caused by their ploughing through the water towards him? He stared at it. Unlike everything else around him, it was getting bigger. It was the lobster boat and it was heading for him. But could they really see him so far away? He could just make them out but they were so much bigger and red while he was grey. Except for his jacket! He whipped it off, took one of the oars out of its holder and tied the arms to the handle. Then, holding the blade, he began to wave it. For such a light coat, it was surprisingly heavy. He waved it and watched. He was now not sure whether the red hull was coming towards him. He could still see it. Maybe it had stopped.

Carefully he stood. He placed a foot each side of the rubber seat and made sure he had his balance. The lobster boat was on the move again. He could see it clearly now. The white was the bow wave. He picked up the oar with the jacket attached and began to bring it back and forth above his head. Suddenly the lobster boat turned sideways and seemed to pick up speed. Doyle waved more frantically. As he waved he began to shout. If he stood on the seat they'd have to see him.

He put one foot on to it and raised himself. It was working – he was higher. They had to see him now. And then he felt himself go and knew, with certainty and dread, that he was falling backwards. Cold raced in around him and salt water covered his face. All sensation changed. He was beneath the surface, weightless, unable to breathe. He spread his arms out like one of the cormorants he'd seen earlier. Then his head broke the surface. Suddenly there was sound and light, and the grey side of the dinghy about two feet away from him. He swam for it and draped his arms over the curved sides. He rested, only his head, shoulders and arms out of the water. He would somehow have to get into the boat. But there was nothing to grab hold of to pull himself up.

As he clung to the side he realised he was getting cold and his arms were aching. He had to get back on board – and soon. He tried to haul himself up. He got his ribcage out of the water but lacked the strength to pull himself up any further. He dropped back, rested, and then tried again. This time it was worse. He was losing strength fast and knew if he couldn't get back in the next minute he might as well let go and drift away, do what Theo had been so reluctant to do.

He decided on a strategy. He would push himself first under the water and then, using the upward momentum created by his buoyancy, launch himself at the side of the dinghy. It had to be worth a try.

He took a breath and pushed himself under. Then, still holding onto the rounded side of the dinghy, he pulled himself up. Straight away he got higher than before. He was well above belly-button level when he threw his arms over the side and lay there panting. He was half in. All he had to do was get his legs over and he'd be there. He inched himself further up and then, in a surge of effort, raised his right leg through the water and landed it on the side of the dinghy. Now he could simply roll himself into the boat. This he did and lay on the floor. The grey water surrounding him felt warm.

After several minutes he lifted himself. The oar with the jacket attached was floating twenty feet away. The lobstermen had continued on and he was now looking at the back of their boat. He lay down and realised he needed to piss. A smooth warmth spread over crotch and thigh.

Well, I'm sorry to be such a disappointment to you, Mr Shackleton, but I'm going to have a little rest now. Yes, I know what you'd say, but you forget there's no one waiting on Elephant Island for me. I'm as free as a canary, only I can't fly. If I could, believe me, I would. Besides, you never gave your friends the benefit of the doubt. They might have woken up of their own accord twenty minutes later and, fresh as a pair of daisies, bounced over the hill to the whaling station on the far shore. You never gave them the chance. And another thing: we have only your word for it. OK, we'll take your word. No need to fight over it. You're a great man, no doubt about it, a Kildare man, can't beat them.

He became aware of a light, a big beam of it in his face, and wondered where it was coming from. Why now when he was so comfortable? Couldn't they just for once leave him alone? He wanted to turn over but they were talking over him now in strong accents. And there was splashing. Why did they not just leave him be?

He felt hands under his arms. Words were being spoken all around him. There was grunting and then he felt his head being raised. Why were they doing that? He had found a really comfortable position. They put him down on a different surface. It was so much harder and there was an awful lot of noise

He woke again and listened. There was an engine. It was under him. He could feel the vibrations. It was dark. He could tell by the motion that he was on a boat. Then a face appeared above him. If this was God, He was a bit of a disappointment. The face stayed staring at him, then turned and shouted, 'He's awake.'

Another face joined the first. The second said, 'You gave us a terrible fright.'

He closed his eyes.

'Just hang on in there, son, there's an ambulance waiting on the quay.' Then he heard the same voice say, 'They said if he woke up to keep him awake ...'

Doyle smiled. Poor bastards, they're half-dead, both of them. A seagull had landed on his chest. He knew the bird had news but, Christ, what did you have to do to get these things to speak?

There were new lights and new voices and a different movement. He felt himself lifted, this time uniformly. He was wrapped in silver. They were going to cook him. More lights, more voices, then a woman with dark hair wearing a green short-sleeved top worked around him. She asked him questions, poked him, shone a light into his eyes but finally she allowed him to go back to sleep.

Eighteen

When Doyle opened his eyes he met Margaret's. He closed, then opened them again: she was still there. Beyond the halo of her hair he saw a bar of bright neon light and, to the side, a string of beds. He closed his eyes. There was the soft hum of electronics, the distant rattle of plates, a telephone and there was talk, indiscernible words whose meaning was lost in the distance but whose sound still reached him. He was on a hospital ward. His head throbbed. He wanted to return to the oblivion of sleep.

'So, how are we feeling?'

Doyle opened his eyes again to see a nurse standing beside Margaret.

'I'll get Dr Raven,' the same voice said.

On this ward it was as though sleep was akin to heroin. The doctor made him sit up, busied himself talking to Doyle, taking blood, taking his temperature, looking at the printouts that were coming from the machine that was making the soft hum. From him Doyle learnt that he was in the Torquay General Hospital and that he had suffered severe hypothermia, also that he was very lucky because another half an hour in that boat and it would have been too late. The nurse returned with pills, which Doyle dutifully swallowed as the doctor continued with his verbal and physical explorations. All this time Margaret stood a little way back, staring at him with an expression of dull disbelief.

When they had gone she sat. 'Desmond, I'm sorry, I'm so sorry. We had to go ahead with the funeral.'

When he had seen her first by his bedside he had known who she was, what she was doing there. There was no moment of confusion, of disorientation. But he had not thought of Daphne, and now her remains were gone.

'Did they find the boat?'

'He brought it around to Brixham, then got a taxi to Totnes and caught a train to London. They picked him up in Paddington. He confessed everything.'

'Do you know what it was all about?'

'Yes.' She began to weep.

'I found some diaries in the old shed.'

'I know. I'm so sorry.'

'Who found me?'

'Fishermen – the dinghy got tangled in one of their pots. You were lying in the bottom of it. They thought you were dead.'

'So did I.'

'Well, you're not.'

Ruth and Garry walked up behind her. They both stared at him without a word. Then Ruth leant forward and kissed him on the cheek. 'We're going to take Mum home now. We'll be back tomorrow. Get some rest.'

'Is there anyone you want us to call?' Garry asked.

'My phone got wet, don't have anyone's number.'

'We'll get you another. Your friend Geoff is here,' Ruth said.

'I'm not sure they'll let him use a phone in here,' Margaret said.

'You're not going to be in too much longer anyway, are you?' Ruth was smiling now.

Doyle felt tears well in his eyes. He blinked and they spilled down his cheeks. Margaret reached for his hand. 'It's all right, Desmond, it'll be all right.'

'I'm sorry but it's not,' he said. 'It's just all so wrong. How could everything be so fucking wrong?'

'Don't talk like that,' Margaret said, kneading his hand in hers. 'You've been through a lot and it's all over now. Soon, when you're better, things will seem different.'

Their retreat was slow and silent. When they were gone he lay there thinking that sleep would come and rescue him, but it did not. And the sights and sounds in front of him grew more vivid. He did not want to make eye contact with the man in the bed opposite, who seemed to be staring at him. To his right, an elderly man, round and bald, had lots of newspapers spread around his bed and on his table.

Doyle lay back on his pillow and was aware that he wanted to go home. Home, he thought, I have no home. I have a flat in Bristol and in the flat is a chair that I parked in front of the window and that is what amounts to my home.

He thought about Theo standing in front of him, holding the gun, and how, later, he'd sworn he would kill him. Whatever he was to do with the rest of his life one thing was for sure: he would not kill Theo Palmer. The man was safely disintegrating on his own, no need to accelerate the process. If he, Doyle, felt the need for revenge, he could read the local newspapers, watch his comings and goings to and from court on local TV. What was he talking about? He himself would be a chief witness – he could watch him at first hand in the dock. Doyle wondered would the arrogance subside. He was sure it would: it was nothing other than a thin layer of ice that, he imagined, had already started to melt. He wondered then what might lie beneath it.

Doyle was surprised by how hungry he was. The smell of the food when they first brought it in had given rise to nausea but when it had landed in front of him he became interested. Pork chop, mashed potatoes and peas. It was while he was eating it that Geoff came in.

'How you doin', sailor?' he said, with a smile that was a foot wide.

'Getting better.'

'Causing commotion on the ocean, I hear.'

'I could do with some rowing lessons.'

Geoff peered at the plate and made a face as though he was about to vomit.

'This is good, Geoff, honestly.'

'You're in bad need of education.'

'I'm in bad need of a lot of things.'

Geoff sat on a chair. 'You're getting out tomorrow, apparently – that is, if you don't give them any cause for concern during the night. Do you know how close you came?'

Doyle continued eating.

'The guys who found you thought you were dead. It was only because the fellow on the radio told them to keep giving you CPR and warm you up slowly that you survived. The doctors were amazed you pulled through.'

'How did they find me?'

'They checked some pots that were right out in the bay. And when they got there they found a dinghy attached to one. Its rope was caught around the line to the pot.'

'You mean the painter?'

Geoff smiled. 'I forgot, you're an old seadog now. I mean, what are the chances? They said when they found you that you weren't breathing, no heartbeat, nothing.'

'I must have had a heartbeat.'

'They said they couldn't find one, and that was when the guy on the radio said, "Don't presume him to be dead, keep up the CPR."'

'So I was out at sea getting mouth-to-mouth from some hairy fisherman?'

'I told you life at sea was fun.'

'How do you know all this?'

'I met them at the funeral yesterday. You're the talk of the town.'

Doyle felt the tears again. What was this? Some tear-duct malfunction caused by hypothermia? They spilled down his face. Geoff handed him a tissue and continued talking. 'Cancelling funerals is a very complicated and expensive business and although Margaret didn't want to go ahead with it she really didn't have a choice.'

Doyle couldn't speak. He wanted to say it was OK, it didn't matter, but the words bounced off each other and his tongue stuck to the roof of his mouth and the tears fell more and more quickly. Geoff pushed the table out of the way, sat on the side of the bed and held his hand. Doyle couldn't stop them now: it was like all the water that had soaked into him needed to come out. He turned away from Geoff and felt his body almost burst in a convulsion of internal heaving. They came in waves, as though they were trying to shift something huge. Then, slowly, they subsided and his breathing was returning to normal. He waited until he could hear the din of his fellow patients. Geoff was still there.

'Christ, Geoff, I'm a mess. This whole fucking thing is a mess.'

'You're not a mess, man, you're a fucking hero.'

Doyle smiled. 'Hero? I can't even row a rubber fucking dinghy!'

Geoff's eyes were glistening now. He wiped them. 'Listen, two members of the constabulary are waiting outside. They want to take a statement. Nurse Ratchet out there told them not to be long so I'll go. I'll come by tomorrow to see if we can get you out of here, OK?'

The policemen stood at either side of the bed, much more polite than their Bristol counterparts. One began asking questions from a list while the other tried to write down the answers. Doyle told them everything he remembered in as much detail as he could. The younger of the two scribbled as he spoke, looking up from his board occasionally as though to plead for a slower pace.

When Doyle finished speaking he felt tired. The policemen nodded their thanks and left him. He lay back and closed his eyes.

When it was confirmed that Doyle was to be discharged the following day, Margaret organised a lunch. She contacted the two fishermen, who said they would look in, say hello, but they wouldn't be eating – too busy. They arrived before Doyle and both stood in the living room holding glasses of white wine, which looked foreign in their hands. When Margaret insisted they sit one of them, the one Margaret presumed was the older, more authoritative one, began to open up a little. Ruth and Garry were in the kitchen. By the time Doyle and Geoff arrived Margaret had learnt more about the EU fishing policy than she thought she would ever have to know.

Doyle did not recognise either of the two men sitting on the sofa with her. When he was introduced he approached and straight away felt the tears surging to the surface. They both stood up and Doyle, as much to his surprise as theirs, embraced them. 'I don't know what I can say to you.'

'Nothing to say,' the older one told him.

'Well, there is – there's thanks for a start.'

'I suppose,' said the other. Both men looked uncomfortable. They emptied their glasses, then turned to Margaret, 'We'll be off, let you people get on.'

'You know you can stay – you'd be most welcome.'

'Thanks, missus, but we have to be gone. Thanks for the wine.'

Doyle walked with them to the hall. 'I wish I had the words to thank you.'

'Listen, mate, we did what anyone would do.'

'Yeah, but I was told I would have died if you hadn't got me warm and all that.'

They looked embarrassed. 'Anyone would have done the same.'

At the door he felt the tears threaten – it was as though they danced just under the rim of his eyes, dying for an opportunity to pop out.

The older man turned to him. 'God knows, the sea takes enough. Nice to be able to pull one back.'

'Tell you what,' said the other, 'you get yourself all better and that and come down again. Just ask for the Garnham boys and we'll have a good old drink.'

He shook their hands. It was a woefully inadequate gesture but it was the only thing that Doyle felt they would all be happy with.

Geoff came out of the kitchen and saw them at the door. 'You boys aren't going, are you?'

'We have to be away, spring tides.'

'OK. I'll walk you to your car – I need a word.'

'I'll be down again and we'll have that drink.' Doyle watched them walk along the path with Geoff, already much more at ease.

He left the door open and went back to the living room. He sat at the table that was set for five, aware that Margaret was gazing at him.

'PC Bainbridge said he would pop by and collect the diaries. You still have them?'

'Yes.' As he said it, he looked at her. Her face was placid, almost stony. He became aware of what she must be going through. 'How are you?' he said.

She looked at him as if to say, That is a very stupid question.

'I'm sorry, I've been so absorbed in myself I—'

'Right now I cannot even begin to describe how I am because I don't know. The awful thing is, the truly awful thing, I think I knew.'

'You mean about Alison . . . and Daphne?'

She was nodding, but not looking at him. 'It's hard to be sure now. I knew he was a vile man. I've always known that, but I ignored it. I ignored it.'

'Margaret, we all do what we must to get by.'

'And then we make a mistake and someone doesn't get by. They die.'

'None of this is your fault.'

'Isn't it?'

'No!'

Geoff came back, looking pleased. 'I think,' he said, 'I've just secured a very good source for fresh lobster for the restaurant.' When Doyle and Margaret continued to stare at him, he said, 'Those guys are fishermen – it was just business. Sorry.'

'No need to apologise, Geoff, nothing wrong with doing business. And, anyway, I think, for the moment at least, apologies are banned in this house.'

The lunch went well. There seemed to be an overall sense of relief. But perhaps it was because Geoff was very talented, when it suited him, at orchestrating a conversation that was light and included everyone. It was interrupted towards the end by a policeman in uniform who turned out to be PC Bainbridge and an old acquaintance of Margaret.

'Sorry to disturb you. Won't keep you long. I'm here to collect the diaries.'

'I'll get them.'

They were where he had left them, in the side pocket of his rucksack at the bottom of Daphne's wardrobe. Downstairs he handed them to the policeman.

'Thanks,' he said. 'I believe you're a friend of Inspector Kneebone up in Bristol, Mr Doyle.'

'We know each other.'

'Well, he's contacted us, asking us to pass on his best to you. He says he'd like to call in on you when you've recovered sufficiently.'

'Tell him he can call in whenever he likes. He knows where I live.'

That evening Geoff and Doyle drove into Bristol. Geoff asked Doyle if he wanted to be dropped off at the flat.

'Where else am I going to go?'

'You can come and have some dinner with me. Did I tell you Gina Harding's keen to see you?'

'Is she?'

'You're wrong about her, you know.'

'How so?'

'She's a good woman.'

Doyle looked at Geoff, who said, 'No! Not like that. She's just a good woman, you know, caring. Stuff you and I would know fuck-all about.' Then, into silence, he said, 'She's agreed to do the opening.'

'Jesus Christ, you don't let the grass grow under your feet, do you?'

Geoff was smiling.

'When is it?' Doyle asked.

'May the eighth, a Saturday. It shall be a most prestigious affair.'

Two days later, Gina came to visit him. It was a pleasant but slightly awkward conversation. She talked about the work she would show at the opening and about how much fun it was all going to be. Doyle thought she was adopting the optimism: it didn't seem to fit naturally on her. As she was leaving, he said, 'Done any more involuntary drawing?'

She smiled and shook her head. 'No, it stopped.' Then she looked at him. 'It taught me something, though. I hope you'll see it at the opening.'

'What?'

'Well . . . to be freer. I was becoming so regimented and that thing changed me, shook me up.'

'I wonder what was going on, I really do,' Doyle said.

'There are probably as many answers to that question as there are people in the world.'

'Probably, and even then none of them might be right.'

A few days later he had a visit from Kneebone. He was quite a different person without an agenda. He sat across the table wanting to know what the diaries said, how Theo had reacted to them and what had happened in the dinghy.

When Doyle had finished the tale the inspector said, 'How did you know to look in the shed?'

Doyle hesitated, then decided against bringing Gina and her drawings into the story. 'Intuition?'

'You,' Kneebone said, pointing a finger at him, 'my friend,

should become a detective. Although my intuition with you was a bit wide of the mark.'

'Not really. You thought I had something to do with Daphne's death. I did.'

Kneebone's eyes widened.

'I think I knew what she was going to do. I didn't discourage her.'

'That's a very different thing from killing her.'

'Is it?'

Kneebone was staring at him intently. 'Yes, it is. Right now you might be weighed down with all sorts of grief and guilt till you don't know one from the other but, believe me, in years to come you'll know there was precious little you could have done.'

Doyle smiled. 'I'm not so sure.'

Kneebone said nothing for a minute. Then he stood and took up his hat. 'For my part I wanted to apologise and, if you ask my wife, she'll tell you that's a rare event.'

'For what?'

'Adding to your burdens.'

'You were doing your job.'

'Yeah, my bloody job . . .'

Doyle looked at him questioningly. 'Nothing,' Kneebone said. 'You really don't want to hear my troubles. I'll see myself out.' At the door to the living room he stopped. 'Look after yourself, Mr Doyle. If you ever need me you know where I am.'

The opening was everything Geoff had hoped. Through friends he had pulled in a top DJ. Wine flowed and the food was excellent. The art was wild with colour and unlike anything Doyle had seen of Gina Harding's work before. He noticed Geoff by her side more than once.

Towards the end of the night Doyle found himself next to her. 'I love the new work,' he told her.

'I'm showing it in a gallery when it's finished here.'

'What's the show to be called?'

She looked at him and smiled. '"Falling Slowly".'

Acknowledgements

Steve Barnes, Hilary Fannin, Karen Edwards, Rynagh O'Grady, Eamon Murray, Giles Newington, Peter Rolt, Aoife Fannin, Ella Palmer, Jassy Conroy, Faith O'Grady, Ciara Considine, Hazel Orme, Liam Murphy, Tommy Foley, Denise Fannin, Marina Baibara, Mike Wynter, Keith Burgess, Leanne Winter, Nick Bedwell, Liz Elliott, Sorcha Moran, Simon Tebbs. And to all those of you who keep me honest, buoyant and sane. Many thanks.